*When hunting vampires,
there will be blood*

BLOOD
BATH

BEST SELLING AUTHOR
RACHEL RAWLINGS

Blood Bath
A Maurin Kincaide Novel
Rachel Rawlings

ISBN: 0692542116
ISBN-13: 978-0692542118

Published in the United States by: R Squared Publishing
www.Hallowread.com

Cover and formatting by Incredibook Design

DEDICATION

This book is dedicated to my family. Thank you for your continued support, for all the FFY - Fend For Yourself-nights, for learning to appreciate Ramen noodles. I love you more than words can express.

A huge thank you to Stephanie Adams, the best Beta and cheerleader an author could have.

I have to thank my editor, Tina Winograd. It's always a pleasure working with you. You not only improve the story but my writing skills.

Patricia Statham, Katrina Hough and Melissa Lewis you ladies are great! Thank you for your support and for loving my characters! And of course the marvelous mad Madam Kelley Kell, thank you for your support and the awesome marketing graphics!

Books By Rachel Rawlings

The Maurin Kincaide Series
The Morrigna
Witch Hunt
Wolfsbane
Ill Fated
Mistletoe Meltdown

Coming Soon
Payable On Death, a Jax Rhoades novel
A Haunted Life
It's All Death To Me

CONTENTS

But first, on earth as vampire sent,
Thy corpse shall from its tomb be rent:
Then ghastly haunt thy native place,
And suck the blood of all thy race;

There from thy daughter, sister, wife,
At midnight drain the stream of life;
Yet loathe the banquet which perforce
Must fee thy living corpse.

Thy victims are they yet expire
Shall know the demons for their sire,
As cursing thee, thou cursing them,
Thy flowers are withered on the stem.

~The Giaour by Lord Byron 1813

ONE

"You have got to be kidding." I cursed a string of profanities that would make a sailor blush as the red and blue lights came into my rear view mirror before pulling to the side of the road. I wasn't even speeding. Well, okay I was going nine miles over the speed limit but wasn't there some unwritten rule about keeping it under ten?

When the all too familiar and unwanted doughy exterior of one Detective Masarelli appeared in my side mirror I banged my head on the steering wheel, managing to blow the horn in the process.

"I don't have time for this shit." I reached across the front seat and pulled the registration out of the glove box. Pairing it with my driver's license, I waited for Detective Dickhead on the off chance this was just a regular traffic stop. Highly unlikely. I was already late for my meeting with Arawn.

After traveling through the between so much, I sort of forgot about all those time consuming things like stop signs and traffic lights. I hadn't allowed enough time to actually drive there hence the sixty-four in a fifty-five.

The reason I was in a car instead of grey fog was Kellen. A member of the Seelie court and new Council chair, he somehow turned my magic against me. He could force me through the between to any destination of his choosing. The more I resisted Kellen the more excruciating he made the jump. He had my magic so screwed up I couldn't jump on my own without throwing up for weeks. So Aidan basically forbade me using the between.

Normally I wasn't one to let a guy tell me what to do but until my father explained Kellen's hold over my magic, the between was off limits. For once I was in complete agreement with my slightly over-bearing vampire boyfriend.

A frustrated sigh escaped me. I had plans that so did not involve a fumbling detective who smelled like greasy take out and stale cigars. The evening's itinerary consisted of a meeting with my father, finding out the source of Kellen's hold over me and whether that made traveling in the between dangerous, followed by dinner with Aidan. And hopefully a few other things having to do with my vampire.

This was only the second night I had with Aidan since he got back from Reykjavik. That was almost a week ago. Unfortunately whatever was happening with the vampires occupied all his time. Iceland could be a synonym for our relationship at the moment. Something I fully intended to change once I got rid of Masarelli and on with the rest of my night.

"Kill the engine." Masarelli tapped on the glass and motioned for me to put my window down. He jumped back when Conry - my ethereal guard dog - poked his head up from the back seat.

"Was I speeding officer?" I handed him my license and registration.

"I'm not pulling you over for speeding, you dunce. Though your lead foot and this car is a recipe for disaster. We need to talk." Masarelli leaned into the Camaro, a low whistle escaping as he took in the fully refurbished interior of the classic muscle car. It really was a thing of beauty - every gear head's wet dream.

"And you thought pulling me over was the best way to do that?" I grabbed my cell phone off the seat and shook it in his face. "Ever heard of one of these? What'd you do? Put an all points bulletin out for me?"

"Thought about it. I knew you'd just send me straight to voicemail."

I thought about the Pink Panther theme song ringtone I gave him. Odds were good I would send him to voicemail. At least I always called back. "What the hell is so important that you had to pull me over?"

"You need to come to the station with me." He moved to open my door, like that would get me into motion. Conry took interest in the detective again and Masarelli quickly removed his hand from the handle.

"Look, I was going to talk to you about the Salem

pack. I'll spare you the bullshit excuses and just admit I forgot. Cash is the new alpha. If I promise to come in tomorrow and tell you about it can I go? I'm already late for an appointment." I glanced at the clock on the radio. It was the only unoriginal thing in the car, well that and the speakers. I was now ten minutes late for my meeting with Arawn.

"It's not about the wolves. It can't wait until tomorrow." He backed up enough for me to open the car door.

"I'm not getting out of the car until you tell me what the hell is going on." I started to put the window back up.

"I am not going to discuss this on the side of the road. Quit busting my balls and get out of the dammed car."

"Quit busting your balls?" I opened the door and stepped out in a rush, thrusting my hand out. "Hello, pot, my names kettle. It's nice to meet you. Why can't I just follow you?"

He ran a hand over his face, across stubble that was too long, even for him. "This is exactly what I was talking about. Because I know you won't follow me. Now would you please get in my car so I can take you to the station and get your expert fucking opinion on something?"

I relinquished any hope of salvaging my night, leaned inside the Camero, put the window up, grabbed the keys from the ignition and whistled for Conry. I glared at Masarelli over my shoulder as I walked to his car, daring him to question me about my dog. Masarelli locked and shut the car door, giving the Camaro one last approving look before heading back to his filthy unmarked patrol car.

Since I wasn't under arrest - at least not yet, the night's still young - I opened the car door myself and slid in behind the driver's seat. "Remember that movie we watched last week, Conry? The one where the dog ate the nice policeman's headrest?" I gave him a big belly rub as he stretched out over my lap and the rest of the back seat.

Masarelli gave me his best cop stare in the rear view and headed toward the station. "So you just forgot about the fact that a black ops merc killed the alpha and took control of the Salem pack? You got papers for this guy?"

"It's a pack not the AKC." I took a deep breath and let it out slowly. "Matthison approved his pass personally."

"It's expired." He blipped the lights and burped the siren to get through the intersection.

"Cash is Alpha now. The paperwork is irrelevant at this point. Unless of course you want to run him out of town on a technicality and create a power vacuum." I gave Conry a little nudge, my legs were falling asleep.

Masarelli spared a quick glance in the rear view mirror. "What happened to Roul? They eat him?"

"Eighteenth century France called. They wanted their superstitions back. How did you get this job again? They buried him, following pack ritual." Not even ten minutes with him and I was already exhausted.

"And his mate?" He couldn't know, could he? Was this what the mysterious trip to the station was really about? He needed my expert opinion on some trumped up murder charge?

"Dead." I didn't elaborate.

"Killing the mate isn't covered under the Meneur de

Loupes agreement." He was fishing for something, anything to get rid of Cash.

My mouth was moving before I thought about the consequences. "It doesn't need to be covered by the Leader of the Wolves agreement since a werewolf didn't kill Olwyn. I did and it was self defense."

"And that's why you didn't bother telling us about it? I have to file a report and take your statement. I don't suppose you have someone to corroborate your self-defense story?"

Shit. "Besides the pack you mean?"

He shook his head. "What do you think?"

"No." If this sounded half as bad to him as it did to me I might actually be in trouble.

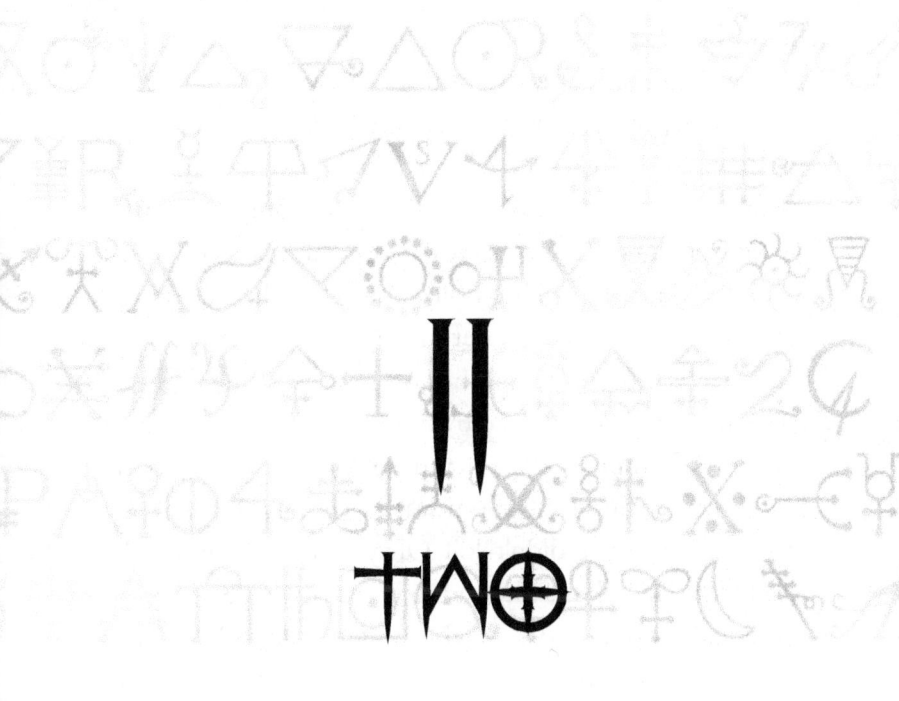

TWO

After years of taking over Masarelli's interrogations, I was the one answering his questions. He asked me how Olwyn died twenty different ways and I gave him the same answer every time - the truth.

"This is bullshit, Masarelli. Just call Pollyanna so I can go home." I locked my fingers behind my head and leaned back in the metal chair.

I knew the eyes and ears behind the two-way would send her in to put an end to this. Even if I was guilty of murder, Masarelli wouldn't get a confession. I knew all his tricks. Hell, half of them he stole from me.

Pollyanna walked in a couple minutes later. She was five foot nine, one hundred eighty pounds of scary ass albino bitch who supposedly gained the ability to sense a lie after being struck by lightning. Apparently the current of electricity that ran through her body fried some synapses and rewired the rest. She was a walking dowsing rod when it came to liars. Her name was plain Anna until she started beating polygraph percentages. Some dumbass thought it would be funny to call her Pollyanna. The joke was on him when she legally changed her name.

I never needed to call her on my cases but I'd heard enough to know being read by Pollyanna was going to hurt. The guys behind the glass must have ratcheted up the thermostat because the room was sweltering. Or maybe it was just nerves. I didn't kill Olwyn in cold blood. She would have killed me. She had to be put down. So why was I suddenly so nervous? Maybe because we didn't have a 'stand your ground' law and it was hard to prove self defense. If Pollyanna sensed how uneasy I was, she didn't say a word. She pulled out the chair across from me and sat.

I knew the drill, my arms were already extended across the table. She latched onto my wrists and dug her nails into my skin. Tiny jolts of electricity shot to my shoulders and through my chest. I instinctively pulled away but she jerked my arms back.

The lights flickered as her power crackled in the air. Pollyanna's skin turned a sickly gray as she sent her energy through my body. Holy crap she was terrifying. Why did I ask for her again? Oh yeah, I wanted to get the hell out of here.

I focused on what happened when Olwyn attacked

me, how she completely lost her mind when Roul died and the permanent claw marks on my stomach. If I was lucky, some of it would get through.

It felt like thousands of fire ants crawled over my body. I fought the urge to squirm in my seat. Resisting her would only make it longer and hurt more. The burning, itching sensation burrowed under my skin using my nervous system to work up to my brain. Her grip tightened more as she picked through my mind. I freaking hated the feeling of things crawling on me. Inside my skull was a thousand times worse.

Sweat beaded on my forehead and ran down my spine as I fought the desire to give Pollyanna a sampling of fae magic. She was so close, her fingers biting into my wrists. I could use the connection to rip my way through her mind, rifling through her memories.

The muscles in my jaw twitched as I waged an internal war over giving her a taste of her own medicine. Something told me she could do this without the pain - she just got off on it. Unfortunately as much as I wanted this to be over, I needed her to tell Masarelli the truth.

If I tore my way through her head, made her feel even a tenth of what I felt now, she could get up and call me a liar. Her word was as good as mine used to be around here. She asked me the same questions as Masarelli and I answered the same way.

Her pallor returned to normal and she relaxed her hold on my arms. I gently pulled free of her grip and rubbed my wrists. A grin that said she knew all too well the position she had me in and loved every minute of it, crept across her face. She glanced at the mirror behind me before walking out of the room.

My phone started playing 'If I was your vampire' by Marilyn Manson from my back pocket. Aidan. I slid the phone out and looked at the message. *'Care to explain why my car is on the side of the road and your father is on my couch?'*

Another text came through before I figured out the best way to summarize what happened. *'Or you could explain why you're with that derelict detective instead of me?'*

I should have known Aidan had contacts in the department. As for my father? I imagine he went looking for me at Aidan's when I didn't show up for our meeting.

Masarelli was back with a manila folder before I got the chance to answer. He threw it on the table, spilling its contents. The face of a young girl stared up from the papers scattered across the table.

"I have four more files just like this. Know anything about that?" He tapped a crime scene photo of what looked like the same girl. Except in this picture she was sprawled naked in a bathtub, one arm slung over the side.

"Is this the part where I'm supposed to ask for my attorney? Do you honestly think I would tell you what happened to Olwyn if I killed five girls?" I pulled the pictures out of the file and flipped through them.

"You want to lawyer up? Same firm as last time?" He smirked, knowing Aidan wouldn't be able to masquerade as my attorney again. "I never said they were dead."

"Cut the shit, Masarelli." I spun the photo of the girl in the tub around to face him. "Even you could have put that together."

"What do you know about these girls, Maurin." He obviously wasn't thrilled about working with me again.

Not that I blame him. The last time we worked together things didn't go according to plan. Sure some of the problem was Masarelli's desire to cling to old stigmas about the Others and his less than stellar detective skills but in the end the jail cells in the station were destroyed, the department shrink was dead and we had to wipe half of what happened from the minds of Masarelli and his team.

I should've had Aidan plant the idea I wasn't just Liaison to the Council but an expert in preternatural activity and a valuable asset to any Salem Preternatural Task Force case. Not that Masarelli would have believed it for long. My fly by the seat of my pants investigating style would have blown that out of the water.

"I don't know anything." I flipped through the photos again, trying to place the girl but I'd never seen her before. I told him as much.

"Any talk about a rogue vamp or werewolf running around?" He sat across the table from me.

"Now that the whole killing Olwyn thing is behind us and we're friends again, tell me something. Where's my dog?" I didn't want to draw too much attention to Conry but I needed to know where he was, especially if I was going to be stuck here for a while. Something told me I was.

"I never said it was behind us. Pollyanna is still processing her report. Your dog is downstairs." He folded his arms and rested them on his stomach.

"Come on, you and I both know she already told you I was telling the truth or you wouldn't be talking to me about this case. And please tell me you didn't lock my dog in one of those disgusting cells downstairs."

"What the hell did you want me to do with him? He looks like a Great Dane that swallowed a mastiff. I can't have him running around the station. We gave him water, and Mike even shared his cheeseburger. The cells have been fully renovated thanks to you. Think of it like a big dog crate." He stifled a yawn.

I chose to ignore the fact he blamed me for the destruction of the jail when he was the one who took the amulet, the only thing hiding me from a demon, before locking me up a few weeks ago. "Fine, can someone take him for a walk later?" I wasn't sure what effect the iron bars of the cell would have on Conry since he was basically a fae creature but it certainly wasn't the time to find out. The less time he spent in the cell the better.

There was a knock on the door. Masarelli got up and poked his head into the hall. He grumbled something to whomever was out there before shutting the door and sitting down.

"Pollyanna says you're clean." He sounded a little disappointed.

I thought he was upset he couldn't use detainment as a threat to get my help instead of not having a legitimate reason to arrest me. "I haven't heard anything about a rogue. vamp or otherwise. What makes you think it's not suicide? Maybe something was going on at school or home?"

"That's what we thought at first. There's one problem. We overlooked it with the first two girls. The lacerations and lack of any defensive wounds all point to suicide. By the third girl we couldn't ignore the evidence. Notice anything out of the ordinary in the picture?" He spun it around and pushed it closer to me.

I shook my head. Whatever he wanted me to see, I wasn't. "Young girl, seventeen, maybe eighteen. Wrist slit along the vein not across."

"What else?" He wasn't going to make this easy and just tell me what I was missing.

"No blood on the floor or outside of the tub. The water was drained. Was forensics already on the scene when this photo was taken?" I had it figured out but wanted to be sure.

"No, that's exactly how we found her." He nodded, confirmation I was on the right track.

"Okay, so if the tub was empty when the girl bled out, where's all the blood? If she filled the bath with hot water to speed up the process and ensure success as the direction of the wound suggests, where's the water?" I knew these were questions Masarelli had already posed to his investigation team. "Let's say it drained on its own before you found her, bad seal on the drain plug, where's the ring from the bloody water inside the tub?"

"Exactly. I'm ashamed to admit we assumed the tub drained and didn't question the lack of any residue on the porcelain. Seemed pretty cut and dry at the time. The girl's parents were a mess, we just wanted to get the scene processed and the body out of there." His expression darkened and I knew he silently berated himself for the oversight. "With the third girl we swabbed the drain and pulled apart the plumbing. We went back to the first scene and we went over the bathroom with Luminal, no trace of blood anywhere."

"Okay, so five girls found in tubs, wrists slit, no water or blood in any of the bathrooms. What else do they have in common? What's special to the killer about these girls?"

"So far just their age. All of them are eighteen, give or take a few months but not one of them is a minor. Different hair, different eyes, different body shape, some with tattoos some without. No patterns in home life or social status either. There's no physical pattern why these girls and not five others."

"Are they witches?" The last time Masarelli and I worked together an extremist group was killing witches. To keep the witches from casting while held captive and tortured, their hands were cut off and cauterized. In one case however, the witch's hands weren't cut off, her wrists were slit.

"No, I already looked into it. That rules out the Inquisitors. Last I checked they only killed witches, not normal girls."

"Maybe random is the pattern."

"Random is by definition not a pattern."

"For lack of a better word, it is a pattern if you're going out of your way to pick girls that aren't alike."

"We call that MO."

"Do you even know what that stands for, Masarelli? Maybe the killer is looking for girls who are different from each other so people won't immediately question the suicide cover?"

"The parents wouldn't talk to each other, let alone know about the others unless someone told them. We haven't released any information to the press. The families don't know we're treating these cases as homicides. You may be on to something, Kincaide."

"Don't sound so surprised. What's next, what do you need me to do?"

"I need you to liaise or whatever the verb is for what you do. Find out if anyone in your community knows anything about five dead girls."

"That's it? You don't want me to get a reading on any of the girls' belongings? You just want me to run information?" I tried not to sound offended.

"You don't have a badge anymore."

"You don't have to sound so happy about it. Fine, I'll ask around and let you know what I find. We done here? I can go?"

"Yeah, I'll have Mike bring up your dog."

"How about a ride back to my car?"

"I'm not your fucking chauffeur. Call someone to pick you up."

"Hey, I said I would follow you but *no*, I had to ride--"

"Fine. Quit your bitching and come on."

A commotion exploded outside the interrogation room. Masarelli jerked open the door to find Conry charging down the small hallway that led to the lower level where the cells were housed. The tow chains they used as a makeshift leash rattled as my dog tried to shake off the patrolman dragging behind him.

I let out a low whistle. Conry slid to a halt, his nails struggling to find purchase on the tile floor. The patrolman leaned against the wall trying to catch his breath. I closed the few feet between us and unhooked the heavy chains around Conry's neck. A normal dog would have struggled under the weight.

"You didn't have to chain him like he's a kraken. He's really well behaved." I rubbed his chest while he nuzzled my side.

Masarelli leaned in. "I'd let it go. Unless you want to explain exactly what he is and where he came from. That's no ordinary dog and he's not registered."

Conry licked the scowl from my face. "We're going home, boy." I had half a mind to tell Masarelli to forget the ride. I'd jump us back to my apartment but it wasn't worth the backlash of exposing my new skill to SPTF. No one, not the council, Aidan, or my father thought it a good idea for the Norms - especially the ones working for SPTF - to find out I could alter reality and with it the potential to change events.

With Conry in tow I followed Masarelli out of the station. I barely made it through the door before my dog bolted past me down the steps. I called after him and moved from behind Masarelli to give chase.

"Looks like I won't be needing a ride after all." A smile crept across my face as I took in the sight of a vampire, feared among his kind for the harsh justice he served, giving my dog a belly rub.

Aidan quickly regained his composure and leaned back on the side of the car. The similarities of hard lines and muscle between him and the Camaro were not lost on me. I did my best not to melt under his smoldering stare. "Thought you might need a lift." His accent was thick and skin was paler than usual. He hadn't fed yet.

"You might start your questioning with him," Masarelli grumbled on his way back inside.

"Some lawyer you turned out to be." I tentatively closed the distance between us. Something besides hunger had him on edge.

"You seem to have a penchant for getting arrested." He pulled me against him and familiarized himself with the sensitive spot behind my ear.

"I was a little surprised you didn't try to bust me out." I leaned back, putting a little distance between my neck and him. Aidan had never asked to feed from me but his agitation was bubbling beneath the surface and I didn't want my jugular to get caught up in it. He's tasted my blood twice. Never as a meal. I didn't want his obvious hunger and emotional state to make this a first.

"As was I, when I learned you confessed to killing Olwyn in order to protect the alpha." The last word came out in almost a growl.

His relentless insecurities over my friendship with Cash were pissing me off, so I fired back. "I simply told the truth. Something that might serve you well in this relationship instead of the half truths and secrets between us lately."

He bristled at my accusation. "I see you've already

resorted to hitting below the belt?"

I glared at him.

"I suppose now you'll stomp your foot and pout those beautiful lips." He ran his thumb along my bottom lip for emphasis.

I swatted his hand away. "I don't pout."

"You do and as much as it pains me to admit it, I find it irresistible."

"Knock it off, Aidan. I know you know something."

"I know a great many things. You have yet to tell me what the detective questioned you about. What makes you so sure I know anything about his case or that this is even a council affair?" His hand found its way to my lower back, stopping me from inching away.

"How about that response for starters? Aidan, we are well past the part where the council tries to keep this a secret. SPTF is asking me about rogues."

"A rogue wolf is a good place to start any investigation given the new regime."

"He wasn't referring to just wolves. What's going on, Aidan?"

He let me go abruptly, preparing himself for the argument he knew was coming and I stumbled back a step. "You know there are things I can't tell you."

"Can't or won't?" Another low blow. Aidan had been nothing but truthful with me - as much as his position allowed anyway. After the coven betrayed me, he knew I would accept nothing less than honesty, a condition testing the bounds of his obligation to the council during more than one of our all night conversations.

He actually looked pained by the question. "I have never lied to you. Especially not when I told you there would be things I couldn't talk about."

"Things like dead girls in bathtubs?"

"Get in the car, Maurin." He was trying to keep the anger from showing on his face and was failing miserably. His eyes and thickening Irish accent always gave him away.

Looked like I over played my hand, pushed him too hard too soon. I should have built up to what Masarelli's investigation was really about. Instead I blurted it out, needing to know everything, to be a part of every council disaster take over. I was never getting him to tell me anything this way. I needed to figure out a way to salvage the conversation and our night together.

"Would you get in the god forsaken car?" he snarled, mistaking my lack of movement as a dismissal. "Why are you so hell bent on ruining our night together? Quite possibly the last night we'll have before the Council sends me away again."

News he would be leaving again so soon was a sure fire way to stop me asking about dead girls in bathtubs. At least for a little while. I'm surprised he didn't say checkmate. "I wonder what's causing the sudden up tic in vampires behaving badly. You've barely been home a week. How long are you going to be gone this time?"

He didn't say anything. The muscles in his jaw, another of his tells, twitched. Something was wrong, something more than chasing down another vampire in the throes of a blood lust.

"How long, Aidan?"

"Indefinitely." He practically choked on the word.

I felt sucker punched in the gut. Sure he was over protective and jealous and stubborn but I had those same endearing character traits as well. In reality we hadn't been a couple very long and time alone had been scarce but that didn't stop him from worming his way into my heart. I wish I had seen the signs before it was too late. I let him in and now he was leaving. The emptiness I felt when I thought Oberon died was nothing compared to the darkness eating into my heart.

"Maurin, I'm sorry." He pulled me into his arms, burying his face in my neck. The chill of his cool breath on my skin matched the cold seeping into my bones, snuffing out the fire that usually roared inside whenever Aidan touched me. "I didn't mean to tell you this way. Will you please say something?"

There were no words. I broke free of the embrace, not allowing myself even a moment of comfort in his arms. How many times had my fears and weaknesses been chased away while he held me? Too many in too short a time. No, it was better this way. I wouldn't let him soothe me as he said his goodbyes. I stepped back, the mixture of sandalwood and spices - of Aidan - clinging to me. I wrapped my fingers around Conry's collar and faded into the between.

THREE

It didn't take long for him to show up outside my door. If I had somewhere, anywhere else to go I wouldn't have come back to my apartment. I barely managed to strip off my clothes and turn on the shower before the pounding started. I thought about letting him in, if only to spare the door any more abuse - until he called my name.

Anger laced with anguish as he demanded I open the door and talk to him. Instead I stepped into the shower and let the hot water hide my tears.

I was still raw from seeing my so called family after a decade of my mutually agreed upon exile and subsequently ending that chapter of my life. It had only been a week since my sister's wedding. I didn't want to go but hadn't had the heart to disappoint Frankie. She was the only person in my adoptive family that I cared about or that seemed to care about me for that matter.

I left the house in Beacon Hill were I was raised as soon as I could. They never looked for me and I never looked back. Until the wedding invitation came in the mail. It was hard to say goodbye to Frankie at the reception - we both knew it was forever- but there was no place for her in my life now.

Now I had to do it again. Except this time there wasn't anything mutual about it. Vampires were typically over protective and territorial when it came to the people and places important to them. Aidan warned me of that on more than one occasion. I took it to mean he'd be around for a while. I guess I wasn't that important because now he was cutting me loose. Sure I knew the Council was the real reason he was saying goodbye but my heart blamed him for it anyway.

I scrubbed, lathered, rinsed and repeated, then stood in the shower until I drained the hot water heater and the cold forced me out. I wrapped my hair in a towel before drying off with another. The pounding stopped. I let out a sigh and then another. I was relieved and resentful all tangled into one. Relieved that he stopped trying to beat down my door and resentful for exactly the same reason.

Half of me wanted him to go the hell away, the other half wanted him to stand out there all night miserable and professing his devotion. I was about to throw on pajamas and crawl under the covers when the sound of another person outside my door made me freeze.

"What are you doing here?" Aidan's voice was so cold I half expected frost to form on the door.

"I'm here for Maurin." Cash managed to insinuate a hell of a lot with those four little words.

Power seeped into my apartment from the hall. The walls and door concaved from their opposing energy. Life and death clashed like two weather fronts. One warm, one cold, creating the perfect storm in the confined hallway. Something, more likely someone, slammed against my door and I jumped. Conry didn't stir from his favorite spot on the couch. Seeing as how they posed no threat to me, he was content to let the two of them wage their little war outside my door.

An image of the two crashing into my apartment, bruised and brawling, flashed through my mind. While some carnal and obviously twisted part of me found that arousing, I had to stop them before things went too far. Cash was a member of the Council, fighting him outside of a sanctioned challenge was the same as treason - even if Cash was egging Aidan on.

I threw the door open, my lack of clothes completely forgotten until one set of eyes raked over my chest barely hidden by the towel and the other scorched their way up my exposed legs. I was immediately assaulted with emotions - rage, jealousy, desire. I clutched the towel with one hand and the doorknob with the other for support.

"I thought you'd get the hint after the first twenty minutes of pounding. You're going to break the damn door."

"With these wards? I hardly think so." Aidan pointed

to something etched into the inside top of the door jam.

Squinting I struggled to see the faint markings. The more I concentrated, the more visible the tiny runes became. Once I knew what to look for I saw them running down the sides as well. Why hadn't I seen them before? I needed to add the strange markings to the ever growing list of things to talk to Arawn about.

Their collective breath, taking in my scent, as I stood between them sent a chill racing down my spine and goose bumps across my skin.

"Well, in that case you can rip out each other's throats for all I fucking care." A bitter laugh escaped me as almost identical looks of shock took up residence on their faces. I slammed the door shut and headed for the vodka in the freezer.

"Maurin. Open the door." Cash's turn to knock.

"Knock until your knuckles bleed. I don't give a shit." I poured a shot of espresso vodka and slammed it back.

I heard the door open and cursed myself for forgetting to lock it. Not that they couldn't have busted it down if they wanted to. It was respect for me, for my space, that kept them on the other side of the door. That and the wards, which apparently only stopped someone who meant me harm. Without thinking or caring which of them entered first, I turned and hurled the shot glass. Cash caught it before it hit him in the face.

"I'm guessing that was meant for you." He cast a smug glance Aidan's way and walked in like he owned the place.

"It was meant for whoever was dumb enough to let themselves in. What good are wards if anybody can waltz in my front door?"

Conry's collar jangled as he jumped off the couch. A low growl building in his throat. Cash tentatively held out a hand. My guardian sniffed, nudged and licked. Apparently satisfied that this wasn't a home invasion, Conry returned to his spot on the couch.

"Hey, you're supposed to be on my side. Some guardian you are." Conry let me know exactly what he thought about that comment by turning around on the cushion until I was literally looking at the wrong end of a dog. I took a swig from the bottle since Cash still palmed my shot glass. "Are you going to tell me what you want?"

"You know what I want." No insinuating there, that was pretty straight forward. A little glint flashed in Cash's eyes. Good thing Aidan didn't see it.

The oxygen was sucked out of the room and replaced with a suffocating amount of testosterone. Aidan finally crossed the threshold and positioned himself between the two of us.

"Stop trying to piss him off, Cash. He and I are managing just fine without your help. Tell me what you want and go home. *Please.*"

For the second time, they both wore similar expressions. Not shock, maybe concern. I don't think it was the please so much as the way I said it. Even I caught the hurt and exhaustion in my voice. I wanted to take it back as soon as it left my mouth.

"Your presence has been requested at Risqué." Cash was all business now.

"You're a councilman not a messenger. They couldn't

get someone else to get me?" Something was up. Aidan was too quiet.

"We did send someone else. He was supposed to have you there forty-five minutes ago." He didn't need to tell me Aidan was supposed to take me to the Council. The menacing glare he gave Aidan said it all.

***

The four walls that made up my cramped bedroom crumbled around me. The worn carpet fading beneath my feet was quickly replaced with familiar nothingness. I decided to take off for my appointment with the Council before either of them offered me a ride. I didn't want to be trapped in a car with either of them right now. Cash would want to know why Aidan was locked out of my apartment. Aidan would force me to talk about him leaving. I'd rather risk running into Kellen than have either of those conversations.

After Kellen hijacked my power and forced me to jump to Cash, I knew he could travel through the between too. I'd been avoiding jumps in an effort to stay off Kellen's radar. Aidan would be furious I chanced it twice in one night but he was leaving so I didn't give a shit what he thought. At least that's what I told myself. I managed to get back to my apartment with no ill effects and no sign of Kellen earlier. Getting to Risqué should be easy.

After driving everywhere I needed to go, being back in the between was a balm to my frayed nerves. Energy seeped into my pores, sinking deeper into tissue, muscle and finally bone. Power I recognized as my own coursed through my veins before pooling in my core. Like cold water pouring into a glass, it rose from the pit of my stomach, behind my ribcage, to the hollow of my throat until it nearly burst from my chest. Holes in my shields were filled. I hadn't known until that moment how off balance I was by shutting myself off from this.

Even Conry seemed to benefit from being here. Symptoms of dehydration and malnutrition I hadn't noticed before faded away. He needed this as much as I did. Roped muscles filled out his frame while his white coat thickened. Fire flared in his red eyes. He looked like the ferocious beast I first saw crossing to Salem with Arawn last year.

Feeling better than I had in weeks it took almost no effort to jump to the seedy night club recently purchased by the Council. Two sets of eyes bore down on me again as I stepped through the veil that separated the dark parking lot behind Risqué from the between. I knew they would both be waiting at the back door for me to arrive.

This time they weren't wearing matching expressions. Aidan's eyes filled with the anger he was trying to hold back. He coiled like a viper ready to strike. So of course I ignored him. I caught the glint in Cash's eyes that was becoming all too familiar as I brushed past him on my way through the door.

"You're so fucking stubborn," he chuckled behind me.

I walked down the stairs to the old speak easy part of the club that served as office and conference room, with a pissed off vampire and a werewolf at my back. This should be interesting.

"I send two of Salem's finest specimen of men to offer to bring you to me and you choose to travel here alone. Your willfulness is becoming a regular source of amusement for me." Agrona was perfectly draped over the chaise lounge in a cream, off the shoulder fitted top and navy blue sailor pants. The tips of a pair of tan leather heels that probably cost more than my rent peeked out under the hem.

I stopped comparing my wardrobe to hers awhile ago. She loved designer labels, luxurious fabrics and over spending. I was happy with jeans, boots - preferably Docs - and a vintage band T-shirt. Tonight's choice, The Ramones. It was appropriate since I would probably want to be sedated after this meeting.

"Happy as I am to entertain you, I get the feeling you wanted to see me for a reason."

"Straight to the point as always. You're being called up again, Maurin. It seems you are destined to be more than just a liaison."

"Masarelli hauled me into the station today to wave some pretty gruesome pictures in my face. Started asking questions about rogues. I don't suppose this is related?"

"Very perceptive." Her gaze slid to Aidan and back to me. "So the detective suspects a wolf?" A hint of the absurdity she felt over that concept was in her voice.

"I kind of got the impression it was interchangeable for him. Vamp or were, makes no difference to him. He's wanting a crack at this case, Agrona. Five is too many to keep under wraps. Maybe if they weren't found in their own homes... You should have brought me in sooner. What were you planning to do? Clean slate SPTF again? You can't go wiping people's minds whenever you want."

"*Hello, vampire.*" The attempt at the modern phrase was at odds with her...well everything about her actually. She waved it off. "The detective has put in a formal request for your services. It would seem they are in need of a psychometric." She watched Aidan again, waiting for a reaction.

His jaw twitched, hands clenching and unclenching at his sides. "It was not a threat, Agrona. I will make good on my word if you do this."

I felt my eyes widen. What the hell was he doing? You don't threaten the Council and despite what he said that's exactly what it sounded like.

Agrona sat up, swinging her legs around to the front of the chaise gracefully. "I have grown weary of this conversation, Aidan. You have nothing to gain and everything to lose should you follow through with your plan. Despite this one blot on your otherwise perfect record you are the best cleaner we have ever had, but you are replaceable. Stay and she is involved, go and she is still involved with no one to protect her. Don't bother protesting, Maurin. I see it forming on your tongue but hear me well on this, you will need someone from my line with you."

Aidan looked about to explode but he didn't argue or question his queen. Apparently Cash had been here the first time they had this conversation because he looked beyond bored. Whatever was going on was definitely a council matter but it didn't involve the wolves directly and that's all he cared about.

Kedehern walked through a door hidden in the wall, dabbing a napkin at the corners of his mouth. Apparently he wasn't alone in the secret room. He stood behind his wife, fingers trailing from her shoulder to behind her ear and back down again. "Maurin will meet the detective in the morning and report back to Cash. Aidan will find you once the sun has set. Understood? She will have one of you available to her at all times. Come pet, your dinner is getting cold."

"She would be safer if you left her out of this." All the venom had left his voice but he couldn't let this go.

"Would you like to test your tolerance for silver?" Kedehern didn't wait for a response from Aidan. He knew there wouldn't be one. "Perhaps I should pack your mouth full of it to see if you truly are immune."

From the days of Hippocrates to the early twentieth century, silver leaf was commonly used in wound care. During the Irish Rebellion of 1798 Aidan was seriously injured, resulting in not only silver sutures but silver leaf to fight the infection. He was turned two days later with enough silver in his system to create an immunity in his undeath - something that hasn't happened before or since.

Agrona stroked Kedehern's forearm, lips curled up in a fiendish, fang exposing smirk. She had an ace up her sleeve and was ready to play it. "Since you're so vehemently opposed to this plan, Aidan, perhaps I should find someone else to take your place. Kellen couldn't join us this evening but he has volunteered his services."

Aidan didn't flinch, his face remained neutral. He wasn't giving her the reaction she wanted but she knew she'd won. I don't know the history between Aidan and Kellen but I was relieved his hatred for that particular fae outweighed everything else.

Something about Kellen scared the shit out of me. I was furious with Aidan for trying to keep me out of this, for his distorted sense of honor and need to protect me. He might not think so, but I was more than capable of protecting myself. Still, working with Aidan while I was pissed off at him was better than being forced to have Kellen at my back.

"What time am I supposed to meet Masarelli?" I heard the beginning of a protest from Aidan and rounded on him. Letting Kedehern pack his mouth full of silver was sounding like a great idea. "I don't need your permission. They asked for a psychometric. Did drinking my blood give you the ability to read objects or people, to follow the memory links?"

"You let him feed from you?" Cash aimed for cool and uncaring but I caught the disappointment in his eyes.

"He probably would have died the first time. I was suffering from blood poisoning, the second time. I'd hardly call it feeding. Not that it's any of your fucking business, Cash."

Another emotion I couldn't place ran across Cash's face. If I didn't know better I would say it was anger, maybe even jealousy over Aidan having a piece of me he never would. I didn't bother thinking about it too long. Cash would be a problem for another day because I wasn't finished with Aidan.

"What do you care? You're leaving remember?"

"I care a great deal more about your safety than you do," he ground out.

"Oh this is too delicious." Agrona leaned forward, her hands steepled in front of her face. "So he told you about his plan then? The maid holds himself in such high regard he thinks threatening me with accepting offers from other families - offers I know full well he's been entertaining for some time - will save you from being involved. But you don't want a savior do you, Maurin? Aidan doesn't understand that about you."

"She wants someone standing by her side, not in her way." Everyone turned to gape at Cash. Everyone except me – I wasn't surprised. He was always right when it came to my feelings. Cash read me like an open book. Aidan acted like I was a Rubic's Cube.

"We'll have to tune in next time to see what happens in the soap opera that is Maurin's life, my dear. The night is young and your dinner awaits. Meet the detective tomorrow morning, SPTF at eight sharp." He drew Agrona up and into his arms. Before she could object Kedehern covered her mouth with his.

The moment the metallic tang from the remnants of his dinner hit her taste buds the predator took over. The two withdrew to the hidden room and their donors, leaving us in the uncomfortable wake of that conversation. The click of the door officially signaled the end of the meeting but none of us spoke. The awkward aftermath of Cash's insightful remark was too much for me. I decided to break the silence. By leaving.

IV
FOUR

SPTF was at DEFCON one. I walked into a police station overflowing with uniforms. Officers from the Massachusetts State Police mixed with Salem's patrolmen. SWAT jockeyed for position in the section usually reserved for Masarelli's team. Concerned citizens gathered where they could, shouting for answers and justice. What the hell was going on?

Masarelli found me in the sea of people, grabbed my arm and dragged me into his office. *His* office used to belong to Captain Matthison - before we worked on a case together and the bad guys put him out of commission. He'd unknowingly been given Agrona's blood, resulting in a miraculous recovery but he still hasn't reclaimed his office or position.

A pang of guilt hit me as I looked at the plants on the desk. Once withered and brown from the neglect of the captain, they thrived under Masarelli's care. I had hoped Matthison would be back by now but it looked more and more like the medical leave was turning into retirement.

"Are you listening to me?" Masarelli slammed his hand on the desk.

"Sorry, what did you say?" I shook my head to clear the thoughts of Matthison and what happened to him on Winter Island.

"In case you didn't notice the three ringed circus on your way in, I've got men from every fucking division out there. The mayor and governor are breathing down my neck. I've got more brass up my ass than a marching band and nothing to go on. Nothing that will find out who managed to kill seven girls in less than a month and God only knows how many more. The FBI is running it through their computers to see if they get any hits."

"Seven? I thought you said the body count was five." This was bad, really bad. This was the kind of shit that had people changing laws and taking away rights. There hasn't been a serial killer case involving an Other since the seventies - not publicly anyway. With this many departments and politicians involved there would be no way to keep it out of the media.

"Try and keep up would you? Two more girls went missing. One from MIT and one from U Mass. Their bodies haven't been found but after the last five it doesn't look good."

"So why aren't the Boston Police handling it?"

"Look again." Masarelli spread the blinds for me to peek at the mob gathered in the station.

"Is that Campus Police out there too? Holy shit, this is a mess." I let out a low whistle. "How do you know the two missing girls are related?"

"I don't, not officially but my gut is telling me it's connected. I've got a leak, Maurin. It got out we have five dead girls and the mayor called the governor for outside support. The next thing I know my station is a command center. The only people missing are Fish and Game. Though I suspect they'll be called in for the search."

"Do they know you suspect a rogue?" I had to get in touch with Cash, he was my daytime contact and the Council needed to know Salem was on the brink of martial law.

"No, I managed to keep that little tidbit quiet." He dropped into the chair behind the desk and leaned back. He was exhausted, this case was getting the better of him.

"What do you want me to do?"

"Get me a coffee." He rubbed a calloused hand over his growing stubble.

"Excuse me? Get your own dammed coffee. I thought you needed a psychometric not a secretary." He had a lot of nerve dragging me down here this early in the morning just to play barista.

"Go to the Daily Grind and wait for me to call. I don't want them to see you touching the evidence. They're going over the details for the search one more time before they head out. Once they're gone you can do that thing you do."

"Why all the secrecy? I used to get paid to do this. Remember?"

"Used to. Now you're just another Council lackey. They didn't want me to bring you in. I'm a hairs breadth away from losing this case, Maurin." He was laying it all out on the table.

"So get another psychic. Every department has one. You don't need me. You need a precog." Someone who saw the future would be a hell of a lot more useful to him than someone who saw the past.

"They're bringing one up from Bristol. He's supposed to be really good but I don't know him. I don't know if I can trust him and he isn't going to get me the stuff I need to catch this sadistic fuck."

"A precog can find the missing girls." I added, "alive" for emphasis.

"I want those girls found alive, I do, but really I want the evidence that'll put this guy on death row." The look in his eyes said he would do whatever it took to make that happen.

"You want a Red Eye?" I decided to give him a break. The mob forming outside his office took the fun out of breaking his balls anyway.

A bit of the stress weighing him down went away when he realized I was going along with his plan. "Black, four Splendas. I'll call you as soon as this place clears out."

On the walk to the Daily Grind I called Cash and asked him to meet me. I've only been to the coffee shop once since Mahalia was handed over to the fae after trying to kill me.

The coven and I didn't see eye to eye on her sentencing. I thought she got off easy and they thought it was my fault they were without a high priestess.

The last time I was there with my sister, some asshole hexed my coffee. I figured having the alpha with me might deter anyone from doing it again. The Daily Grind had the best coffee in Salem and I was seriously jonesing for their espresso. The closer I got the more I felt like a junkie looking for their next fix. I was leaning against the side of the building anxiously drumming my fingers on my leg when Cash finally got there.

"You look like you're detoxing. Let's get you inside before your shakes turn into the sweats." He held the door open and gave me a wink.

Amalie had my order waiting for me. "I saw you outside. I didn't know you were waiting for someone." She gave Cash the once over before throwing me a questioning look.

I just shook my head. We hadn't talked in a while. I missed her and I was starting to believe what she said about not being involved in Mahalia's plot to get rid of me. Plus she basically came to my rescue the last time I was here, serving me when everyone else wanted to toss me out. I just wasn't ready for a heart to heart, especially not in front of Cash. We'd work out the problems in our friendship. It was on my growing 'problems for another day' list.

"Why don't you grab a table while I order?" Cash's timing was impeccable. He took in Amalie's broken expression and gave me the stink eye.

"I need a Red Eye and four Splendas too." I turned to

find a seat. I could tell Cash was talking to Amalie about more than how he took his coffee. I sighed. *They're not talking about you.* I was getting better at deluding myself. I zig zagged through the tables until I found an empty one by the windows.

I opened the white paper bag and picked a corner off the warm croissant waiting inside. Flaky, buttery pastry perfection. I washed down the first bite with a swig of the best coffee in town. This time it tasted like espresso, steamed milk and a dash of cinnamon, instead of something scraped off the inside of a chimney flu. I closed my eyes, barely stifling a moan of pleasure.

"Is that the same face you make when you're whoring yourself out to the Council? How much does it cost to get you on your back?" It was the same asshole as last time. "Waste of a fine piece of ass if you ask me," the guy sitting next to him said. "Fucking dogs, fairies, and corpses? That's what she chose over a coven member? She's just a worthless psychic, not even a precog, just another Council whore. Hope she gets fleas or maybe she'll get a rash from the fairy dust on her p..."

I flashed through the between, popped up behind him and smashed his face against the table with one hand and vice gripped his balls in the other.

I tried really hard to let the fact he didn't hex my coffee out-weigh his mouth. I wasn't a whore and normally I wouldn't care what some loser with a limp wand said about me but enough was enough. It was high time somebody taught him a lesson.

"Marcus, Marcus, did you, did you see that?" the

friend stammered.

"The only person to treat me like a whore was your precious priestess. Call me anything except my given name again and I'll make you a fucking eunuch. You have no idea what I am or what I'm capable of. Do we have an understanding?" When he didn't answer right away I squeezed harder between his legs. Marcus let out a groan and attempted to nod his head in between my hand and the table. "I'm sorry I didn't hear you?"

"Yeah, fuck," he ground out through clenched teeth.

"Now say you're sorry." I squeezed again. I practically felt my thumb touching my fingertips through his, well you get the idea. I was giving new meaning to blue balls. If he didn't apologize soon he'd need more than an ice pack down his pants.

This time he cried out. His friend and several other men in the room winced in sympathy. More than one hand moved into a protective cup in front of their zipper.

"Close enough."

Cash grabbed my arm, wrenching it from Marcus's manhood. Not the smartest move since I hadn't opened my hand yet. Marcus screamed like a little bitch. I let go of his neck and he slid out of his chair to the floor. Cash shoved me away from the table, his hand firmly clamped on my forearm. After using my body to open the door he loosened his grip. "What the fuck is the matter with you?"

"Me? What's the matter with me?" I shrieked. "That guy calls me a whore, not once, not twice, but like six times. Then proceeds to say I'm screwing a corpse - which is disgusting and I think physically impossible - , a were, and,

and a..." I couldn't bring myself to utter the last part. Kellen terrified me. He was gorgeous but a sadist through and through. No way, no way in hell would I get involved sexually with him. I'd be screaming the safe word before he closed the bedroom door.

"As much as I enjoyed watching you hand that guy his ass, and believe me I enjoyed it, it was pretty hot actually--"

"Having a guy's balls in a death grip is hot? I'm worried about you."

"No, you totally in control, kicking ass, all raw power. That is fucking hot." He jerked me against him. He was on fire and I don't think it was just because he was a wolf. His gaze could melt panties. Too close, he was too close. I pushed against his chest, putting space between us. Big mistake. He laid his free hand over mine, pressing it to the hard plane of his chest. His heart pumped a steady rhythm beneath my palm.

I needed to defuse the situation. "So you dragged me out here like my ass was on fire to tell me that?" Okay, mentioning my ass was not the best idea. His lips curled in a devilish half smile and he let go of my hand. I could tell he was fighting the urge to slide his hand around and into the back pocket of my low rise jeans.

Holy hell, I needed space. This was rapidly moving into not just friends category. There was a line and he was about to cross it. Don't let him. *Maurin, don't let him cross it!* I shouted in my head. Cash was the best friend I had. I couldn't lose that.

The bell on the door to The Daily Grind chimed as

Amalie came out with a drink carrier and a white paper bag. "Remade your order. On the house of course." She gave me a knowing look and I hoped the one I returned conveyed my thanks.

Cash stepped back and I grabbed the cardboard tray. Relief surged through me, relief and other emotions I wouldn't acknowledge.

"You showed a room full of others you can jump. We agreed you were not going to do that, remember?" He went from sexing me up to dressing me down. My brain was having a hard time keeping up.

"Oh, yeah." I didn't have a witty comeback. He was right. I let my temper get the best of me. I hadn't registered my new abilities with SPTF or any of the other Norm organizations that oversaw interspecies relations because as far as we knew there wasn't a classification for me.

I'm unique and in this day and age that wasn't necessarily a good thing. Tensions ran high and it wasn't just the murders causing the widening divide between Others and Norms.

Factions of the government wanted stricter regulations, more testing. There was whispering of a campaign to create super soldiers, genetically altering the troops by harvesting specific strands of DNA from Others. The Council did not want me in the hands of the extremists. Neither did I. We needed to stop the killer before this case became one more talking point in the argument for the war mongers.

I gave Amalie a sideways glance and headed back to the station. Masarelli hadn't called but I wasn't hanging around outside the Grind. A couple benches sat up ahead. We could wait there.

"You should find a new place to get coffee." Cash took the tray from me and wiggled his cup free.

"Why? I'm not going to let some asshat run me out."

"If you're not going to work out things with Amalie, you should find somewhere else to get your caffeine fix."

I stopped walking and stared at him. I hadn't expected him to lecture me on mending my friendship but it looked like that was where this conversation was headed.

"You really should give her a chance to tell her side but if you're not ready to listen then give that new place a try. She feels bad enough, you ignoring her makes it worse. That and you can't afford to let every, what did you call him, asshat, piss you off to the point of using your magic or whatever you call it. Not unless you want to be the first of us to end up in a lab." He kept walking and I jogged a couple steps to catch up.

He sat on the bench and took a swig of coffee. "All these years I thought the Council was bullshit. Old creatures clinging to the old ways. What I didn't know, what you don't know, is how necessary we are. Cohabitation is such a fragile thing. All it takes is one charismatic whack job and the next thing you know everyone's drinking the Kool-Aid and we're second class citizens. The thought of... Just do me a favor, don't expose yourself like that again."

"Okay."

Cash's body jerked forward. I thought he was choking. Or would that be drowning since coffee was a liquid?

"Okay? Just like that? You definitely need to find a new place to get coffee because Amalie is obviously putting drugs in yours."

I gave him a sharp jab in the ribs. "We've been friends long enough and you've been on the receiving end of my temper on more than one occasion. It doesn't seem to have the same effect it used to. Maybe it's time for a new approach." I chose to ignore the furrowed brow and downcast eyes over the word friend. "I'll try. It's the best I can do."

He looked like he wanted to say more but I wasn't ready to hear it. I might never be ready to hear it. Avoidance was working for me so far, no sense changing tactics now.

"New topic. Well, not really new. Actually it's kind of related."

"Related how?" He scrambled to catch up.

"The case. I had a bad feeling when I walked in the station earlier, what you just said confirmed it." I could tell his mind was still on the things he hadn't said but my next statement would bring him back to reality. "Salem looks on the brink of martial law."

"Over five dead girls? There's no evidence of foul play." He was back on track. Thankfully.

"Probably seven if Masarelli's hunch is right. The M.E. hasn't said murder but he hasn't said suicide either. The station was wall to wall with uniforms from every division in the state. They're about to head out on a search for the two missing girls. As soon as they clear out I'm looking at what they've got. We're waiting for Masarelli to call."

"Why are we waiting for him to call? Is that normal? I was under the impression you still had pull as liaison."

"I do, well I did. This case is getting away from him thanks to a leak. A leak I think might be working for the politicians pushing for more testing. So far Masarelli's rogue theory hasn't gotten out but he's going to lose the case if he doesn't get his house in order. They're running info though the FBI database. And the so called search and rescue looks more like search and destroy with all the different departments involved.

"The only thing keeping it with Masarelli and SPTF is the proximity of the five bodies and the psychics on his payroll. Imagine what they'd be doing if they thought they were looking for an Other.

"Plus, someone doesn't want me working this case either. They're bringing a precog up from Bristol. I mean if there's any chance of them finding the two girls alive they need a precog but Masarelli said *they* didn't want to bring me in on this. Who's they and why don't they want me involved?"

"Maybe the rogue theory isn't so secret after all and they don't want the Council involved."

Before I had time to chew on that interesting tidbit the Pink Panther theme blared out of my coat pocket.

Cash laughed as I read the text. "All clear. Let's go."

V
FIVE

Masarelli led us into the interrogation room. I was spending more time in here than when I was on SPTF's payroll. I wasn't sure I would call the items spread over the table evidence. It was more like a few personal effects. No weapons or bloody clothes, just trinkets and a couple pieces of jewelry.

"Is this it?"

"They were found naked in their bathtub. What did you expect?" Masarelli had a point.

I didn't know what I expected but staring at the table I knew I needed more. I wasn't getting more help so I had to do my best with what I had. I picked up a necklace first. It was old. Older than the girl who wore it when she died.

A tarnished Gothic cross hung from a simple silver chain. A small diamond chip adorned the center of the cross. I took a deep breath, pulled on the energy that made me a psychometric and got nothing.

What I felt was Masarelli's eyes boring into my back. I grimaced as wave after wave of anticipation hit me. I closed my hand around the cross, the points digging into my palm, and concentrated on the girl. The precog would know I handled it now but I needed a stronger connection. There was no memory link to the dead. Sometimes the residual imprints were clear and other times, like now, muddled. I blocked out Masarelli's emotions - and the undercurrent of power from Cash's wolf - and focused like a laser beam on the first memory rippling to the swampy surface of the dead girl's imprint.

The images didn't make sense. The town, the people, everything was different. The roads unpaved, the houses further apart. Women passed in long skirts, their shawls wrapped tightly to keep the offending cold at bay. Men with buttoned down coats followed men dressed for work in the field with a sense of purpose I knew had nothing to do with crops.

Either this girl was obsessed with nineteenth century New England or this memory was old. I was betting the latter. I let the past consume me again and silently caught up to the men through the eyes of the original owner of the necklace.

My hand instinctively covered my mouth to stifle a gasp. Shovels upturned the fresh grave. The farmers piled dirt on both sides as they dug deeper into the earth under the watchful eyes of two other men.

Finally a box was lifted from the ground and set at the foot of the grave. At the insistence of the two well dressed men, the farmers pried off the lid.

I almost cried out for them to stop but feared the repercussions of being discovered. What form of wickedness had taken hold of these men that they would defile the resting place of the newly dead? I had known them since I was but a child. I would no more think them capable of this than the pastor. Who were those two devils dressed in their finery, come to lead our townsfolk astray?

Leaves crunched underfoot as someone approached. I stilled my breath and crouched behind the tree, praying whoever it was didn't see me. More devils or misguided neighbors? The sound of my beating heart roared in my ears and I hoped it did not give me away.

I pressed my hands into the cold ground to keep from falling over as I saw who broke through the tree line. The man I had planned to go to for help! Pastor Wilkes shook hands with the well dressed devils before enthusiastically thanking them for coming. A man of God was responsible for bringing this wickedness to our doors? I wanted to scream to the heavens but instead sent a silent plea to God that the innocent be spared and these men find their way back from this devilry onto the path of righteousness.

The horrors continued to unfold as the men pulled hammers and short stakes from a worn leather bag, like one was accustomed to seeing a doctor carry. The farmers stepped away from the casket holding the corpse of young Henry Wilkes, upon seeing the instruments held by the two strangers.

One man held a stake over Henry's chest as the other drove the hammer down. The stake was pulled free, stained with what remained of the heart. The hammer came down again, this time slamming into the ribs, breaking bone. I forced my eyes shut at the sound of a saw working through bone and prayed again for an angel to save us.

"Not an angel, my dear, but I will spare your innocent eyes from witnessing any more of this." The stranger gestured to the grisly scene.

Had I said my prayer aloud? Could this be the deliverance I asked for? I didn't know this man but what choice did I have. I couldn't trust the people I knew and respected. How could I be in any more danger with this gentle stranger than the crazed men of my community.

He held out a hand to me and I let him pull me up. I knew instantly it was a mistake as his cold hand closed around mine. This was not the cold of the oncoming winter that clasped my hand but the eternal cold of death. I gripped the cross around my neck as if somehow it would save me from the monsters that surrounded me.

His eyes were entirely black. Sharp teeth extended from his gums as he smiled. I opened my mouth to unleash the scream building inside. He had me pressed to the tree before I could make a sound. I was stupid to come here. What did I hope to accomplish by following these men? No one would have believed me anyway and now I was going to die.

I could only hope my body wasn't desecrated the way Henry Wilkes's was. Agonizing pain ripped through me as those terrifying sharp teeth pierced my neck. With his hand pressed against my throat and his crushing weight pinning me to the tree, I felt my life draining as he suckled my neck.

Darkness crept into my vision, my limbs felt heavy and my heart slowed. I knew, despite the fog in my mind, there were only a few seconds left of my life. My heart would stop beating and I would die here in the woods. Perhaps my body would be ravaged by wild animals. It seemed a better alternative than having stakes driven into my corpse. So long as my soul was spared.

Just as the darkness was to completely engulf my vision he withdrew. My body felt like it weighed a thousand pounds as I hung limply in his arms. The monster pulled me from the tree and hurled me through the air. I landed in a tangled heap at the bottom of the grave. The last thing I heard before death finally took me were shouts of vampire *from the men I had followed.*

I collapsed against the table holding the few items. My hip slammed into the steel chair before my knees made contact with the floor. The cross fell from my hand. I clawed the vinyl until I felt the chain and grabbed hold of it before someone else picked it up. I couldn't shake the feeling there was something else I should have seen. I tried to call up the vision again but all I saw was the blackness of her death. It swamped my mind and weighed on my body. My breathing slowed.

I came to, cradled in Cash's arms on the floor in the interrogation room. Masarelli loomed over us. I knew he was fighting the urge to bark orders and demand answers. Maybe it had something to do with the alpha at my back. He handed Cash one of those paper cones from the cooler filled with ice cold water and waited for me to come all the way around.

Cash passed the cup to me and with slightly shaking hands I took a sip, and then another. Cash brushed the stray hair from my face and tucked it behind my ear. I felt weak and cold, like death himself reached through the veil to claim me like the girl in my vision.

I curled into the warmth of Cash's body and tried to ignore the inaudible sigh, the rise and fall of his chest that told me he was aware of the intimacy of the moment. I should protest the small circles he was rubbing on my back or to the soft whispers he didn't think I heard. If I wasn't so tired. So very tired...

The white walls of the interrogation room faded. I was back in the woods, but looking through my own eyes instead of a dead child's. I watched the men at the grave hammer a stake through the heart of the corpse. My heart pounded in time with each strike. I heard leaves rustling. Someone was behind me.

I moved around the tree, pressing my back against it, arms firmly at my sides, willing myself to disappear. I held my breath, made no sound but he knew I was there. He silently stalked around the tree and was on me before I screamed for help.

I looked into the eyes of my attacker. The longing gaze of a lover, replaced with the cold, hard stare of the predator I should have known he was all along. I wanted to ask him why. Why was he doing this? Wasn't it enough I had given myself to him? Why would he take by force what I would give freely if he had only asked?

My mouth moved, the questions perched on my lips but no sound came. Locked in his terrifying gaze I stayed when I should have run, my feet unresponsive to my silent screams for them to move.

I was a fool to love him. I saw that now and cursed my stupidity. It never made sense that he would fall in love with me but I was desperate enough to believe the lies. He was the spider and I the fly.

A few sweet words and tender caresses was all it took to ensnare me in his web. How easily I had become the prey. His fangs extended and my traitorous body responded despite knowing he didn't love me. I had secretly wanted this, to be his life blood. To give him the last piece of me, what I had never offered another. Something flickered in his eyes and I knew, even pressed against that tree, that he had no intention of drinking from me. He wanted nothing more than to be free of me. Aidan. His name came out in a rushed whisper as his hand pierced my chest and ripped out my heart. The last thing I saw was him squeezing what blood remained in the chambers into his mouth.

Thick, grey fog rolled around me and I sank into the familiar comfort of the between. I wouldn't be rejected here. Through the veil where realities were created, changed or simply left to unfold, I was rejuvenated. This was my seat of power, this world between worlds. I could stay here and build a new reality or I could focus on someone, something until I transported myself to that reality. I was more than the crumpled mass lying at the feet of my - well he obviously wasn't my anything, not anymore.

The heart ripped from my chest only moments ago beat steadily behind my unbroken sternum. Had my subconscious managed one last hurrah, whisking me away before the last drop of blood left my body? I felt my life slip away when Aidan tore out my heart but here I was - safe and sound in the between.

I focused on my father. I needed to know what the hell was going on. I put all of my energy into picturing him and where he was. I knew I was well and truly fucked when instead of Arawn, dressed in one of those tunics he loves so much, I saw Thomas Kincaide, my adoptive father. And no, he was not painting some whimsical cottage with a water wheel. He was pouring an eighty year old scotch and preparing for one of his famous "Maurin, you need to try harder to be normal" lawyerly speeches.

He was a respected and very well paid corporate attorney. The kind who helped big businesses dismantle small businesses. He was not the artist nor did he have an appreciation for the arts.

He looked at me over the rim of his glass, like he had a thousand times in high school. His eyes flicked left before focusing back on me as he slammed a scotch aged for appreciation not frat boy binge drinking. Like a deer sensing the hunter, I knew my adoptive mother was behind me. I looked down at my favorite worn pair of chucks, my Beastie Boys shirt. I fought the urge to squirm under the weight of her disappointment, fidgeting with the hem of my jean shorts.

It was the shirt that finally brought me out of the dream - out of what was obviously my subconscious mind's version of a horror show, like watching all five Saw movies back to back.

Now, that particular shirt had been washed and worn so many times the cotton was practically see through and shrunk to a size just above obscene given my abundance in cup size. I couldn't be wearing it because it was tucked neatly in my pajama drawer. Of course there was still the chance I was in fact dead. Being a teenager and living at home again could certainly qualify as hell.

I felt the fog of sleep receding, my heart beating, air

filling my lungs. I was definitely alive. And not in my own bed. My hand slid across sheets with a higher thread count than mine to find the other side of the bed thankfully cold and empty. My fingers found the butt of a gun that also wasn't mine under the unoccupied pillow. I palmed the grip as I tried to figure out whose bed I was in and what the last thing I remembered was.

I felt a headache coming. The more I tried to recall where I was before waking in a strange bed, the more my head hurt. At least it wasn't a gaping hole in my chest courtesy of my ex vampire boyfriend. And I didn't need a Freudian analysis to figure out what that dream was really about.

I smelled cedar, lime and the earthy scent belonging to Cash. If there was any doubt about my heart actually being ripped out, the hammering in my chest from that realization confirmed its whereabouts. Why was I in Cash's bed? And not wearing my jeans. While I contemplated all the painful ways I would make him tell me what happened, something tingled at the edge of my awareness. I was not alone in the room. It wasn't Cash. His scent was all over the sheets but not the cloying scent of an alpha wolf sitting a few feet away.

I pretended to be asleep on my side, tightened my grip on the gun under the pillow and tried to sense exactly where the other person in the room was. I had a thirty-three point three three percent chance of getting it right. In front of me--beyond the empty side of the bed, at the foot or behind my back which faced the rest of the room. Instinct and a pretty decent horror movie repertoire had me picking the last one.

Before I could contemplate the fact that the voyeur could have killed me while I slept, I rolled to my knees swinging the gun around in a move that would have been totally bad ass if not for the worst case of bed head in my entire life. I found my target and didn't bother lowering the Walther p99.

"The safety is still on."

"Easily remedied."

"Before I can disarm you?"

"Wanna find out if vampires are faster than a silver bullet?"

"Given the fact you are sleeping in a werewolf's bed," his eyes dropped to the black lace with strategically placed cotton that made up my boy shorts, "I highly doubt the bullet is silver."

"Funny, that's what makes me think they are. Not that it would have the desired effect on you. What are you doing here, Aidan?"

"I could ask you the same thing. Given your state of undress it seems your wolf was entirely truthful." His tone was entirely too accusatory for someone so willing to walk away from me. "Are you going to put the gun down?"

"He's not *my* wolf and I'm still thinking about it." Seeing Aidan sitting across from me was a little unnerving after the dream I just had. I fought the urge to rub my sternum and lowered the gun.

"Your wolf went to fetch your laptop, coffee and clean clothes from your apartment. He seemed to think you'd want a shower and your favorite blend before googling this latest problem to death."

"Stop calling him my wolf," I growled. "And why couldn't I do all of that from my apartment one flight up?"

"I think he enjoyed the idea of me finding you half naked in his bed with your scent clinging to his sheets." The jealousy darkening his gorgeous features hurt my already aching head and had my heart skipping a beat.

I flopped down on my back and slipped the gun under the pillow. "Why do I feel like I'm getting over a pandemic flu?"

"You've been out for eight hours, after you blacked out twice at SPTF. You..." He shook his head. "I can't... I need you to get out of his bed. I know you're exhausted but I can't stand the sight of you in just your underwear tangled in his sheets."

"I'm wearing a shirt and my bra." I gave a quick feel for confirmation. "Son of a bitch! How did he get my bra off?" I thought about making him uncomfortable a little while longer. He deserved it. Then I thought about how I would feel if I saw him in some other woman's bed, innocent or not and had one of those Kill Bill flashing red light, wee woo siren moments.

Once the red cleared and I could see straight again I decided he had suffered enough watching me toss and turn in Cash's bed, missing half my clothes- which Cash and I would discuss later.

I barely had both feet planted on the floor before Aidan had me crushed against him. He tucked my head under his chin and muttered something about wet dog before sniffing under my jaw. He brushed back my tangled hair and buried his face in my neck, his lips resting gently on my pulse. I felt him relax as he inhaled my scent. I tried to back up to get his face off my neck and understand what he was saying. I didn't know it was possible to be pressed this tightly against someone without merging into their body.

"I know you haven't been with him. His disgusting scent is all over you but it's faint. It's not in you."

"Umm, first eww. I don't think I want you to confirm if that meant what I think it means. And second, does he really smell disgusting to you because I think he kind of smells like cedar and lime, like the forest after a storm." He growled and if I didn't know better I would have thought he was a wolf too. "Right, sorry. Jealous vampire. Got it."

"Any man's scent on your body would disgust me." He feathered kisses down my neck while his hands crept lower on my back.

"I wouldn't have expected this reaction from someone who could just toss me aside like yesterday's garbage." I almost said *rip my heart out* but decided against it.

His hands froze below the waistline of my boy shorts. "I did not throw you away like a piece of trash. I was trying to keep you from getting hurt."

"Well guess what, I did get hurt. By you."

"I was trying to protect you, to keep you safe." He wasn't pawing me anymore but he didn't let go of me either. I think he was a little afraid of the increased pitch and decibel of my voice, which often led to flailing arms and flying objects.

"News flash, Neanderthal, you don't dump your

girlfriend to keep her safe. You stay firm--" My tirade was cut short by Aidan crushing his lips against mine. His tongue traced my bottom lip before prying its way into my mouth.

His cold touch set my skin on fire as he backed me against the wall, pinning my hands above my head with one hand. His free hand slipped under my shirt, over the curve of my hip toward my ribs. I gasped as he familiarized himself with my neck and his hand slid higher.

"I was wrong. Agrona was right, you were right. No matter what I do to prevent it, you will wind up involved and in danger. Like you always are. I was an idiot. From the first time I saw you, that night at Mahalia's, I knew. And then you gave me your blood. My fate was sealed with the first drop, a chuisle."

I shushed him. "Too much talking. You had me at *I was wrong.*" I hooked a leg around his hip, just as the front door opened. We both groaned and not in a good way.

Aidan let me go and nudged me toward the master bath. "Take a shower, it'll help."

"If you're referring to the olfactory onslaught, I doubt it." The front door slamming confirmed my statement.

"The olfactory onslaught will help the wolf remember you're mine but I was referring to the fact you're still not running at top speed. You'll feel better after a shower." He laid a gentle kiss on my temple.

"I'm feeling better already." And I meant it. I wasn't normally the needy, dependent kind of girl but Aidan cut me when he decided it was better for him to leave without so much as discussing it with me.

Hearing his admission that I drove him crazy, that he wanted me as much as I wanted him, did a lot to mend the wound. Hearing him say he was wrong practically had me undone. This did not mean I was trading in my sword for an apron to live in domesticated bliss with my vampire.

I traced a finger down his jaw, satisfied for now that he was my vampire again, before closing the bathroom door. I turned the hot water on and decided to stay in the shower until the pissing contest about to take place in Cash's kitchen was over, or the cold water drove me out.

VI
SIX

Cash had coffee waiting and my laptop fired up by the time I got out of the shower. I padded out of his bedroom barefoot in a pair of black yoga pants and the perfectly worn Beastie Boys shirt from my dream.

I knew Cash had simply thrown open a drawer and grabbed the first thing he saw but it still freaked me out. Not as much as the time he obviously spent picking out my underwear, however. No wonder I was dressed like I was going to clean my apartment instead of using my crime solving skills and general bad assery to figure out who was killing these girls. He spent the whole time in my apartment digging in my underwear drawer - because this set was definitely not on top.

I was surprised to see them both sitting at the kitchen table waiting for me without ice packs or bandages. They looked up when I came in, with similar expressions of possession and desire. The look Cash gave me was directly related to the matching black lace bra and panty set he picked out.

Aidan's was because he knew he would be the one to actually see me in them. Although this dammed shirt was thin enough to give Cash an idea of what he was missing. Actually that might explain why Aidan had a smug look on his face instead of fighting with Cash again.

The last time the three of us were together was at my sister's wedding reception. There was dancing, the silent declaration of both men's intentions, fighting. You know, the usual. I had been ignoring the strain on both of my relationships - friend and boyfriend - ever since. If nobody else was in the mood to discuss it tonight, I was happy to continue to ignore it.

I poured a cup of the Starbucks eighty-twenty blend, wishing Cash had grabbed my French Press too. I switched to a press a couple weeks after swearing off the Daily Grind, and was hooked. Of course the need to feed my caffeine addiction meant I would gnaw on coffee beans if that was my only option. Aidan slid my laptop to his side of the table while I mixed in the perfect amount of sugar and cream. It was obviously going to be one of those passive aggressive battles. This was going to be a long night.

I took a sip from my mug, relishing the taste of the magical brew, and thought about the best keywords for my search. My companions new better than to pester me with questions about passing out at the station or what I had seen when I held the necklace until after my second cup of coffee.

I would have to call Masarelli soon but he'd have to wait until after my refill and a little bit of googling. I needed something more substantial to tell him because *I saw a murder but it was like a hundred and fifty years ago and then I had a bad dream*, was not super helpful.

New England vampires would probably bring up a page of useless websites but I didn't have a better starting point. Imagine my surprise when the first thing to come up was a link to a newspaper article and the History Channel's website for a corresponding show based on its findings. I started with the article.

1892 Exeter, RI- Mysterious illness claimed life of nineteen year old Mercy Brown and her mother. When it appeared her brother was doomed to suffer the same fate, Mercy's body was exhumed. Upon examination, doctors discovered pink flesh, longer hair and nails than the girl was known to have in life and she was subsequently deemed a vampire. Her heart was cut out, burned and the ashes fed to her brother who died two months later.

1896 Willington, CT- Dr. Grant, deemed a snake oil salesman by modern medicine, sent a letter to editor of local paper offering a cure for vampirism. According to Dr. Grant, to determine if the recently departed had indeed become a vampire, one should look for vines growing through the grave site. If vines had over taken the grave, the remains should be dug up and burned. Upon hearing word of Dr. Grant's advice, Isaac Johnson dug up his two children, Amos and Elizabeth, and performed the cure.

19th Century Griswold, CT- in an undated and relatively unmarked grave researchers discovered grisly remains of who they affectionately call J.B., the only thing etched into the tombstone. Upon examination it was determined that the head had been posthumously removed and placed in the grave facing west. All of the ribs were broken and the femur bones crossed over the torso to form an X- the symbol for death. With no full name, or written record of anyone with the initials J.B. living in Griswold, it may never be determined who this person was and why his remains were desecrated.

Researchers now believe the rampant fear of a vampire den living in New England during the late 1800s was in fact a wide spread infection of tuberculosis. Symptoms of fatigue, pale skin, coughing up blood -which often left the sick with blood on the corners of their mouths- was cannon fodder for the superstitious, leading to the belief that vampires had invaded and corrupted their communities.

Damn. Interesting but not very helpful. Aidan had been reading the article as well and went sort of rigid when he got to the end.

"Tell me what you saw that made you search for this?"

"I didn't search for this. I searched for vampires in New England."

"Maurin." Aidan's tone said he wasn't in the mood for games. "That would have garnered all sorts of ridiculous results. Why this article? What about it called to you?"

I spun the laptop around so Cash could see what we were talking about before I answered him. "It felt like the right time period. I got something from the necklace, from a girl but not the right girl. I was hoping I could make some sense of what I saw before I talked to Masarelli."

Aidan's hand clasped mine. "Tell me what you saw."

I told them both in vivid detail about my reading from the necklace. Cash looked confused. Aidan looked stricken.

"Mercy Brown."

It was a whisper but I heard it. My stomach dropped. I gave Cash a cursory glance to see if he was keeping up but he just shrugged. I squeezed Aidan's hand, prompting him to continue.

"She wasn't dead when he threw her into that grave. They thought he killed her but while the townspeople were out looking for him he came back to finish the job. I think he may have actually loved her."

He was there. He didn't need to read the article. Aidan saw it firsthand. He wasn't newly turned, of course I knew that but I'd never really seen him as anything beyond the thirty year old man he appeared to be. We spent a lot of time getting to know each, our likes and dislikes but as he told us about Mercy Brown I realized how seldom he talked about his past.

For the first time I was getting more than a glimpse of Aidan's history, of the events that shaped the vampire I had grown to love. I had a million questions that I knew would break the spell Aidan seemed to be under. I needed to let him tell the story on his own.

"She rose the next night with an insatiable thirst and no comprehension of what she had become. He warned her not to go but she was afraid. Of him. Afraid of the monster she realized he was and what she had become. She went to the only place she felt safe, home. Her brother was there and she succumbed to her thirst. She drained him. Once her blood lust was sated the reality of what she was, what she had done lay like a withered husk at her feet. He found her muttering about the devil and her soul while rocking her brother's corpse and took her back to his home. He would never save her. Not that night or the night the necromancer came.

"Mercy was not the first he sired, not after centuries of walking the Earth. He was insane, a tyrant in life and no better in undeath. I think he thought she could save him. Instead he spent the next four years keeping her from walking into the sun.

"I was there waiting, watching. Dr. Grant was no doctor. He was a necromancer, hired by Willington to rid their community of the demons hiding among them." He laughed. "Demons, if they only knew they truly existed, but we were terrifying enough."

I didn't miss the fact he said *we* and wondered what Aidan had done to include himself. Cash apparently heard it as well and gave me a *fucking vampires* look. I gave him a swift kick in the shin under the table. I held my breath, afraid even the sound of air filling my lungs would bring him back to the present and the story to an end.

"He shouldn't have left her alone but he had no choice. There was no one to look after her. He slaughtered every vampire he recently sired. At first I thought he did it to save himself, even back then I had a reputation. His little nest had drawn far too much attention from the town and the infamous Dr. Grant. Years later I understood why he destroyed his line.

"He wanted no evidence of the true monster he was for Mercy to find. For their lives to be untouched by the ferocious vampires he had created in his likeness. So when she refused to hunt, the only thing he could do was bring blood to her. Grant discovered his identity and sought him out. Perhaps it was a rare lucid moment or a shred of her humanity responding to a familiar task that made her open the door- either way, it was to be her end.

"I should have intervened, stopped the necromancer but I thought it would be an entertaining way for my task to be completed. So I waited. I watched Grant work until the horrific acts were too much for even me to witness. Do you know why we hate them, why most vampires fear them?"

I wasn't sure if I was actually supposed to answer. He looked at me expectantly, like he already knew what I was going to say and it would be wrong. "Because they can raise the dead, they can control us.

"Not just control our minds but our flesh and bone. Grant tortured her, breaking bones, tearing flesh as fast as she healed it. Until her lack of feeding and blood loss finally took its toll. And still he did not kill her.

"Unable to stomach more I intervened. I think he would have left her that way, unrecognizable, unable to feed or heal herself but unable to die. I had Grant by the throat, ready to finish him, when Gaius came back with a young man no more than fifteen years of age in tow and under his thrall.

"At the sight of his beloved, distorted and disfigured beyond repair, he became enraged. A newly made vampire in the throes of a blood lust could not hold a candle to the vampire charging toward us. I had gotten lazy and over confident, I didn't know the history then. I knew this vampire was old but that didn't necessarily mean strong. He was using a different name. I had no idea who I was up against until he hit me.

"He didn't bother to ask who was responsible for what had been done to Mercy, he'd see us both dead. What he didn't know was that Grant was a necro. Pain racked Gaius's body and he crumpled to the floor. With power unlike any I had seen in his kind before, Grant held him, writhing on the floor and focused on me.

"Never faced a vampire immune to necromancy before, he stumbled when I stepped toward him. I grabbed him by the lapels and wasted no time draining him of his power and blood with the screams of a no longer enthralled young man in my ears.

"Weakened and vulnerable from the effects of Dr. Grant, Gaius could no longer control the mind of the young man so I was left to deal with the human. I turned to him, my shirt stained and no doubt mouth red with blood. Some things cannot be wiped away. I picked him up and did my best to ignore the fact he had soiled himself. I let the blood call to the predator within me and feasted upon the young man.

"After making myself presentable and locking up my charge, I found the pastor. I brought him the now decapitated body of the young man and proclaimed he was a vampire. The parents protested but their young daughter was already showing signs of tuberculosis. The blood stains around her mouth were enough to convince their father, Isaac Johnson. We burned and buried the Johnson boy, and young Elizabeth followed a week later.

"Dr. Grant was buried with his head facing west, ribs broken, femurs crossed in the shape of an X, as was the custom for necromancers, under an incomplete marker bearing the letters J B and nothing more."

"But what about the vampire? What happened to him," I asked, feeling like a child being told a terrifying bed time story.

"I brought Gaius Caligula Caesar before the Council. Agrona planned to make him personally responsible for Mercy's care for all of their unnaturally long lives but the other members, even Kedehern, demanded release for the innocent girl forced to become a vampire. Caligula was made to take her to meet the sun. He stayed with her longer than he should have. It took years to heal the burns."

"Where is he now? I need to talk to him."

Cash had been busy, his fingers flying over the keys on the laptop. "I think we should all have a history lesson before we talk to this guy."

"He's our only lead. We *are* talking to him."

Cash swung the laptop around and tapped the screen. "I didn't say we weren't, just that you should gather your intel first. You need to know who you're dealing with in order to know how to negotiate."

"I'm not a noob, in case you forgot, I used to interrogate people for a living. This is what I know how to do."

"And how's that been going for you lately? Because I kind of remember picking you up off the floor today only to have you pass out again in my arms." Cash didn't even glance at Aidan. He didn't have to. He hit his target.

I needed to figure out a way to stop this love triangle before it got started. Ignoring the problem would only make it worse. I had to talk to Cash. He deserved to hear it from me and I was going to tell him. As soon as we found the missing girls and our killer.

"I think that's because the girl was dead. I don't do so well with dead things." I closed my eyes. It was too late to take it back.

"That's what I've been trying to tell you." Cash gave me a wink and leaned back in his chair.

"Ah, yes. You'd much prefer she shopped at Pet Smart, in the werewolf section, no doubt." Aidan glared at him.

Ready to get the conversation back on track I started reading aloud from the profile Cash pulled up on Caligula from the Council's files. "This can't be right. Gaius Julius Caesar? Like ancient Rome? That would mean he's..." I tried to do the math.

"Incredibly old and powerful. Which is why we are going to be sure he is involved before we barge in with guns blazing." I wasn't sure why Aidan was looking at me when he said that. Okay, maybe I deserved it a little.

"The necklace is enough to connect him to at least one of the girls. We have to talk to the crazy bastard." Cash slid his chair closer so we could both look at the file. "Scroll down. See if there's an address."

"I said he was crazy not stupid. The words are not interchangeable. He has not seen two millennia of sunsets by being the village idiot. And despite his past transgressions he is well received in vampire communities today, even the Council seems to have forgotten the incident in Willington. Though I doubt he has."

"So what's your plan? You want to invite him over for dinner and see if it comes up in casual conversation? How've you been Caligula? Things are good. I've been draining girls and leaving them in their bathtubs. Would you please pass the o-neg?" Cash grabbed the mouse.

I couldn't help it, I laughed. For some reason I pictured Caligula in a toga, complete with sandals and olive branch crown sitting at my kitchen table. Aidan didn't seem amused. Maybe if I described the whole toga and sandals thing, nope even then he wouldn't have seen the ridiculousness of it.

"Do you trust me?"

I wasn't sure if that was a trick question. Did I trust him? With everything but my heart. I was happy he had come to his senses and that we were back on. Still, it was going to be a while before I stopped wondering if he was going to find another reason why walking away was better than being together.

"Yes." It was the only answer I could give but we all heard the hesitation in my voice. I saw the pain in Aidan's eyes and then the determination to undo the damage to our relationship. Cash sat back content to let Aidan set himself up. I sat up a little straighter and tried to convince everyone I meant what I said. "What do you have in mind?"

"Can you get us into the morgue?"

VII
SEVEN

"This is a terrible idea, Aidan." I hated being in the morgue.

"You said you trusted me."

"I do, but you weren't here when I tried this previously. It kind of cemented the fact that I can't read dead people," I whined. During that whole debacle, I attempted to read a dead witch, whose hands and tongue had been cut off. Needless to say, it didn't go well.

"Not to mention I had an appointment to be here last time. You didn't tell me we were breaking in."

"We're not breaking in. We're sneaking in."

"Semantics. I don't think the police will see much of a difference. I'm warning you, Aidan, it was really bad last time."

"The reason is there's too much death in a morgue for you to be effective. Your power is centered in the living world. You need to connect with someone whose power isn't."

"How do you know that?"

"Cash can't keep the technician distracted for long and Conry can't remain in his ethereal form forever. We don't have much time. I promise I'll explain later."

"Aidan." I hoped that one word conveyed the trouble he was in if he didn't answer me.

"You're not going to do anything until I tell you are you?" He pinched the bridge of his nose and sighed. "I was doing research about the Kellen factor and sort of stumbled across it. I was hoping to confirm it with your father."

"And you were going to tell me this when exactly?"

"I found out around the time Agrona told me they thought you'd outgrown your position as liaison and were considering making you a permanent part of my team. I just haven't had a chance to tell you."

"Oh I understand, not a minute to spare. You've been so busy making decisions and planning my life. How could you possibly find the time to discuss any of it with me?"

"Maurin, please. I'm happy to let you berate me for something I have already apologized for, after we find out if Caligula truly is involved. Personally I find it a little too convenient for the necklace to be found among the girls belongings."

"We're definitely not done talking about this, you can bet on that. And for the record, you apologized for dumping me without having the decency to talk to me about it. This? This is a completely separate mistake. That requires its own apology. And groveling. Lots of groveling. You know, you've been around a long time; I expected you to be way better at this relationship shit."

"Indeed. I can't help it. I lose the ability to think clearly where you're concerned." He pulled me into his arms but I didn't give in to the embrace. Well, not right away. "Are you ready to give this a try?"

"Just tell me you didn't call Kellen." The fact that Aidan wanted to confirm anything with Arawn told me everything I needed to know about the Kellen factor. He kissed the top of my head, before walking down the hallway to the emergency exit and pushing on the bar to open it. "I'm warning you, if Kellen walks through that door I'm staking you at sunrise."

When I saw who walked in I almost wished he had called Kellen. Graive came through the door with Oberon in tow, their hands clasped. Well weren't they just the picture of perfect coupledom. I fought the urge to roll my eyes.

I had gotten over the fact that Mahalia - former high priestess and convicted attempted murderer - convinced Oberon to pursue me romantically to ensure my allegiance and the coven's seat on the Council. Graive had obviously gotten over the fact that he broke things off with her to do it.

But we were all far from friends. I was still kind of hung up on the "killing me by demon" plot Mahalia concocted. The Council was convinced of their innocence in Mahalia's master plan but I was pretty sure if Graive knew about it she wouldn't have done anything to stop it. I think we all agreed Oberon's ethics were questionable at best. The coven's blind loyalty to Mahalia was why I had avoided them since her incarceration with the fae. That and some of her coven loyalists decided to shun me.

Amalie slipped through the door just before it closed and I was actually happy to see her. I knew she didn't have anything to do with Mahalia's plans. She declared it often enough and I was being a royal bitch by lumping her in with the rest of them. I thought about what Cash said and how she had stuck up for me twice in the Daily Grind, even if it meant the shunning extended to her. I walked over, gave her a hug, and whispered an apology for being such a jerk in her ear. She squeezed back before letting go and wiped a gloved hand over her eyes.

Aidan grabbed my hand and led me into the morgue ahead of the others. "I thought you could use a friendly face tonight."

"It's a good thing I wanted to mend my friendship with Amalie or I might be a little pissed about you and Cash meddling like two old ladies." I gave him a little nudge in the ribs to let him know I was teasing but he seemed to be brooding over the fact that Cash had also made the effort to save an important relationship in my life. "Let's get this over with."

Aidan nodded to Graive and she stood next to the wall of steel drawers. Her fingers just barely grazed the surface, the temperature dropping as her power oozed out seeking the right body.

She stopped, palming the face of a drawer before pulling it open. The track on the drawer clicked as it extended to expose the girl sealed in the body bag. There was no point checking the tag on the outside of the bag to confirm it matched the one on her toe, we knew this was the right girl. I reached for the zipper, expecting my hand to shake. My nerves held up as I undid the zipper and folded the top of the bag over.

This girl didn't even look like a corpse. There weren't the typical signs of trauma when homicide is suspected, just her slightly upturned slit wrists. Looked like the diener already weighed, washed and taken samples from her body for the coroner.

Her brown hair was combed and tucked neatly beneath her head. Obviously, the medical examiner hadn't performed the autopsy yet. Lividity, a purple discoloration from blood in the body settling, was absent from her body. She had been completely drained. She looked more like a porcelain doll than a dead body.

Graive grabbed my wrist, avoiding the palm of my hand and reached for the girl. I thought she would take the girl's hand but instead she placed her index and middle finger over the cut in her wrist like she was checking for a pulse. I was seriously hoping we weren't reanimating another corpse. The last time Graive did, the zombie's head got blown off. That might be a little hard to explain to the ME.

There wasn't the telltale moaning and groaning of the waking dead. Instead a rush of images flooded my mind:

The girl at the movies with her friends, glancing to the

shadow in the corner of the lobby.

Alone in the college library, checking behind bookcases where she was certain she had seen someone.

At a local sandwich shop, peering out the window at the street lamp to catch a glimpse of the person standing there.

I gasped in unison with the girl in my mind's eye as fangs pierced the sensitive skin on her inner thigh. Strong hands kneaded her flesh, careful not to bruise. Her back arched and I fought the urge to do the same. I clamped my jaw shut to prevent mimicking her moans of pleasure while feeding her vampire. Holy hell.

The teen knew what he was and wasn't afraid. The pleasure switched abruptly to pain but not how I would have expected. The vamp walked away. The girl's crumpled expression, her arms folded as she tried to stop the sobs that racked her body.

I watched the vampire turn as if to give the girl a glimmer of hope, only to snuff it out forever as he moved away faster than her eyes could follow. She fell to the ground, utterly destroyed. Something moved in her peripheral. Was he back, had he changed his mind? Hope sprung eternal in the young girl's chest for the return of her vampire and the promise of immortality. She turned and let out a terrifying scream, which now poured from my mouth.

Graive let go of us, breaking the triangle of power. I swayed, exhausted from reading the dead girl. Graive on the other hand hadn't so much as broken a sweat. She channeled my abilities through the dead but the energy expelled to make it work had come from me. Aidan wrapped an arm around my waist and I leaned into him. I heard Conry barking and knew we were out of time.

A voice came from outside the door. "You're not with the paper. That was Ed Clancy, homicide reporter at the Times, on the phone and he's never heard your name. You can't go back there. I'm calling Detective Masarelli. Hey man, call off your dog." The technician was in a panic.

I glared at Aidan. "The paper? Really?"

"We needed to gain access to their files, or at least see what they knew and if any identifying marks had been found by the diener."

I gave a whistle for Conry -he probably wouldn't listen to Cash's command to back-off if he thought the technician was a threat. "Aidan, do you're vampire Jedi mind trick and wipe this disaster of a reconnaissance mission from his mind. If you wanted to see the files I could have gotten them from Masarelli."

"Masarelli won't be getting a copy of the files."

I pointed Aidan toward the guy manning the morgue. "We'll talk about that later."

With the morgue attendant taken care of, we settled on going back to my apartment. All of us. Fun, right? Not. My apartment overflowed with head strong, powerful sups. The air was thick with magic and attitude. I opened the window behind the couch so I could breathe.

When we left the morgue I sent Amalie to raid the Daily Grind. I wished she'd hurry up because I seriously needed to feed my addiction and there wasn't enough coffee in my pantry to do it. Plus, I wanted croissants. I needed protein after a reading like that but right now it was all about comfort.

I couldn't quite shake the sadness I felt from the girl. Maybe because it brought back feelings I had when Aidan said he was leaving, outside the station. For a second I wondered if I had made the right decision to trust him.

As if sensing my thoughts, he looked at me. Something in my expression must have given me away. He dropped his gaze but I caught the disappointment in his eyes. I refused to feel guilty for my wavering emotions. No, Aidan and I were definitely not out of the woods yet.

Cash caught the exchange. Thankfully Amalie hit the buzzer for the door just then. Cash helped her with what I declared essential items to solving our case, but I caught the look in his eye as he brushed past me.

"One thing's for certain," I said around a mouth full of croissant. "We know Caligula is involved, was involved with the girl."

"I thought you knew that before going to the morgue."

I glared at Graive as she mumbled something about it being a waste of her time. I may not have been sure if Caligula killed these girls, but I knew for certain she was still a bitch. "Now we know he knew her and that the necklace wasn't a plant. It's enough to get us an audience with him."

"*We* aren't going to talk to him. *I* am."

Everyone backed out of the kitchen. Everyone but Aidan. He glowered, daring me to argue with him. "*You're* not going anywhere near him."

"Like hell I'm not. I. Am. Going. With. You. End of conversation." He obviously hadn't learned anything. Not that I should expect someone as old as him to change his ways in a couple days. Old dogs, new tricks and all that. Still his attempt to order me around kind of undermined his apology.

He grabbed my arm when I moved to storm out of the kitchen and gently shoved me in one of my chairs. He fired up my laptop. The anger and frustration in his eyes had me glued to my seat. His fingers flew across the keys ferociously before he spun it around. Mercy Brown's face stared at me.

"Notice anything?" When I didn't answer, he bellowed, "Look at her!"

The others started to creep back in the kitchen to see who I was supposed to be looking at. I heard the collective breath but refused to acknowledge what they thought they saw.

"I mean it's not identical or anything but the resemblance is there," Amalie whispered. Realizing the fragility of my emotional state and our recent reconciliation, she quickly covered her mouth to prevent further outbursts.

More pictures flashed across the screen. A slide show of pictures he found online of the victims. All of them having some physical attribute in common with Mercy Brown. The slant of the eye, the curve of the mouth, bone structure but none of them had as many similarities in appearance as I did.

I knew where Aidan was going with this but I would

not be deterred. He thought it put me in danger. I was convinced it would give me an edge. The fact they all looked a little like Mercy Brown was enough to have the Council charge him. I was going to make this vampire confess to murdering these girls and then watch him meet the sun.

"Maurin."

"Don't Maurin me. I'm going."

Amalie stepped up. "Take Graive with you." If the elbow to the ribs Oberon gave her was any indication, she was going to regret that suggestion.

"That's not a bad idea actually," Cash said.

"No, it's a fantastic idea. Why hadn't I thought of it?" Cash lost the smug expression as Aidan went on a rant. "I'm sure he'll take one look a Maurin - the spitting image of his dead lover - with a necro and the vampire who took him before the council and invite us all in for a drink. From the vein most likely. He has slain more necros than any other vampire. Bringing Graive will only incite his hatred for me and stir his passion for a long lost love. It would be a bloody disaster. Literally."

"Hey, fuck off, fanger. If you had killed him the first time five girls wouldn't be dead and Maurin wouldn't be at risk of being kidnapped by some sick fuck bloodsucker."

I moved between them before a fight broke out in my cramped kitchen. Nothing, not the cabinets, the fridge or my new gas stove would survive them. "You're assuming the worst will happen, Aidan. Maybe we can use the fact I look so much like her to get him to talk."

"No, I won't risk it. He's stronger now than he was

the first time I met him. If he is on a killing spree, he will meet the sun but I won't give him the chance to use you as leverage."

"I can go without you." If he wouldn't listen to reason, I wasn't going to listen to anymore of his misogynistic bullshit. I backed away, pulling the veil around me.

Aidan felt the shift in my power and grabbed me before I disappeared. "Damn it, woman. I am only trying to keep you safe? Why won't you let me protect you?"

"Because you're idea of protecting me is locking me away in a tower."

"That's not a bad idea actually." Acutely aware of my blood pressure rising, he gave in before my head exploded. "You will wear my mark when we speak to him. This is not negotiable."

I heard of weres marking their mate but not vampires. Did fang marks really look that different? I guess if you can be identified by dental records in life, you could be in undeath. I wasn't exactly sure how I felt about being marked. Again.

I still bore a demon's mark branded into my neck. The fact I was having any reservations probably meant I shouldn't do it. Strings were definitely attached. Cash saw me warring with the decision and was about to object. I think he knew a little more about the commitment than I did and had reasons beyond my uncertainty for stopping it. I squared my shoulders and stepped forward before he could talk me out of it.

"Fine. I'll wear your mark."

VIII
EIGHT

"I would be a liar if I said I hadn't thought about giving you my mark. This wasn't what I had in mind." Aidan paced the floor at the foot of my bed.

"I've never been big on flowers but I think I have a bottle of wine if it makes you feel better."

We were alone for the first time in days. Everyone had gone home. There was nothing to do until the next sunset - except for Aidan to mark me. I was on the bed, leaning back on my elbows, watching him wear a path in the carpet.

"You didn't even question the mark or what it means. You just agreed. You only said yes because you want to challenge Caligula." Frustrated, he ran a hand through his hair.

"You want me to wear your mark, I want to question Caligula. Isn't this a win win?" My fingers were going numb so I sat up.

"Did it ever occur to you that I would want you to want to wear my mark?" He tugged at his hair again. "Christ, did that even make sense?"

"Okay, maybe you should explain this whole marking thing to me after all." I reached for him. "Aidan."

He stopped pacing and looked at me. "Now you want to know what it means? Second thoughts? Good, because I don't want you anywhere near Caligula."

"I am not having second thoughts. I would like to know why you are freaking out."

"I do not freak out. I am the Cleaner, a highly trained and deadly assassin. I. Do. Not. Freak. Out."

I waved a hand, gesturing to his pacing and waited for his behavior to sink in. He was *so* freaking out.

"It means you are mine."

"Wh, what?" I cleared my throat, my mouth suddenly dry. "Like your wife? Holy shit! Did I unwittingly agree to some kind of vampire marriage ritual? No wonder Cash wanted to stop me. Damn it, when am I going to learn?" I was too busy berating myself to hear the growl forming in Aidan's throat.

"Don't make him the hero when his reasons for stopping you were selfish."

"He's my..." I was about to say Cash was my friend and for that reason alone he wouldn't want me making a decision without all the information but the look in Aidan's eyes stopped me cold.

"He's your what? What is he to you exactly?" He was trying and failing to reign in his jealousy.

I wasn't sure what answer would upset him the least so I remained silent. Big mistake.

His eyes burned with so many emotions- anger, confusion, hurt. "This is about us, not the wolf," he yelled.

I didn't bother to tell him that if he kept yelling it was probably going to be all about the wolf since Cash could no doubt hear him. I cringed at the thought of Cash rejoicing in the fact that he was suddenly the topic of conversation while Aidan and I were in my bedroom.

Aidan caught my movement and mistook it for something else. He dropped to his knees in front of me. "I'm sorry. I shouldn't have yelled at you." He raised a hand to cup my face. "I just, I don't know if my mark will even be enough. If something happens to you..." he rested his forehead on mine.

"You've lived through worse than the prospect of losing me." I brushed the barest of kisses across his lips.

He pulled back, slipping a finger under my chin and raising my head until our eyes met. "I would not survive it." I tried to look away, anywhere but his eyes, it was too intense- like he was examining my soul. "Before you say it, let me make something perfectly clear. If leaving you ensured you would not be involved, I would have done it because it meant you would live.

"I would be a miserable bastard without you. I'd leave a trail of blood and ash in my wake but I would have left because I could rest during the day knowing you were out there somewhere raising hell. But your death? I would not survive it. And I am afraid because for the first time in centuries I have something to lose. My god woman, what have you done to me?"

Before I answered his mouth crashed into mine. Aidan pushed us back onto the bed, his lips never leaving mine. His tongue demanded entrance and I opened to deepen the kiss. He was so close, holding his body mere inches from mine with an arm on both sides of my head.

My chest brushed against his. Wrapping a leg around him I closed the distance and pressed our bodies together. I let out a small moan and he growled before devouring my mouth again. I wanted this, wanted him. He released my swollen lips, trailing kisses down my neck, over my scar and then stopped.

"Aidan, if you stop now I am going to open every curtain, every blackout shade in this apartment and welcome the sun while you sleep."

"I would like nothing more than to erase this, the memory of this, before marring your perfect body with another mark. So many have already tried to claim you. The coven, a demon, even your own magic is marking you and now I would force you to do the same."

"You're not forcing me to do anything. Tell me about the mark, Aidan," I said with a sigh knowing even my threat of turning him to ash would not sway him from this train of thought.

He rolled off me and collapsed on his back. "Servus non habet personam - a slave has no personality. In the beginning it was used simply to mark feeders. A brand, like ranchers marking cattle, we marked our property much the same way." He raised a hand to stop the flood of protests he knew was coming at the mention of property. "We haven't had blood slaves for centuries but there are some who still see the mark as a sign of ownership. Very few marks are given nowadays.

"With the awareness of vampires, blood banks and the endless lines of willing donors there isn't a threat of losing your food supply. In modern times it has come to mean something else. Yes, you still belong to me but I don't own you. You are under my protection, and the protection of my line. It is seen as a sign of value, with or without romantic attachments. If a vampire marks someone today it means they are important. It is given with respect. With love. It can elevate the bearer above all others in the vampire's line."

"How many people bear your mark?" Jealousy worming into my head warred with the calm I forced into my voice. Why was I afraid to hear the answer?

"None."

"None? Surely there was someone, in all your years there must have been at least one?"

"None. I have satisfied every need, every desire. Fed from them, bedded them but not once in my existence has someone stirred a passion in me so strong that I want to give them my mark."

"But you've thought about it with me?"

"I have thought of little else lately."

I was through talking, thinking. Pulling my hair back, I exposed my neck to him. His lips brushed the sensitive unmarked skin on my left side before his fangs pierced my neck.

Desire -spread through my body like wild fire, my back arched and he slipped an arm beneath me pressing our bodies together. With each pull on my vein Aidan brought me closer to the edge. Every nerve ending, every cell in my body was engulfed in the flames of our passion.

Before I begged for release he poured all his feelings for me into the connection. Emotions swirled with pleasure overwhelming my senses until he took us over the cliff. I wanted to scream his name and weep with joy at the same time. He withdrew his fangs as aftershocks racked my body. Instead of licking the small wounds to heal them, he busied himself with kissing my collar bone and lapping up the blood that pooled there.

Rolling onto his back he pulled me on top of him. Aidan took me to heights I had never known but I needed more. I wanted to make him feel the same things, make him writhe with desire until he screamed my name. The wounds barely seeping, I stood and did my best to ignore the dizziness. I didn't want him to stop me out of fear he'd taken too much blood.

After making a tantalizing show of removing the rest of my clothes, I slowly undressed my vampire, trailing kisses over newly exposed skin. Suddenly in touch with a seductress I never knew existed within me, I pushed him back onto the bed. I crawled slowly across him, every inch of our bodies touching.

His hands slid down my thighs, kneading, gripping. My own desire building again, pooling almost painfully inside, I wouldn't be able to tease him much longer. I gave myself to him completely for the first time, taking us both over the edge as he moaned my name.

IX
NINE

I was well into my second cup of coffee when I called Masarelli. Something occurred to me while I was in the shower. Aidan said Masarelli wasn't getting the coroner's report. Why? Was he off the case already and if so, I needed to know more about who was in charge. We weren't going to see Caligula until after sundown. I had plenty of time to find out what was going on with SPTF.

He answered on the third ring. "It's about fucking time you checked in. I've had brass on my ass since your little blackout. You gonna tell me what happened?"

Shit. I pinched the bridge of my nose and braced myself for the words I was about to speak. "You're right." I cleared my throat, fighting the gag. It was physically painful to admit Masarelli was right about anything. "I should have checked in."

There was a thud, then silence. "Hello? Masarelli, you still there?" Maybe I gave him a heart attack.

"Sorry, dropped my phone. I thought I heard you say I was right."

"I'm not saying it again. Do you want to hear what I have to tell you or not?"

"And there's the Maurin we all know and loathe. Yeah, what have you got?"

"I got something off the necklace but not from Caroline Sousa. It was old, really old. It didn't make sense at first. I mean how did the girl get it and why wasn't there any residual memories from Caroline?"

It was weird to use her real name. I usually preferred to keep it as impersonal as possible. They were bodies, never people. I don't think I would have made it three years with SPTF, seeing the things I'd seen, if I let myself make a connection to each victim.

I knew it wasn't like that for Masarelli and he probably wouldn't appreciate me referring to her as the girl or the body. And if I wanted to get under Caligula's skin tonight I would need to say her name repeatedly. I needed to get comfortable with the words.

"Isn't that your area of expertise? Maybe she got it at a yard sale or something and hadn't worn it yet."

"Maybe or maybe it's misdirection."

"What the hell is that supposed to mean? Stop talking nonsense. I don't want to hear what you think you know. Tell me what you actually do know."

"If you're going to be a dick, maybe I should talk to the person in charge of the case. We both know that's not you anymore."

He cursed my name and just about everything else. "How'd you find out?"

"So it's true, you're off the case? Aidan said something about it but I didn't think they would have done it."

"I'm not off the case. I'm just not running it anymore or SPTF for that matter. Sent in some big shot fed to take over."

"So they know about your suspicions? That it's some sort of rogue?" I was hoping to use Masarelli to reign in the Norms. Stop the interference before it really got started. A massive search party involving every branch of police in the state for the two missing girls was bad enough. I didn't need them getting in the way of catching Caligula. We'd hand him over to the Council and figure out exactly what to do about the Norms afterward.

"Yeah, but it hasn't left the new chief's office. He's got a call into the Council already. Since we found those two girls and nobody else has turned up dead, things have settled down a little."

"You mean they're alive?"

"One of them anyway. She decided to take off with her Southie boyfriend without telling anyone and the other, well seems the reason she was able to work two jobs to pay her way through school and still make the grades were the daily doses of Adderall and Ritalin. Combine the weight loss and insomnia from the drugs with her previously undiagnosed heart condition and you get a dead college student. She was already DOA when she got to Mass Gen. She didn't have any ID on her so it took a while to figure out who she was and contact her next of kin."

"That's something to be thankful for."

"A person dying, no matter the circumstances, is nothing to be thankful for, Kincaide."

"I can think of a few circumstances where I might be more than thankful someone died but I was talking about the fact our rogue has stopped killing."

"There is something seriously fucking wrong with you."

"Probably. I'll see you and the new chief later."

"Don't threaten me." He laughed.

"You said he had a call into the Council. Who do you think is going to answer it? Like I said, I'll see you later." I hung up before he could come back with another comment.

So a former fed was running SPTF now. That could seriously complicate things. What if he didn't want the Council handling Caligula? The last thing we needed was a crazy serial killer vampire paraded in front of the media and the very public trial that would go along with it. Agrona better have a plan to contain this or we were all going to be in deep shit.

I slapped a pb and j together and settled in front of my laptop. I was glad I wolfed down the sandwich before I got too deep in Caligula's file, otherwise I would have lost my appetite.

Keeping the sandwich down was a challenge. His rule of the Roman Empire was one thousand four hundred days of torture, murder and sexual depravity - some of those happened at the same time. Bet the Senate regretted plotting and then executing his murder only to have him come back as a vampire. Not that I could understand who would actually want a guy who literally fed people to lions and slept with his sister to live forever.

Before I got to the section on his undeath, my father appeared, looking none too happy with me.

"Daughter."

Conry licked Arawn's hand before settling at his feet. "You have kept me waiting. Again."

I dropped my head. Damn it. I totally forgot about meeting with him. "Sorry. You obviously know why I wasn't able to make it."

"Obviously. I had expected you to contact me when you were released. I've felt you in the between twice since then and neither time did you reach out to me."

"I said sorry. I am, okay?" God, it felt like I was apologizing all the time lately. I wasn't any better at it though, practice was not making perfect in this case. "Do you know what's been going on? I mean why I haven't gotten back to you?"

"I am aware of the mortals' deaths. Among other things."

"Like the runes on my door?"

He raised a brow. "Show me."

He examined the door frame, scrutinizing every mark scrawled into the wood. "Looks like Fae handy work to me."

"What?" I shrieked. "You mean Kellen? He knows

where I live? How does he know where I live?" Arawn gave me an incredulous look. "Did he followed me through the between?" I cursed myself for being so stupid. Aidan was going to flip when I told him.

"He could easily follow you in the between but I was referring to someone else. Don't worry, dear, if he wanted to harm you, he wouldn't have bothered with the runes. It seems you've piqued the hunter's interest."

"Fantastic. Just what I need. Another admirer."

"Yes, you seem to have more than your share of suitors. Still, having gained his attention will help you in your lessons."

"My what?"

"The hunter has agreed to teach you how to defend yourself from fae magic. We are not the only ones who can move through the between, you know."

"Actually, no I don't know. You and Aidan never tell me anything. Who is this hunter?"

"All the more reason for you to train with him. I don't recall his first name. But Hunter is more than a surname. It is what he does. After centuries with the Wild Hunt we stopped calling him anything but Hunter."

When I groaned and flopped myself onto the couch in a rare but totally justified grown up temper tantrum, he conceded to postpone the training until after I had wrapped up my murder case.

"But you will train with him. You will learn to master the between and your powers under his skillful hand. Worse things than Kellen could follow you home through the between. The wolf is at the door."

While I was trying to figure out where I heard that saying before, a wolf in fact knocked at my door. I let Cash in and went to make more coffee, trying not to think about what could be worse than Kellen.

"You didn't go through with it." The relief in his voice cut me. I had gone through with it and I knew it was going to hurt him when I told him.

"Go through with what?" Arawn sat at the table looking at Cash and then me. When I didn't answer he leveled Cash with a gaze that would have had lesser men pissing in their pants.

"The mark. Aidan was going to give her his mark but she didn't go through with it."

One hand flew to my exposed neck while the other fumbled to release the hair clip. Instead of freeing my mass of hair all I managed to do was get the clip knotted up.

Arawn flew out of his chair. "Absolutely not. I forbid it. You will not be bound to anyone outside of the fae."

"Relax, Arawn. I said she didn't go through with it." Cash leaned against the doorway to my kitchen.

My fingers nervously traced the skin along the left side of my neck, hoping to hide the marks until I made my father understand why they were necessary. Except they weren't there. I spun around and looked at Cash. He dropped his head when he realized I had in fact gone through with it but something had gone wrong.

"Don't tell him."

"It's a little late for that, don't you think?" Cash wouldn't look at me. Now he knew that while there might be a little physical attraction he was already too far into the friend category for me. Once there, it was nearly impossible for a guy to make it back into the potential boyfriend category.

"Not him." I jerked my head in the direction of my father. "I mean him!" I pointed to my bedroom where Aidan slept. "If you tell him he won't let me near Caligula."

"As if that would stop you."

I moved across the kitchen, closing the distance between us. "You're right, it wouldn't stop me. But, you also know it would be better if I didn't go alone."

"You don't have to go alone."

"I need a vampire, Cash."

"You've made that abundantly clear."

"*Cash, please*," I pleaded.

"Fine. I won't say anything but he's going to find out sooner or later. My money's on sooner."

"Maurin." I turned slowly to face Arawn. The fact he called me Maurin instead of daughter meant he was pissed. I backed into Cash selfishly taking the support he offered. "You will explain yourself. Make me understand why my daughter would allow a vampire to mark her or worse, claim her?"

"He wouldn't let me question Caligula unless I agreed to wear his mark. I need to question this vampire, Father. I'll do whatever it takes to bring him down. What's one more mark if it gets me closer to finishing this?" There was more to it than that but I thought appealing to his practical side would be the best course. He wasn't interfering in my relationship with Aidan but I knew he wanted me to find a nice fae to settle down with.

"What's one more *mark*? You would compare what he tried to do to you to the mark of a warrior you bear on your neck?"

"It's not the mark of a warrior. It's the mark of a demon." Cash's fingers closed on my hip, stealing a caress in the name of friendly support.

"It is the mark of a survivor. The one who gave you that mark is dead and you live. Some would say that makes you a warrior. And what about the marks of your power? Would you compare that to the mark of a slave?"

I stepped away from Cash. It would be wrong to take comfort in the warmth of his caress, to accept his support, when I said this: "Aidan told me what the mark used to mean so you can stop trying to shock me by throwing the word slave around. He also told me what it meant to *him*. I'd be under his protection, nothing more. Unless I want it."

"Because you'd belong to him. I doubt all vampires have romanticized the mark in such a way." I rolled my eyes but it didn't bother him. "I wonder how liberal he would be the first time you did something he disagreed with. And if your protector should meet his true death? Then what? Will the next in his line inherit you along with the rest of his holdings? Never let someone put themselves above you. If someone seeks to claim your heart let it be as your equal, not by offering yourself and the power to control you."

I sank down in one of the kitchen chairs. "It doesn't matter anyway. It didn't work." I was hoping this wasn't an omen for our relationship because despite what my father said about the mark, I knew it was different for Aidan. I wanted things to work between us with or without the mark. Still, there was a small part of me that felt like I dodged a bullet.

"Its disappearance, I can only assume, has something to do with your rate of regeneration. A mark was traditionally given to humans. Very few fae are willing to give themselves to a vampire in such a way. The cost is too great. I believe this vampire has honorable intentions today but forever is a long time to live with the scales tipped out of balance.

"I told you before I was tolerating your little love affair because a suitable match has yet to be made." His eyes slid to Cash, letting him know even if I hadn't squarely placed him in the friend column he wouldn't be a suitable match either. "But heed this warning, daughter, do not pursue the mark again. You will not like the outcome."

"I appreciate your concern but you don't need to worry. And you definitely don't need to arrange any marriages." Gods, my dad was so old school.

"You are my daughter and very soon you will understand what that means. Remember what I said about the mark." He took my face in his hands, rubbing his thumbs along my cheekbones. "You are just like your mother. Her stubbornness was her undoing. I pray every day you don't fall to the same fate." He kissed the top of my head before fading away.

"Is he always that intense?" Cash spun the other chair around before straddling it, arms resting on the top.

"Unfortunately, yes."

X
TEN

Too afraid Aidan would notice the marks weren't on my neck before we questioned Caligula, I decided to head over to Risqué on my own - well not entirely on my own, I had Conry with me. The less time Aidan and I spent together the less likely he was to notice.

It was a couple hours before sunset but I knew Agrona would be up. The ancients weren't bound to the sun like the younger vamps. Sure they'd still roast like a campfire marshmallow if they got caught in it but one of the perks of living past six or seven centuries was not having a bed time so long as they stayed indoors. I left Aidan a note explaining my conversation with Masarelli, my plan to talk to Agrona about the new chief and that he should meet me there.

The face that greeted me at the back door of Risqué caught me off guard. "Nolak, I thought you were headed back to Boston."

He nodded his head in greeting. "That was before the Council position. Now I'm heading up security." Nolak was massive, easily pushing seven feet and all muscle. His Native American heritage was more pronounced under the security light behind the club than when I first met him on Winter Island. He wasn't GQ gorgeous but had a rugged quality that made him attractive. He must have been a beautiful wolf. "Nice dog." He gave Conry a scratch behind the ears.

"Thanks. A gift from my father." Nolak eyed my guardian warily, truly seeing him for what he was. "So, manning the door? I'm going to have to get you cleared for permanent residency."

"No need. It's already been taken care of. And I'm not manning the door I'm waiting for you, to escort you."

"Well then, by all means lead the way." I followed him through the door and down the stairs even though I probably knew my way around here better than he did. Well maybe not if he was now head of security. "So who filed the paperwork and how'd they get it back so fast?"

Nolak held the door leading to the Council chambers open for me. "I don't know, new liaison I guess."

"What?"

He shrugged his massive shoulders and nudged me inside the room before I could pump him for more information. The door bumped my ass, knocking me further into the room as he closed it. I turned and scowled even though he couldn't see it.

"There she is. See, darling, I told you not to worry. Maurin always finds her way." Kedehern was behind the bar again, mixing something that looked like a tequila sunrise- I bet that wasn't grenadine. He looked like Hugh Hefner in his heyday, smoking jacket and all.

Agrona looked up from her paper, devoid of the worry my appearance was supposed to wash away. "Something to drink, dear?" She took the highball glass from her husband, swirling the stirrer before taking a sip.

"Vampire." I eyed the vampire king slide behind the bar and mix the vodka, Chambord, cranberry and lime just to be sure of no funny business.

"Interesting choice given your latest assignment." Agrona gave a small laugh and then set her drink on the small end table beside her settee. She swung her satin pajama covered legs around and leaned in. "Unless of course you're craving blood. Feeling the side effects of the marking?"

"How did you know that? What side effects?"

She laughed, a full belly laugh. "I didn't need anyone to tell me he would try to mark you. He fears what you will become, daughter of Arawn. As for the side effects? Well, it's been said that the marked feel their master's hunger. It's what drives the slave's desire to feed the master, to quench the burning thirst and ease the pain."

Kedehern handed me the drink, it was a dark red color, suddenly turning my stomach. I hesitated, the glass perched on my lips but before the delicious concoction could pass over my tongue I set the glass down. With a little wink, he picked it up. "Perhaps an Irish coffee instead."

"Thanks." It was weird, their domesticated bliss. They both looked like they were settled in for a relaxing Sunday morning but I knew what they were capable of. I wouldn't be surprised if brunch was tied up and waiting in the room hidden behind this one.

"It didn't work," I said taking the coffee from Kedehern. I waited until he was seated beside his wife before I continued. "The mark, it didn't take."

"Of course it didn't. Once again Aidan failed to read up on his history. Your magic, fae magic, has already claimed you. To be claimed by another you would have to forsake your lineage and power." Kedehern stroked his hand along Agrona's thigh, skin sliding along silk.

"Arawn didn't tell me that. Are you sure?"

Agrona gave her husband a sideways glance. "I think he was concerned what you would do with the knowledge that it could be possible. You've been known to look before you leap."

I swallowed my denial with quite possibly the best Irish coffee I have ever had. "With or without the mark, I'm going to talk to Caligula."

"You see, there's that stubborn streak." Agrona smiled, settling against her husband's side as he wrapped an arm around her. Their warmth, for lack of a better word, was seriously throwing me off. They were up to something, trying to disarm me with their cuddling. I shuddered. "So you believe it is Caligula then? He has been getting restless but I chalked it up to age. The ancients have been known to struggle with keeping their sanity after a millennia or so."

"So this happens a lot then? Slaughtering women? Any more ancients who need a lithium drip or a lobotomy that I should know about?"

I caught the glance Kedehern gave his wife. They were holding back. "Look, if you know something now's the time to tell me. There's a fed running SPTF now. None of my people are in charge and that's going to make my job a lot harder as liaison. I'd like to get off on the right foot with this guy especially since we have to keep him away from the case and sell some bullshit story about how these girls died."

"They were never your people. It doesn't matter. The cleanup is no longer your concern. You've been alleviated of those responsibilities."

"What? Kedehern, you can't be serious. You can't take me off this now. I'm close. I can get a confession. You can mete out whatever justice you see fit, just let me bring him in."

"I am well aware of your record with SPTF and your unharnessed power, daughter of Arawn. Which is why you will be taking up the position as Regulator for the New England region."

"I didn't know we had a Regulator. Is that like a sup sheriff? What would I be doing exactly?"

"You will no longer be responsible for acquiring passes for the pack or reporting new registrations to the authorities. Otherwise your position will remain basically the same."

"So let me see if I'm following you here. All of the ass kicking and none of the paperwork?"

"That would about sum it up." He chuckled. "Does this mean you accept?"

It was my turn to laugh. "Oh, I'm under no delusion I had a choice, but yes I accept. Aidan said you put me on his team. I assumed it was in addition to being liaison. So does this promotion come with a raise?"

"You're not joining Aidan's team. You'll be leading it."

And there it was. The reason they were so sweet and affectionate. What did Mary Poppins say, a teaspoon of sugar makes the medicine go down. Agrona smiled, all fang, and I knew there was more to my new position. This was about keeping Aidan in check and her royal highness seemed to think making him report to me was the way to do it.

"You'll have a team of two cleaners and two investigators working under you. They will report to Aidan and he will report directly to you." Agrona waited for my usual temper fueled reaction but she was going to be disappointed.

I was sick of pushing paper anyway. I liked the action and I've been ass deep in it since the Council first came into my life. I was finally coming into my own, a little later than most but I'm good with a blade, come equipped with a scary fae dog and a unique skill set perfect for chasing down bad guys. I wasn't about to let vampire politics ruin the moment.

"So do I need to meet the new captain at SPTF?"

Kedehern pulled his wife's legs across his lap and

proceeded to rub her perfectly manicured feet. I think I would rather watch them eat from live donors. Something was seriously creepy about watching them like this. The look on his face said they knew it too. "The new liaison will take care of the initial meeting. She will keep him abreast of your progress. Meet with Caligula."

"I was headed there after this. So who's the new liaison? I'll need her contact info."

"You already have it. We chose Amalie as your replacement. She'll be expecting your call." I started to walk out but he called me back. "And, Maurin, try a little finesse. Caligula can't tell you anything if he's dead."

Aidan still hadn't shown. Did he know something was wrong with the mark? Was there some connection between master and their marked that was missing, tipping him off? I really didn't want to have it out with him but if he tried to stop me from going because of a failed marking, it was on like Donkey Kong.

Actually, he couldn't stop me now that the Council made me team lead but this was about us. He said he wanted to protect me but I wasn't used to having someone at my back or at my front blocking every move I tried to make. It was a little suffocating to say the least.

I leaned against the wall next to the rear entrance, the cold bricks leeching my body heat. The longer I stayed the longer I stewed. I'd developed a terrible habit of hashing and rehashing things. Someone would do or say something and I would turn it over in my mind, analyzing every detail. If I didn't pull the information myself it couldn't be trusted.

So the longer I waited, the longer I had to think about everything that had happened on the case, with Aidan, Cash and even the hunter's wards. Conry was pacing, gravel crunching under his paws, as he tried to shake off my anxiety.

By the time Aidan pulled up in the Camaro I was well and truly pissed. I watched him get out of the muscle car, and my mood soured even more. Something I wouldn't have thought possible. While I counted stars to kill the time waiting on my vampire, I obsessed over my failed marking and the likelihood it was more than my protection that had him attempting it.

Aidan was always gorgeous with impeccable taste and designer clothes, but seeing him in jeans, untucked white button down and leather jacket had my brain screaming we were mad at him to the more traitorous parts of my body. He had stopped to feed before coming here. He crossed the parking lot with casual determination, his sights set on me. A crooked grin ignited a fire low in my body. This would be easier if he hadn't dressed like my fantasy Aidan. I couldn't let it distract me. I had to know if there was more to his attempt to mark me.

"I'm glad to see you at least had the sense to wait for me instead of going off to Caligula's on your own."

"Only because I didn't have his address." He was teasing, I wasn't. If I knew where Caligula lived I would have left fifteen minutes ago.

He leaned in, pressing me tighter against the bricks. I bristled as his hands slid up my hips and his lips worked their way along my jaw. "What's wrong? I feel the tension rolling off you."

"Nothing," I lied. Everything was bothering me.

Aidan's lips moved down my neck and I froze when he reached the spot where his mark should have been. He jerked back. "That's why you left without me. You hoped I wouldn't find out."

"Why did you really want to mark me?"

"Did you think I wouldn't get close to you, touch you?" He brushed my hair back, exposing the unmarked skin.

"Why did you really want to mark me, Aidan?"

"What does it matter now? It didn't work."

"It matters to me."

"Have I ever given you a reason to doubt me? Have I ever done anything but care for you? And still you rush to think the worst of me. Someone says something, plants a seed of doubt and you let it grow into a gnarled hedge of mistrust that I must once again hack my way through. Just to get close to you. All those nights I spent with you, getting to know you, did you learn nothing about me? About the kind of man I am?"

"You still didn't answer the question." My heart was pounding. I wanted to believe the words flowing from his beautiful lips. He was saying all the right ones but there was more to his driving need to mark me. He had to have known about my new position with the Council. Agrona had said he was afraid of what I would become. How many times had they called me daughter of Arawn. Why would he ask me to do something that could sever me from my fae lineage? He knew more last night before he sank his fangs into my neck than he bothered to share with me. He was keeping something from me.

"Didn't I?"

"Did you know last night that I was going to be Regulator? That I was basically in charge of your team?"

"You have got to be fucking kidding me? You think I was trying to what, hold sway over you with my mark? It couldn't possibly have anything to do with the others seeking to claim you. Your wolf, the stranger marking your door, even your father is making moves to find you a match. Did you know that?

"Christ, Maurin, even the Council is trying to claim you. Caligula could lay claim to you. I want to show the world that you are mine and you assume I only want to control you. That my mark gives me power over you. I sought to win your heart and mind. But I haven't, have I? Last night you let your guard down, truly let me in but I see the walls are back up and thicker than ever."

My throat was tight, my voice wavered as I held back tears. He was right. I had already fortified the walls around my heart. "Did you know that being marked by a vampire is forbidden among the fae? That in order to be marked I would be giving up my lineage, the thing that gives me my power, that makes me, me?"

"If I thought such a thing was possible I wouldn't have tried. Were you the daughter of Arawn when I first met you? Were you my superior when I first kissed you? I don't give a damn about your power or position. I wasn't asking you to give up anything but your heart.

"You know, I used to find all your little insecurities

endearing. Now I see them for what they really are. A handicap. You will always look for the worst in others. You don't value yourself, so why should anyone else. You don't see what everyone else sees when they look at you, when I look at you." He walked toward the car. "Let's go. The night isn't getting any younger and we still have Caligula to question."

I didn't say anything, just numbly climbed into the passenger seat as Conry sprawled out in back. He called me an emotional cripple and he was right. It wasn't like my life had been over flowing with love and support. I couldn't accept the fact that Aidan wanted me, that his desire to mark me stemmed more from his feelings for me than anything else. So I let Agrona, master manipulator, plant doubt in my head- for her own enjoyment no doubt. Combine that with my father's declaration that a vampire mark was like the scarlet letter for fae and I had enough to question everything about Aidan and his intentions. I had royally fucked up.

"Aidan?"

"Don't. You've said enough for one night."

"Aidan, I just, I..."

"You just what? Want to offer some half hearted apology? Spare us both. It will offer little solace after hearing what you really think of me."

"A lot's happened the last couple of days. I admit it, I let my insecurities get the best of me. I was overwhelmed, I didn't know what to think."

"Let me know when you do."

The rest of the ride to Caligula's was in painful silence.

I watched the city morph into suburbia and tried to piece myself together enough to get through the questioning. I had planned to confront Aidan about his ulterior motives, but there weren't any. In exchange Aidan laid me bare, exposing all the self esteem issues I typically kept hidden behind a sharp wit and sharper tongue.

I closed my eyes and worked on breathing. I'd tried meditation before. I couldn't sit still long enough. Since I was stuck in the car I tried it again. I couldn't afford any chinks in my mental armor when I talked to Caligula. I needed some serious repair work after the argument with Aidan.

Caligula lived in an unassuming two story Cape Cod with grey shaker siding, white trim, red shutters and door. It was the quintessential upper middle class home, one you found anywhere along the New England coastline and totally not what I expected.

Spring was far from making an appearance but the yard was neatly kept. Boxwood hedges trimmed the grass in place of a fence and two birch trees stood on each side of the walk, the stark white bark a contrast against the grey backdrop of the house. I half expected a mother to pull up in her silver suburban, dragging three kids from hockey practice home for dinner. It was hard to reconcile this house, this home, with a killer-vampire or otherwise.

Aidan hadn't said another word to me on the way over and stood as far from me as possible without actually waiting in the car. How could we work together like this? I tried to get his attention, to get him to look at me. I needed reassurance we were going to be all right, not for the future, just right now- that we were going to walk out of here.

Despite what was said between us earlier, Aidan was excellent at picking up on my emotions. He didn't so much as check me in his peripheral. The hard clipped sound of his voice when he reminded me that he was a professional and despite my new title I was a rookie compared to him, left me colder than the wind blowing off the Atlantic. He stepped in front of me and knocked on the door. The man who answered was as unexpected as the house.

"Well, isn't this a pleasant surprise. I heard you'd been spending more time state side, Aidan. I'm disappointed you haven't called before now." Caligula was dressed in a charcoal grey v-neck sweater with white under shirt, jeans that looked broken in but definitely came that way and black Vans. He looked like he belonged in this neighborhood, hell in this decade, except for his eyes. Something in those dark chestnut orbs showed his age. He may have fooled the elderly couple next door but the power cresting against this suburban facade was obvious to me.

"Aren't you going to invite us in?" Aidan still dwarfed me with his body but Caligula wasn't surprised when Aidan said us. He would have sensed my heartbeat.

Caligula opened the door wider. The house was like something out of Garden and Gun magazine. Rich brown leather couches and overstuffed chairs were positioned around the fireplace. Small wooden tables heavy and worn were on sides of the chairs supporting lamps with stretched leather shades. An old wooden chest with iron straps and lock was a makeshift coffee table. His built in bookshelves were stocked.

The whole room was a contradiction with what I knew about this vampire. He was a madman in life, turned after a vicious assassination attempt and created scores of vampires in his likeness. Finding the love of his life soothed him, and losing her seemed to completely destroy his desire for life. He had quietly assimilated back into vampire society. Powerful in strength and years, socially accepted but never really living. Something had awakened the beast inside him. I was determined to find out what.

Caligula gestured to the living room and we followed. He sat in the chair to the right of the fireplace and waited for us to be seated. Aidan sat on the couch, the middle of the couch, forcing me to take the chair on the left. I caught the intake of breath as I walked past Caligula and felt his eyes burn every inch of me until I sat. I would have preferred sitting next to Aidan, he had a calming effect on me but he wasn't offering any support in that department tonight.

He'd flipped the switch and we were just business as far as he was concerned. Fine. I could do this, I wanted to do this. I was an interrogator. It didn't matter if I couldn't use my abilities, I still knew how to get information. I stamped down my nerves and mentally prepared myself for the game. Getting a confession from Caligula was going to be a battle of wits and wills.

"Aidan, aren't you going to introduce me to your friend?" He talked to Aidan but his eyes never left me.

"Caligula this is Maurin. Maurin this is Caligula." Aidan had no interest in the pleasantries.

Faster than I thought possible, faster than I have ever seen Aidan move, Caligula was standing in front of me. He swept my hand up in his, pressing it to his mouth. His lips were cold, not the icy fire of Aidan's touch, more like frostbite.

"A pleasure to make your acquaintance. Please call me Gaius. What brings you to my home? I am not in need of a cleaner, so this must be a social call. Come to reminisce about the old days? I could tell you stories from my time in Capris that would make every inch of your porcelain skin blush, my dear. Or perhaps you'd like to hear the story of how Aidan and I met. Not as solicitous but riveting none the less."

He knew why we were here. There was no point in beating around the bush. If I let vampire formalities run the show we would be here until sunrise. "We're here about the five dead girls. I'm sure you've heard about them."

"Yes, yes. On the news. Tragic business, suicide pact is what the reporter said. I didn't know such a thing existed. Have you ever heard of such a thing? But I don't see why that would have brought you here." Caligula draped himself across the other chair, one foot casually swinging over the arm.

Of course I knew what a suicide pact was and I'm fairly certain a vampire over a millennia old did too but what I didn't know was that's what the media reported. Now I really wanted to meet the new fed. I bet he was behind that leak to reporters. "Let's not start off on the wrong foot, Caligula. I know..."

"Please, call me Gaius."

"Okay, Gaius. Does the name Caroline Sousa ring any bells?"

"Of course it does, my dear. Lovely woman, we had a brief affair. She wanted me to turn her. I refused and that was the end of our time together I'm afraid."

"She was eighteen, I'd hardly call that a woman. You don't think that's a little young for you? Like a few hundred years too young?" I probably shouldn't provoke him this early in the conversation. I spared a glance at Aidan expecting to see a scowl on his face but all I saw was indifference. His arms were casually stretched out over the back of the couch and he had no intentions of intervening. Not yet.

Caligula wistfully stared off. "In my day women who weren't betrothed by eighteen had little prospects. I love their vitality. It re-ignites my passion for life. But like all good things, the affairs are often short lived. They begin to yearn for the same passion in a partner and once again the fire in my heart is snuffed out."

"That's all very poetic but I find your choice of words intriguing. Short lived, snuffed out? Fascinating turn of phrase, especially since Caroline is dead."

"What? How? Surely you don't mean she was one of those girls?"

"When was the last time you saw her?"

"Two or three weeks ago." His phone rang. "Excuse me. I need to take this call." He stood and walked away.

I leveled Aidan with a fierce glare. "What the hell is the matter with you?" I mouthed afraid Caligula would hear me.

"I could ask you the same thing." He didn't even bother to whisper. I knew Aidan wasn't talking about my very direct line of questioning.

I flipped him off as Caligula came back in the room. He held out his cell phone. "It's for you."

I stood, panic gripped me for a moment. Who the hell would be calling to talk to me on his cell phone? He was certifiable. What if someone I cared about was tied to a chair, held hostage and tortured on the other end of that call. Good thing that was a very short list of people and all but one were Others.

My hand was steady, giving nothing away. We were only testing the waters, trying to see how far we could get with a simple visit. If Caligula had changed the rules of engagement so soon we were in serious trouble. "This is Maurin Kincaide."

Aidan watched me with renewed interest as my brow furrowed and my eyes darkened. A storm brewed inside me but I couldn't let my anger show. A few more mmm hmms and I snapped the phone shut. I fought not to slam the phone into Caligula's palm. It wouldn't have hurt him anyway.

"I appreciate you speaking with us this evening, Gaius." I wanted to tell him what I saw, that I knew he was there the night she died. That he killed her, but it wasn't the time. He won this round but I was going to ensure I got a rematch. "We're trying to piece together the last few days of her life. The news is reporting a suicide pact but we suspect blood magic may be involved. In light of the state of the local coven, I'm not entirely surprised." I reached for him, gently squeezing his forearm, my fingers stroking the soft sweater. "Of course you know that information is not being released. I trust you'll keep this confidential."

He looked at my hand, watching my fingers glide along his arm. He cleared his throat. "If I think of anything helpful you'll be the first person I call."

I pulled an old business card from when I was still with SPTF out of the inside pocket of my leather jacket. God only knew how long it's been in there. "I recently changed positions but my cell is the same."

He smiled with a little fang and held my hand longer than necessary. I thought I heard him say something about positions but decided not to ask him to repeat it. I was sure it was meant for Aidan's ears not mine.

We both knew to wait until we were inside Aidan's car with the radio on before we said anything. Caligula watched us from the door until we were halfway down the street.

Aidan was furious but I don't think it was all directed at me. "Let me guess, his lawyer was on the phone."

"How the hell did he pull that off?"

"He probably called his lawyer before we ever knocked on the door. You weren't meant to ask all your questions tonight."

I was quiet, trying to figure out what Aidan meant by that, an awkward silence filled the car. I watched the houses pass in a blur as my breath fogged the window.

"What are you thinking?"

"That all those romance authors have obviously never met a real Roman because I'm here to tell you that nose is not what they described."

I could tell he wanted to laugh, the little crinkles around his eyes gave him away, but he didn't. I knew he wouldn't say anything until I actually answered the question he asked. I sighed. "I was thinking how much I wished he was a witch or a shifter. At least then I could get a read on him."

"We all succumb to our gifts but you handled yourself without them. It was smart to misdirect him. You were very convincing, though I would advise you against touching him the next time you speak. You seem to be immune to vampire persuasion, especially mine, but he is an ancient. Touching will only strengthen the connection making it easy for him to coerce you."

It was the only compliment he paid me tonight and I couldn't help but wonder how long it would be like this between us. He sat right next to me but I missed him. I missed the easy banter and fireworks that always went off when we were together, even if it was just our tempers. He completely shut down. I didn't know if I could give him everything he wanted but I ached for things to be normal between us. I just didn't know how to undo what had been done. "Are you planning on stopping the jabs anytime soon?"

"Not tonight."

The ride back to my apartment was silent and painfully long. When he finally pulled up in front of my building, I all but ran from the car. It hurt more than I expected to see Aidan and me in ruins. I had cut him deep with my suspicions and general lack of trust. I would say serves him right for what he did but I knew deep down he had my best intentions at heart. He may have gone about it all wrong but it was never malicious.

Deep down all that lingered were self esteem and trust issues. The people in my life so far had either barely tolerated my existence or manipulated me for their own gain. Aidan was different. He was the only one interested in me for me. Well maybe Cash was too but I was too tired to dwell on that tonight.

I grabbed a bottle of wine and went into the bathroom to fill the tub. I'd finish the bath when I finished the bottle.

XI
ELEVEN

I cursed the sun as it broke through the clouds. I vaguely remember opening the blackout shades I'd installed for Aidan, hoping to see him outside keeping watch. If he had been there I probably would have gone to him, begged him to forgive me and lured him to my bed. He wasn't. I lived upstairs from an alpha, who just so happened to be my friend, if I was in trouble Aidan knew I'd have help. He was giving me space. In the excruciating light of day, I realized it was the best gift he could give me. He wanted me to figure out what I was willing to give him. I hoped he was willing to accept it when I did. But first I needed coffee and Tylenol.

I stumbled into the kitchen still cursing the sun like a

true creature of the night and wished I had one of those single cup coffee pod machines. I loved the French press but coffee in under a minute started to sound better and better. Wine is a creeper, the effects sneak up on you. A bottle later and you're in for a headache in the morning. I contemplated eating the grounds when the buzzer for my door went off like an alarm in a firehouse. I hit the intercom and grumbled a greeting. I stopped listening after I recognized Amalie's voice and buzzed her in. That voice guaranteed coffee. She never came empty handed.

Amalie was outside my door when I opened it. She balanced a glorious coffee tray and white paper bag in one hand while she bent to pick up a box resting against the door. It was a plain brown shipping box, totally innocuous, except for the fact it shouldn't be there.

I stopped Amalie, I didn't want her to get hurt if the package was booby trapped. Or spill the coffee, the tray was dangerously close to bending in half. I ushered her inside the apartment and gave the box a little nudge, and then another. When nothing seeped, oozed, misted or erupted out of the box I brought it inside. Amalie set us up with coffee and croissants while I opened the box. She peered over my shoulder by the time I cut through the tape and pulled out all the brown packing paper. Inside the box was another box. This one rectangle and beautifully wrapped with mat black paper and black ribbon. I took the box out and opened the card tapped to the top.

Dine with me. I promise the evening will not only be entertaining but informative. I'll send my car for you.

Until sunset,

Gaius

"Who's Gaius?"

I filled Amalie in on my meeting last night while I carefully unwrapped the box and peeled back the tissue paper. He may be insane but he had impeccable taste. The dress was beautiful. Deep plum silk with black lace overlay. Little black crystals adorned the lace. I held it up by the thin straps and noticed the high slit, which would just cover the tops of my thigh high stockings. Everything important would be covered but I could tell the dress would fit like a glove and leave little to the imagination. Something told me Caligula was up to more than ogling my lady parts. If I accepted the dress and his invitation I wouldn't be able to carry my sword or any other weapons for that matter. I had a sneaking suspicion if I showed up in something a little less form fitting Caligula wouldn't be so forth coming.

I put the dress back in the box and sipped my coffee. I needed accessories. "Amalie get the captain on the phone."

Five minutes later I had an appointment with the new captain of SPTF and Amalie was on her way to class- not before making me promise to call her with an update after the meeting.

She may be the new liaison but she hadn't given up her advanced studies. Especially not since she was so close to mastering ley lines. When Mahalia ran the coven she had chosen Amalie's path, making her a healer. Finally out from under the high priestess, thanks to her incarceration, Amalie chose another way to focus her magic. She would have made an excellent healer but she was a natural at harnessing the lines.

I decided to dress to impress for my first meeting with the new captain. I had never laid eyes on him but I would bet good money he wore a three piece suit every day. My jeans and tee shirts probably wouldn't win me points with the former fed. And I definitely wanted to win him over. Especially if I was walking out of the station with Mercy Brown's cross. It would push all the right buttons with Caligula. I couldn't leave the captain's office without it. The long black sweater hugged every curve and could almost pass for a dress. Black leggings and knee high leather boots completed the outfit. Satisfied with the clothes, I ran a brush through my hair until the black waves cascaded down my back. I did a couple turns in front of the mirror. Bad ass chic.

I headed back into my closet and pulled out a garment bag from the back. The plastic zipper bag held a coat that cost almost a month's salary when I worked for SPTF. It was my one and only designer purchase. I splurged, more like emptied the savings, when I got a new job and a pay raise. I had yet to wear it. Should I?

It was ridiculous to have a coat this expensive and never wear it. The odds of getting blood and guts on it seemed relatively low, so I undid the zipper and breathed in the waft of leather and wool smell. I wasn't usually one of those girls who went crazy over clothes or even enjoyed shopping - I did most of mine online - but when I saw it on Fashion Finder I knew I had to have it.

I pulled out the Rag and Bone Falcon coat and slipped into it. Dressing like this every day in my line of work wasn't practical but it was just the ego boost I needed. I was going to have the new guy eating out of the palm of my hand. Hell, he'd probably put the necklace on me if I asked.

I dug in my purse for the keys to the Camaro and remembered I didn't have the car anymore. I got hit with a serious case of separation anxiety. Aidan and the car were a package deal. I dug in my junk drawer for my car keys. Little pangs hit my chest when I went out to warm up my car.

It wasn't the Camaro, not even close but I couldn't chance being caught walking out of the between at SPTF. I opened the door to my convertible VW Rabbit, cringing at the loud creak in the hinges. I'm pretty sure my car was the inspiration for Adam Sandler's Ode To My Piece Of Shit Car.

It was supposed to be a Cabriolet when I bought it, turned out the seller changed all the badges on the car. Hence forth called the Rabriolet, the windshield wipers didn't work right if the radio was on, the headlights dimmed if you used the horn, the rag top leaked and on occasion flames shot out of the passenger side vents. So it was no surprise I fell in love with the Camaro or that the Rabriolet had refused to turn over. I looked around, making sure the little parking lot beside my building was empty and slipped into the between. Not willing to chance being seen walking out of thin air, I chose a little alleyway a couple streets down from the station.

Confident the coast was clear I stepped out of the alley and right into Masarelli. He grunted a greeting as I checked my coat for grease stains from the impact. The way my day was going I wouldn't be surprised to find the remnants he wore of his lunch stuck to the front of me.

He didn't ask and I didn't offer a reason why I came out of that alley, so we walked in silence to the station together. We parted ways at his desk but I felt him watching me as I made my way to the captain's office. I looked over my shoulder as I knocked on the door. Masarelli didn't look away. His expression was flat but his eyes said he knew I was up to something and he was going to find out what. I would have to cover my tracks. I didn't need him or the officers he was no doubt going to put outside my apartment tailing me.

I was still locked in a staring contest with Masarelli when the captain opened his door. He cleared his throat in an effort to get my attention. I turned and blinked a couple times adjusting my focus. If the FBI had a calendar, this guy would be February. No one should look that good in a suit.

The classic cut and black fabric of his jacket only emphasized his rugged good looks and the small scar on his upper lip. The buttons of his white shirt stretched across his broad chest. With the top button undone and his grey tie pulled loose, he oozed boardroom sexy but I don't think he knew it or was comfortable with it. I thought for sure he would be a pencil pusher but this guy had obviously spent more time in the field than he had behind a desk. So how did he end up in Salem running SPTF?

"You must be Maurin Kincaide." He extended a massive hand. I kept my cool, praying there wasn't drool on my chin, and shook his hand. My hand practically disappeared inside his but I kept a firm grip. "I'm Mason Hunter. Have a seat." He let go of my hand to point to the chairs in front of his desk. I caught an undercurrent of power as my hand slipped from his. Damn, I should have tried to get a read. There was more to this fed coming to town than just replacing Matthison. He hid his power well, he seemed as surprised as I was that I felt it.

I was so glad I chose to dress up for the occasion. I unbuttoned the Falcon coat and draped it over one of the chairs. His eyes moved from my boots to my eyes, taking his time taking in every inch. This should be fun. I sat down and crossed one leather boot clad leg over the other, while he settled himself behind his desk.

It was weird how Masarelli sat behind that same desk a couple days ago and all I thought about was Matthison. But Hunter was different. Whatever the power rippling beneath his skin was it gave him an edge. He had pretty big shoes to fill with Matthison's retirement but I got the feeling he was man enough for the job.

"So what's this meeting about, Miss Kincaide." The chair groaned as he leaned back, arms crossed over his chest. I couldn't help but notice the biceps stretching the sleeves of his jacket. Which was probably the point.

"I thought it would be a good idea for us to get acquainted since we're working the same case."

He unbuttoned his jacket, eased to an upright position and then stretched across his desk. "Don't you mean size me up? See if I'm willing to play ball."

"I'm not the only one sizing someone up, Captain.

And I knew you were willing to play before I came here. If you weren't you would have run with Masarelli's rogue theory instead of suicide pact. That was pretty imaginative, by the way."

"Just because I don't want unnecessary panic gripping my town doesn't mean I am going to turn this investigation over to you."

"So it's your town now is it?"

"From the moment I accepted the job."

"Still, you could have said it was a norm."

"A serial killer is a serial killer. It doesn't matter if it's vamp, were, or norm. People panic and then do stupid things."

"Some people might say lying about murders your first week on the job is a stupid thing to do."

"And what about you? Are you one of those people, Miss Kincaide? Something tells me you're not very good at playing by the rules either."

"Rules are made to be broken, is that it?" Shit, why was I goading him? I was supposed to be winning him over with my sparkling personality and dazzling detective skills. Not antagonizing him. I couldn't seem to help it and he seemed to be enjoying it as much as me. I'd almost say he was flirting if we weren't here to talk about murders.

"Sometimes things aren't always black and white. You have to find the grey, the in between. Don't you agree, Miss Kincaide?" Something about the way he said between convinced me he wasn't speaking metaphorically. He knew about me. But how? No one here, not even Matthison and especially not Masarelli knew what I could do. Oh my god,

I was on the government's radar. I was in so much trouble when the Council found out.

"Please, call me Maurin. You seem to know so much about me it's only right we're on a first name basis."

"Then you must call me Mason. Everyone else calls me Captain or Hunter."

Hunter, hunter. Where had I heard that? It was something important, something... My eyes widened as I realized who was sitting across from me. The Hunter. His eyes crinkled with amusement as the realization spread across my face. "You marked my door!"

"You have a tendency to attract a lot of enemies. Consider it a token of my friendship."

"How did you manage to get this job?"

"I transferred."

"You transferred? But you're with the Hunt. So you did what? Just put in a request, someone signs the form and voila you're here running SPTF?"

"Not quite. I'm still very much a part of the Hunt."

"So you're a Huntsman and a fed?"

"Not any more, now I'm a Huntsman and a captain."

I tried not to roll my eyes, I really did. "I already told my father, I'm not starting any lessons until after I take down the murderer."

"Of course. I don't want anything to distract you. There is so much I want to show you, to teach you. When you're with me I want your full attention." Now he was definitely flirting.

The thought of his undivided attention made me more than a little nervous and set off a flock of butterflies in my stomach. He was filled with power, confidence, sex, just sitting there behind his desk. If we were away from prying eyes and ears and he concentrated all of that on me, my panties would melt for sure. And what about Aidan? This would test more than one kind of power during our lessons. He looked at me the way a lion might a gazelle. The hunter found his prey and was stalking it.

I cleared my suddenly dry throat. "If we could get back to the reason I asked to meet with you." He waved me on, smiling wickedly. He knew he got to me. "We can help each other. You have something I need and I have something you want."

I sucked in a breath. That sounded perfectly reasonable in my head but I heard the double entendre as soon as the words fell from my lips. I thought his last smile was deliciously wicked but this one actually went to his eyes and hinted at what he'd like to do with the things he wanted. The small dimple in his left cheek practically had me fanning myself. I was in so much trouble.

"I have information and you have one silver cross on a chain I'd like to borrow."

"Something tells me there's more to this exchange."

"I want you to keep your men out of my way. Masarelli is probably setting up a tail right now but you're going to tell him it's a waste of man power. You're going to block him at every turn."

"You used to be a part of this team, is it so difficult to work with them? I would think you would have use for them on your investigations."

"You're new here, so I don't expect you to understand

that the only person who wanted me on that team used to sit behind that desk. I do fine by myself."

"You won't have to worry about Masarelli. We've already publicly closed the case. The girls were all victims of cyber bullying, they met in a support group on Facebook that quickly changed tone. The girls fed off one another's suffering until they agreed it would be easier to end their lives."

"Is any of that true?" I knew what had really happened to those girls but my heart ached to think that classmates, coworkers and sadly family were as cruel to these girls as the monster who killed them.

"Unfortunately, yes. The only deception is the means of their true death. These girls, all of them, were already touched in the head. They most likely would have ended their lives without the help of our killer.

"Fucking tragic." I wanted to weep, for the dead girls, for their families for the loss of our humanity and compassion for others. For the part of myself I saw in them.

"Life is full of tragedy. We see more of it than others because we live in the darkness, chase the monsters. It makes the light burn that much brighter on the rare occasion it touches our lives. Now, tell me what is so important that I shouldn't return the necklace to the girl's parents with the rest of her effects?"

"What if I told you Caligula looked good for the murders?"

He walked around to the front of his desk, leaning against the corner. "I'm listening."

I told him about the reading - on the necklace and at the morgue. His eyebrows went up a little in amusement when he heard how we managed to get in. I finished with the visit Aidan and I paid to the ancient last night, the delivery to my apartment this morning and my dinner plans for tonight. I could tell Caligula was someone he wanted. Maybe for a very long time. Had he managed to elude Hunter?

"I'll be right back."

I sank back in the chair, all the tension leaving my body when he left the room. I was exhausted from explaining everything that had happened and thinking about everything I still had to do but I was going to bring that bastard down tonight. He wasn't going to lure any more young women into his sick fantasy of recreating Mercy Brown and then killing them when the psychological transformation failed.

The Council should have killed him when Mercy died. It was a miracle he hadn't gone back to his monstrous ways before now. He was a sick fuck, in life and in undeath. I don't care about his years of good behavior, the history he's seen, the knowledge and power he possesses. He was killing women, girls really, none of them old enough to legally drink, and I was going to kill him. If the Council expected any other outcome they should have assigned someone else. All I needed to do was figure out how to hide my sword while wearing that dress.

I almost jumped when Hunter dangled the chain in front of me. I had been so engrossed in my thoughts I hadn't heard him come back in. I couldn't afford to do that tonight. Caligula had the upper hand choosing the location of our date. He'd know the layout. I needed to be on alert. Hunter waited for me to lift my hair out of the way before hooking the clasp on the necklace. His fingers brushed the nape of my neck and goose bumps erupted all over my skin as a tingle ran down my spine. If he could do that to me with the barest of touches I was in bigger trouble than I thought when my training began.

"If you need backup you can reach me in the between." His lips were so close to my ear, his breath hot on my skin.

I shivered. He was so different from Aidan. Aidan was slow and deliberate. Each touch, kiss was drawn out pushing me to the edge with anticipation of his next move. Mason Hunter was unbridled passion. He coiled up, waited, watched his prey and then ravaged them with unbidden desire once they were caught.

"I think Caligula might suspect something if I flicker in and out of view, don't you?"

"You don't need to send your body. Open the connection to the between with your mind's eye and you'll be able to reach me. Go on, try it."

I focused on the between, felt the familiar pull and then slipped into it. I cursed as I felt the chair slip away and the weight of the grey shift around me. Strong hands gripped my arms and I gasped as he pulled the power from me.

When Kellen used his magic to force the between into me it was violent, excruciating. This was different, almost erotic the way Hunter caused the power to caress every inch of me as he pulled it out of my body and focused me back on the chair.

My head fell back against his lower abdomen but my eyes remained closed. I wouldn't look at him, not like that. I felt the lust he stirred in my body and knew it would reflect in my eyes. I couldn't. Not with things like they were with Aidan. If I was smart maybe never.

"You're pulling too much in. You're so powerful, Maurin, you don't even realize how much of the between you draw into yourself when you shift through realities. I've never seen someone hold that much. You could quite literally change the world with that kind of power. Our lessons can't begin soon enough." His voice was etched with concern. "For now, let's focus on communication. Your father taught you how to focus on anyone person, place?" When I nodded he continued. "Focus on me, but this time use the part of you rooted to your psychometry. Our bodies are here on this plane but our minds are open. Go to that place in your mind that lets you connect to someone's memories, their mind and fill it with the between. Once you've spindled the energy in your mind, focus on the connection."

I followed his instructions, pulling my energy from the between and storing it in that place in my mind that links to someone else's. I focused on the imprint I felt Hunter leave in the between right before I felt him in my mind. Not all of him, just his voice. It was deep and sensual, like running my fingers through the softest fur. He praised me for successfully transmitting on my second attempt and offered a few tips. Useful things like not giving myself away by looking like I was about to orgasm every time he spoke inside my head. Really helpful.

"I think that's enough for today. I've got to get ready for tonight."

"You can reach me any time. I'm at your disposal."

I got up to leave, ignoring the fact he was talking about more than tonight. "I don't think it will come to that. Like I said, I do just fine on my own."

"Maurin, be careful. If that necklace is as significant as you think it is, it might push him over the edge."

"I'm counting on it." I knew he wasn't buying the bravado. We both knew how dangerous my plan was.

XII

TWELVE

I may have told the hunter I worked better alone and Agrona may be right about my tendency to go off half cocked but I didn't have a death wish. I wasted no time calling in the cavalry when I got home. Amalie and Cash were already at my apartment when Aidan arrived. I sat on my kitchen counter with a cup of coffee trying to explain my plan.

"I can do this. I think I've proven that already. I'm only asking for your help."

"To help you on your suicide mission."

I groaned, shaking my head. "Aidan, would you listen to me for a second." I waited for him to stop bitching about my pig headedness before I continued. "I'll have

Conry with me, he'll be in stealth mode. Caligula won't even know he's there. Cash will wire me up. I can't take the Retaliator but I'll have obsidian daggers and my silver covered rowan wood stakes strapped to me. Amalie made me a special pill with colloidal silver that will keep the particles suspended in my blood. I'll be stunning, literally."

Something occurred to me and I focused on Amalie. "How concentrated is the silver? I'm not going to turn blue, right?" She assured me I would not look like the guy I saw on the Today Show a couple of years ago, so I continued. "And you'll be right outside, watching and listening with Cash. It's a good plan. Our only plan and we're going with it. I'm going to get ready. I suggest you do the same."

I knew Aidan wasn't happy. He might be giving me space but that didn't mean he was any more comfortable with the idea of my blood being spilled than before. I heard him outside the bathroom door while I blow dried my hair. I stopped, opened the door and motioned for him to come in. I readjusted my towel and turned the dryer back on while he perched on the edge of the tub.

"We're alone. Well for the most part. Speak your mind." I didn't really have to shout over the dryer. Aidan could hear me just fine. He hesitated. "I promise not to get mad at you. I need you focused tonight. Go on, say what's on your mind."

"You're going to wear the necklace?"

That caught me off guard. He started with a question instead of an order. "Yes." I shut off the dryer and turned to face him, resting on the edge of the sink.

"I don't think you should. What if you pick up residual memories? It's too much. You look too much like her. With the necklace."

"There aren't any links left to follow on the necklace. And looking like her is the idea. It will throw him off, make him stumble. And when he does, I'll have him."

"Right where you want him?" He shook his head at my devious smirk. "You're not ready to take him." I started to object. "You said you'd listen." He waited a moment, until satisfied I wasn't going to interrupt again. "This isn't like the Afrit. You're not locked in a circle fighting to the death. You need to wait for him to leave an opening. For the right moment. He won't give you one. He spent adolescence surviving Roman politics and his adulthood polluting the system even further. You look at him and see a crazed villain. He is a madman but he isn't a stupid man. His lawyer tells you to back down and he suddenly invites you for dinner? He has anticipated every move. He has prepared for the possibility you are coming to kill him."

"He didn't anticipate his assassination. He slipped up before. I'll get him to do it again."

"Didn't he? Do you think some vampire stumbled upon his body? Couldn't pass up the bleeding buffet and then decided to turn him?"

"He knew?" It had never occurred to me that Caligula would hire a vampire to save him from his fate. I hadn't thought about it at all actually. It certainly shed light on the mind of the man I hunted tonight but I wasn't backing down.

"Of course he knew. The man was shrewd,

calculating. Even in the end, at the peak of his madness he had the clarity to assure his survival. To assume he hasn't tonight would be a tactical mistake. One that could cost you your life." His voice was strangled with emotion.

I closed the distance between us, taking him in my arms. His head rested on my chest, his ear above my heart. Our relationship was strained but that didn't mean our feelings for each other had changed.

"Each heart beat is different. Murmurs, stints, tiny defects in the capillaries. So many little things that make each person's unique. Your heart beats the drum of war. So strong, my beautiful warrior. I have no choice but to follow you, a chuisle mo chroi."

It wasn't the first time he called me that. I still didn't know what it meant. I hadn't gotten around to looking it up on a Gaelic translation site yet. "Tell me what it means."

"Perhaps I'll tell you tonight."

"Maybe I'll google it."

"If you could spell it." The Irish lilt was back, the mischief in his eyes that I loved so much.

Why couldn't it be like this all the time? Because we both had a stubborn streak wider than the Charles River. But we could be good together. I wanted us together.

"The only reason I'm going along with this idiotic plan is because you called in a team. You are at least taking precautions."

"The only reason you're hand is still sliding beneath my towel is because you decided to talk to me instead of telling me what not to do."

I felt his smile fade and his hand stilled, no longer

caressing its way up the back of my thigh. "I can't tell you what to do anymore. Not that you'd listen anyway."

I put a finger under his chin, tilting his head back, forcing him to look me in the eyes. I knew the gold had swallowed a little more of the dark brown in my eyes. It always did when my emotions ran high. "I'd never pull rank on you unless you forced me to." I kissed his forehead. "Come on, help me get dressed."

By the time I was in the gown with my hair pinned up in a nest of curls Aidan looked ready to rip it off of me. Who knew helping me into my clothes could be as much of a turn on as when he took them off. I swear if it didn't take so long to pin all my hair up I would have thrown him to the floor when he slid the stockings up my legs.

"The dress is going to have to come off."

"In your fucking dreams, wolf." Aidan's growl could give any wolf, even this alpha, a run for his money.

"There's no way I can run a wire but hey, if you want I'm more than happy to slip my hands under that silk and give it a try." Cash gave me that devilish smirk, the one that said he was joking but his eyes belied the humor. He wasn't convinced about us or the "no us" in this case. He still wanted me and while he was going to play it cool he wasn't quitting the game.

How in the hell had I gotten here? Years of an uneventful love life, a dry spell worse than the Australian droughts and suddenly there are three men vying for a place in my life. I was starting to think my birth mother was a succubus and not a witch.

"Turn around." I glanced at Aidan, making sure we

weren't about to have a pulling rank moment already. He unzipped the back of my dress as Cash averted his eyes. Once the dress fell to the floor I stepped out of it in nothing more than thigh highs and lace panties. I didn't own a thong but the thin barely there lace didn't leave any lines. The dress didn't allow for a bra so I covered my breasts and told Cash to turn back around.

He froze, even his breathing stopped. Everything but his eyes, which took in as much of me as they could before I put the dress back on. Aidan cleared his throat in warning and he jumped to work. I noticed the slight tremor in his hand as he placed the small transmitter, no bigger than a nicotine patch, on my abdomen.

His fingers lingered on the scars running across my stomach from the last Omega of the Salem pack. He was lost for a moment, back to that night I was bleeding out from the gashes in my stomach on the hanger floor.

I felt Aidan's agitation rising and gently touched Cash's hand. He snapped back to the here and now, quickly getting back on task. The wire was different than I had expected. Instead of the small insulated round wires I was used to seeing, Cash ran a sticky strip up my ribs and then around to the side of my left breast. Small prongs on each end of the tape connected the transmitter to the mic, which was smaller than a Q-tip and would be hidden by the seam of the dress.

He wanted to run it up the front but the low cut of the dress and press of my cleavage would leave it exposed or the sound muffled. Satisfied with his handy work and with no reason left to draw it out Cash declared me wired up and ready. I was informed for the tenth time that I wouldn't be able to hear them but they'd be able to hear everything that happened. I slipped my dress on, turning so Aidan could zip me up. Cash moved to pat me down checking for the wire but Aidan grabbed his hand.

"I can take it from here." His voice was ice, menacing, warning Cash without actually having to verbalize the threat.

Cash stalked off to check the rest of his equipment but not before shooting Aidan a dagger filled look that said bring it on fucker. I resisted the urge to sigh. If it was bad now, wait 'til they met Mason Hunter. Actually, their respective hatred of the new competition might unite them in an attempt to rid the playing field of one more competitor.

Aidan slipped cool hands up my dress and strapped the obsidian daggers to my specialized garter. The two stone blades were as sharp as any of my silver ones but would go undetected if Caligula's guards used one of those security wands on me. If they frisked me and he allowed their hands that high up the slit in my dress they'd certainly find them. I'd be forced to rely on the rowan wood stakes disguised as hair sticks fixed into my curls. The silver wove its way around the sacred wood in an ancient design I didn't recognize. They were a beautiful and deadly addition to my arsenal. A gift from Aidan that I appreciated even more tonight than when he gave them to me his first night back from Reykjavik.

The lights from Caligula's hired car illuminated the dark lot outside as I put the last coat of gloss on my lips.

"That's my ride." I reached for my Falcon coat, it didn't go with the dress but it was the nicest coat I owned. I don't know why it mattered. I was putting down a vampire not going to prom.

Aiden looked away. "Amalie bring me the bag I asked you to get out of my car." She handed Aidan a garment bag and he pulled out a black coat. He slid it up my arms and fastened the one hidden clasp in front like a cloak. "Armani's tailoring is still impeccable after all these years."

I blanched at the mention of the designer label but before I could protest and slip out of the insanely expensive coat he reminded me that certain appearances were expected to be kept in vampire society. The layered Ottoman coat accentuated my body with its slim silhouette, instead of cutting my height despite its knee length hem.

"Time to go." With no reason to delay and anxious to get on with it, I walked out of my apartment knowing my backup would be right behind me.

***

"Where are we going?" The driver held the car door for me without a response. "A surprise then," I muttered. I slid across the seat and felt Conry at my side. The driver got in and closed the glass divider, subsequently closing any further questions or conversation.

Eyeing the small bar on the other side of the limo I decided one drink wouldn't hurt, besides I needed something to wash down the colloidal silver. I unstopped the crystal decanter and poured a small glass of scotch. The whiskey was perfectly aged and smooth, taking the capsules with it as it warmed its way down to my stomach. With nothing else to occupy me, I added a little more of the no doubt expensive liquor and settled back into the supple leather seat.

"Right behind me." I whispered to myself in reassurance, not wanting to risk being seen by the driver repeatedly glancing out the back window. Once again I felt Conry. I couldn't see him but he made his presence known by nuzzling my legs.

The scotch did nothing to calm the nerves that had taken over. My team consisted of a highly trained and deadly vampire, an alpha werewolf and a powerful witch, not to mention one kick ass ethereal dog. With backup like that there was no reason to worry. I trusted them with my life. If something went wrong they'd move in. I was about to mentally chastise myself for thinking that way, when the car accelerated.

Had the driver picked up the tail? A sharp turn had me sliding across the back seat. Bracing myself against the door, I chanced a look behind us. Headlights beamed in through the glass, illuminating the back of the limo, making it hard to determine the make or model of the vehicle. I could only assume it was my backup. We took several turns, none of them as hard as the first, before getting on the freeway. Wherever I was meeting Caligula it wasn't going to be in Salem. I pulled my phone out of the little black clutch and tried to open the GPS app. Of course, no signal.

The realization that Caligula was taking me out of state had my heart pumping. Was he taking me to the place where he killed all those young women? Did he plan to kill me the same way? He could try, but I wasn't like the Norms he took there. I would kill him and if I failed, if my team failed, I would jump out of there. He couldn't hold me like the others. He didn't know who he was dealing with. It was the advantage I needed. A reminder for the part of my brain that had spent so long functioning as a human, I had an escape route if things went to hell. With renewed confidence I tried to at least enjoy the rest of the ride in the limo.

The car finally came to a stop lasting longer than a red light. The engine cut off and the driver got out to open my door. I didn't bother waiting. I jerked the door open, almost knocking him over in the process. Anxious to see where we were I climbed out of the back seat, ignoring the proffered hand from the driver. Stubborn? Yes. Graceful? Definitely not. I barely made it out of the limo without giving the driver an eye full of more than my lace panties. I tugged at the slit, barely keeping the daggers hidden. Conry hopped out behind me, the driver still unaware he was there.

"Master Caligula's beach house." The driver made a sweeping gesture to the residence nestled on the edge of a cliff overlooking one of Newport's private beaches.

Beach house was a loose interpretation. It was more like a beach mansion. The area was littered with them from the Rockefellers to the Roosevelts, estates with mansions turned museums lined the Newport coastline.

I'd taken the tour on more than one summer trip with my adoptive family. I was always awed by the expansive marble, the very accurate Japanese tea house in one yard used to meet with foreign dignitaries and the overall grandeur of the era. I shouldn't have been surprised to find Caligula had taken up residence in the affluent area. Perhaps the cliffs and the ocean, the wealth and excess stirred up memories of Capris.

I made my way up the stone walk, about to knock on the front door when it seemed to open of its own accord. Moving through the doorway I was greeted by yet another of Caligula's servants. I bit back the *thank you, Jeeves* on the tip of my tongue as the butler took my coat. This place was as far from the unassuming Cape Cod as you could get. And I wasn't talking about distance. While the small suburban home said normal and content, this place screamed manic opulence. The high ceilings and black veined marble made the place feel cold despite the fires roaring in the parlors on both sides of the grand hall. Caligula came down the right side of the double stairway and I realized this was his home. The house in Salem was just a front, a place to troll for and then court his victims. Is this where he drained them of every last drop of blood?

Gliding across the floor he was suddenly in front of me. My hand was in his and against his lips before I could pull away. "Maurin, you are a vision tonight. Please join me in the parlor for drinks before dinner."

Vision, huh? I was going for more of a ghost of girlfriends past kind of thing. He slipped an arm around my waist and pulled me close as he led us into what would have been the woman's parlor when the house was originally built. Two ornate velvet chairs were situated near the fire. A small table with two champagne flutes on top was between them. A stand holding an ice bucket with an open bottle of champagne inside was behind the table. Caligula let go of me long enough to fill both glasses. I sat as he handed me mine, with Conry only a few feet away.

"Thank you." There was no reason to be rude, yet. I needed him to think he had me fooled. "I must admit I was surprised you contacted me after your lawyer warned me off. You said you had some information for me?" I fingered the necklace, sliding the cross back and forth along the chain. I watched his eyes follow the movement.

"That was before you informed me of the Coven's involvement. If you wish to know more about the dark arts there is plenty I can share with you. For now let us enjoy our champagne. We can discuss everything else over dinner."

Seeing he wasn't going to tell me anything until he was good and ready I had no choice but to keep up the charade. I demurely emptied my glass and got up to get another. Caligula smiled and quickly moved to refill it. This had to be the most bizarre experience of my life and I had a lot to compare it to. My life was pretty bizarre. But sitting across from a man who was once in charge of the largest empire of the ancient world, had tortured and killed in both lives, and drinking champagne as if being properly courted was insane. The cool, slick obsidian pressed against my thigh kept me rooted to the real reason I was here. To kill a killer.

The second glass went down smoother than the first.

My fingers tingled like the bubbles in the wine. I felt the crystal stem slipping from my fingers and tried to tighten my grip. Something was wrong. The glass slipped, spilling the champagne on the floor. I watched as the cascade of wine fell from the crystal flute before splashing against the Persian area rug, followed by the delicate glass which shattered into little pieces.

My vision began to cloud, the room spun. He slipped something in my drink. But how? I watched him while he poured. Could he have moved so fast I didn't see it? It was already opened when we came in. Shit, I was an idiot. Of course he would put whatever he gave me in the bottle, as a vampire he was immune to most poisons.

I felt him move closer. He leaned in, watching my eyes, waiting for me to pass out. I had a few seconds at best. I drew a dagger from beneath my dress. I knew I nicked the tender flesh of my inner thigh by his intake of breath. There was no sting from the blade as it cut my skin. I lost sensation in my lower body and the blackness was closing in. I swung wild, my arm heavy and sluggish.

He grabbed my wrist but not before I nicked his chin with the tip of the blade. The back of his hand connected hard with my face, splitting my lip. Blood bloomed on my mouth. With a hard tug on my hair he forced my head back and sucked my bottom lip into his mouth. I couldn't pull away. My stomach churned, from his touch and the need to purge the poison from my body. My vision was gone, my body totally immobile but my ears hadn't failed me yet. Conry let loose a growl that rattled the tall windows. He had made his presence known and was going to rip Caligula apart.

I heard someone shout. A woman? And then Conry yelped. His pain radiated through me. I tried to reach for him mentally. I needed to shift us out of here but the drugs were thick in my mind. I couldn't pull enough of the between into me. Could I call for the Hunter or my father? Would either of them reach me before the others? My mind struggled with the simplest thoughts. The others! People were coming. Aidan. He was coming for me, with Amalie and Cash. If I could hold on long enough they would bust through the door, kill Caligula and save me. Before I felt the satisfaction of knowing the monster trying to kill me would meet his end I was gone. Everything stopped. No sound, not even of my own heart beating. No feeling, no more heavy limbs rooting me to the velvet chair. Nothing. I was in a suspended state of nothingness. And no one came.

XIII
THIRTEEN

I don't know how long I was like that. I struggled to open my eyes. I wasn't sure I was successful because the room I was in was pitch black. With heavy lids I blinked again. Still no light but the cool air stinging my tender eyes confirmed they were at least open.

My tongue was thick and my mouth made an audible sticky sound when I tried to open it through the cotton that had taken up residence. The pain I hadn't been able to feel when the drug took effect came rushing in, overloading every nerve ending in my body. Tears rolled down my temples as my body shook from the drug wearing off.

Cold warred with the pain for dominance of my senses

and I realized I had been stripped of my dress, my body exposed. I still had underwear on. The lace wasn't really keeping anything from view but it made me feel better knowing they were there. Sharp pains speared my side but I didn't think it was from an injury I suffered. No, this was more like an intense phantom pain.

Fear gripped my heart as I realized it was Conry's pain I felt and I remembered his yelp. Someone hurt my dog. Not Caligula, someone else. My mind struggled to piece together what happened. A woman, I remembered a woman. She was the one who attacked Conry. She couldn't be human, another vampire? Had to be, and an old one if she got the jump on my ethereal dog. That fucking bitch was going to meet the end of a stake. If I made it out of here.

Anger fueled my body, coursing blood through my veins. With each fierce beat of my hate filled heart I felt a little more, heard a little more and saw a little more in the dark.

My senses came back but my confidence was nowhere to be found once I finally took in my surroundings. I was in a dark room, underground? No, under the house. The walls were made of stone and there was the distinct hum of fluorescent lighting. A soft whir and click, followed by another. I struggled to get up, to find the source of the unusual sound but couldn't.

I was strapped to a metal table, iron shackles on my wrists and ankles. I turned my head in the direction of the sound. Faint blinking lights, joined beeping of machines. Medical equipment. I followed the lines from the machines back to my body, noticing for the first time the needles and tubing stuck in my arms. I watched my blood run out my arm through the tubing into the machine and back again. Dialysis? What did they do to me? What did they do with my blood? For the first time in a long time I succumbed to fear. My voice cracked on a sob as it tore from my chest, drowning the anger that resided there moments ago.

Conry whimpered in response to my cries. He was down here. He was still alive. I didn't want to think about not having him with me anymore. Some of the despair released its grip on my heart when I heard him. He saved me when Olwyn attacked me in the hanger. If it wasn't for him I might have suffered more than scars on my stomach that night. If he was still with me, even with both of us injured and weakened, we could get out of here.

"Hey, boy, you okay?" I cooed, despite knowing he was anything but okay from the pain I still felt in my side. I strained to see him. He was in a small room across the hall behind iron bars. We both were, I noticed. I also took note of the iron bar sticking out of his side. What was it, was that a handle? Fire poker? She stabbed him with a fucking fire poker.

I was going to kill her, death painful and slow by a thousand toothpicks dipped in holy water. He tried to stand, to make his way to the edge of his cell and closer to me but only made it a few steps before collapsing. The iron weakened him. And me. They knew we were fae, that I was enough fae to be effected by the iron. We weren't going to heal any faster than a mortal. Infection was suddenly a very real threat. Anger and frustration took over again. I roared, thrashed, screamed for my jailers. I wanted them here, to know what their plan was so I could start plotting my escape.

The IV ripped free while I flailed on the table. Blood seeped steadily from where the hep lock ripped out. I wasn't making any progress with the straps or iron cuffs. In fact the more I fought, the more the iron cut into my skin, the weaker I felt. I forced myself to calm down. I had to keep my head. Conry and I wouldn't make it out of here if I totally lost my shit. I stilled my body, letting out a frustrated sigh, before my mind followed.

"Tsk, tsk." The woman was outside my cell. "What have you been doing? You're going to hurt yourself. And we can't have that. Not yet."

The sound of keys jingling and the lock turning was followed by the sound of her shoes clicking against the stone floor. The sound of her footsteps was simply for my benefit. She hadn't made a sound as she approached. She shut and locked the cell door before stepping into my line of sight. A vampire I had never seen before and she was old. Not as old as Caligula or the vampire king and queen but closer than any I have come across before.

"Are you going to be a good girl while I fix the IV? Or do we need another dose of the henbane?" She moved in to reinsert the hep lock. "You made a mess of that beautiful vein. We'll have to move it."

The machines stopped. Silence filled the room. My heart raced with nervous anticipation. Her hand slid along my thigh. Would I be able to work it free if she tapped a vein in my leg? I was strapped spread eagle, my legs held down tighter than my arms. She moved around, tracing the outline of my body with a finger while she decided where to start a new line.

"Who are you?" I didn't recognize my own voice. My throat was raw from screaming and dehydration.

She didn't answer right away. "This is going to hurt." She jammed the needle in my neck, slowly pulling it out to leave the tiny plastic tube for the hep lock behind. My back arched involuntarily and I couldn't hold back the groan. "Don't strain, it just makes it hurt more."

"Who the fuck are you and where's Caligula?" I ground out through clenched teeth.

Little daggers stabbed my ear drums as her laugh bounced off the stone walls. "My sire would no doubt be delighted by your desire to see him. He has thought of nothing else since you came to see him a couple days ago. He barely had the restraint to wait for the henbane to take hold. And then he tasted you. I feared he'd keep you all to himself. It took some convincing, he's quite mad you know, but he has never refused me. Not once since the day he turned me. You may look like his love but I am his kindred spirit."

The machines kicked on again and I felt a tug on the IV in my neck as the blood was drawn out. "I had to promise not to kill you. Not like the others. But you're not at all like the others. I needed them to get to you."

I tried to listen to everything she said, I really did. I knew the importance of every word that fell from her evil lips could be critical to my survival but the only thing I heard in her villain tirade was *a couple days ago*. I tried to hold back the well of tears but it was no use. I felt them running back down my temples into my hair. I had been down here, wherever here was for more than a day. No one came.

The reality of my situation hit me. I hadn't realized I still held on to the hope that Aidan or my father, that someone would get me out of this until she clued me in on how long I had been down here. The tears fell faster as a horrible thought took hold of my mind. Had they killed them? Or worse, chained them in some torture chamber like mine? When they heard the scuffle, before the mic no doubt went dead, did they try to charge in only to be out maneuvered by Caligula?

"Ah, you've figured out no one is coming to rescue you." She wiped away the tears as if genuinely concerned about my breakdown. She brought her fingers to her mouth, licking the salty fluid away. "This is always my favorite part."

"What do you want with me?" My voice broke through the tears.

"I thought it would be obvious." She waved a hand in front of the dialysis machine like she was practicing for The Price Is Right. "Your blood, the key to your power. The silver was a nice trick." She ran her fingers along her lips and I noticed the blisters for the first time. They were almost healed, looking more like cold sores than the seeping pustules they would have been when she first tried to drink from me.

"I waited a full day for the silver to work its way out of your system, it took a lot of henbane to keep you under and out of the iron so your body would reject the metal. I under estimated the witch who stirred the potion for you. I didn't drink straight from the vein the second time, for obvious reasons. You know, the dammed silver was actually suspended in your blood? Clever witch. But not one to be outdone I procured this device and had it modified to purify your blood."

"You could drain the life from anyone, why me? Weren't the five other girls you killed enough?"

"They were an appetizer. Barely enough to wet my whistle. I have an insatiable appetite. In my past life I lured the young maidens to my chambers under the ruse of being hired as a hand maiden. The blood of nearly six hundred girls filled my baths before they locked me in that tower.

"It was Caligula who freed me of course. He recognized himself in me after spending only days with me at court. Rumors had already begun to spread, I made the mistake of hiring an aristocrat's daughter. I told myself I wouldn't have her but her youth called to me. My body sang with the need to soak in her blood. I could absorb their vitality, you see. My own beauty, my own youthfulness extended by theirs. There is no sensation like bathing in warm blood, even now I prefer it to drinking. Caligula became aware of my gifts and rescued me the night before my execution." She made adjustments to the equipment, punching buttons, changing cycles.

"It took us sometime before we realized my gifts had expanded. I had only been satisfying myself with humans until he met Mercy. The assassin he sent was his greatest mistake and my greatest blessing. She was so young, too young. I became a feral beast. I had to have her, had to feel her against my skin. I had denied the creature inside me too long and she was just the opportunity I needed.

"She was gifted with the sight, for a time I was too. You can imagine my surprise when I saw what would happen to my sire. I wouldn't save his woman, not after he tried to cleanse his line for her, but when the Council was through with him I nursed him back to life. He wasn't the same and I tired of watching him barely exist. Europe called to me, I hadn't been home in ages." She sighed, a little shudder crossed her body as if she remembered something arousing. "They were glorious times, watching the modern age take hold. The mind of man grew darker and my life was easier for a time."

She was on a roll and I had no intention of stopping her. I was pretty sure I had figured out who she was. Caligula was crazier than I thought for turning her. No wonder he wanted to kill off his line and keep his children a secret from Mercy Brown. If the Blood Countess was an example, he'd sired a line of monsters. I was in some serious shit. I had an idea of what she had planned for me and none of it was good. The colloidal silver didn't stop her but it bought me time. There was obviously enough left in my system that she wouldn't risk it touching her skin again.

I needed to take advantage of however long it gave me. The henbane had almost completely worn off, the fog in my mind had lifted so I tried to focus on the between. I called out to my father, desperate for him to hear my plea. The weight of the iron was as heavy in my mind as it was on my flesh. I hadn't regained enough strength. I could only hope she'd keep talking or the silver would stay in my blood a little longer. I was working on a way out. I needed more time.

"The blood lust was always my curse, even after all my years I could still lose myself in it. I got sloppy. The European Council sent for a cleaner, that fucking vampire has haunted my every step. I thought I lost him after Reykjavik.

"I came here knowing my sire couldn't refuse me. Caligula took me in and for awhile I was able to satisfy both our needs. How the hell was I supposed to know the assassin actually lived near here?" She let out a small chuckle.

"He led me to you, did you know that? I was watching him the first time I saw you. The other girls looked like Mercy but you, you could almost be her doppelganger. The girls were the only thing that kept Caligula from meeting the sun. When I saw you, I knew I could have it all. The freedom to move undetected, the power to take the blood I need without being hounded by the fucking council and the one thing that would save Caligula."

Oh hell no. No fucking way was this bitch going to use my blood to get into the between to track down victims and my body to bring back her sire. I tried again, tried to force my brain to remember what Hunter taught me in his office. He said I was powerful, that I could spindle more of the between in my mind than any other fae he knew. I had to push through the iron blocking me. I might not be able to jump Conry and me out of here but by the gods I would bring someone to us.

No matter how hard I tried I couldn't reach my father. I'd only met him in the between in the flesh before. I wondered if not having created a mental link to him was why. Mason said not every fae had that gift but he was my father, surely he could hear me. I tried again. Nothing. Damn it! I almost let my disappointment and frustration out on a scream.

"What are you doing?" She hovered over me, then fussed with her equipment, then hovered over me again.

One of the alarms on the monitor beeped furiously. All this shit I was hooked up to gave me away.

My heart raced, my head pounded and I dripped with sweat. She knew I tried to pull on my power. I felt the warm rush of drugs through the IV. She doped me with more of the henbane. I had seconds before I was out again. Ingested, it only took minutes to put me out, intravenously it worked faster than anesthesia. I called out to the only person with the ability to see inside my mind. Over and over I silently called out to him.

"Don't get any ideas pet, no one is coming to save you. They've searched both of my sire's homes and found no trace of you. I didn't think the glamour would hold up on the ghoul, you would have seen through it with your fae blood no doubt. Good thing iron was such a popular building material back in the day. It'll keep the fae bottled up inside you, makes your blood more potent too." She stroked my arm tenderly. For being a completely insane, murderous bitch her bedside manner wasn't half bad.

I sank back into the abyss of nothingness. Calling out for my hunter as I continued the downward spiral. I could almost feel the bottom. It rushed up to meet me. The sound of my heartbeat slowed. Seconds ticked by between beats. Thump. Thump. With a lurch the last audible thump sounded in my ears. I was weightless, suspended in a black sea. Cool velvet coursed across my skin, in my mind. And then I heard it. A whisper, *Maurin.* My name had never sounded more beautiful. It was the last thing I heard.

XIV
FOURTEEN

The voice of my captor split my skull as she screamed, over and over again. There were words in there somewhere but I couldn't make them out. All I heard was the ear piercing shrieks. Elizabeth Bathory tore the room apart. Equipment clattered to the floor, something big crashed against the wall. I tried to fight off the effects of the henbane but I'd been given so much in such a short period of time. My eyes were not even trying to open. My ears and a small part of my brain fired on less than one cylinder.

Something happened. Had Caligula decided she'd kept me long enough? Was he coming to take me? I didn't want Bathory to have any more of my blood but I really didn't want Caligula to take me when I couldn't fight him off. The thought of his hands on my body, living out some sick fantasy while I was mentally aware but physically unable to stop him terrified me. Faced with two deadly fates I found myself choosing the physical death of the Countess draining my blood to bathe in, over Caligula using my body, slowly killing my soul until I finally withered away.

My neck burned and I felt something run down my shoulder. The IV was out, probably yanked out by the amount of blood I felt puddling beneath me. Some sensation came back but not nearly enough. I heard her fumbling with the leather straps, she wasn't unlocking the iron cuffs yet. Either she was forced to move me or Caligula was really taking me away.

Please let her be taking me somewhere else. If we moved I had a chance to get away during transport. I didn't think I'd get the same opportunity with her sire. Elizabeth was a bit of a hot head. Her rash actions and blood lust could work to my advantage. Caligula on the other hand had probably run calculations on all the ways he could secure me, including the ones where I tried to escape.

Wake up, Maurin. You've got to wake up. I fought off the henbane by sheer will. *Open your eyes. Open your eyes damn it.* My right eye twitched. *That's it, a little more.* My right eye fluttered open, followed by the left. Searing light assaulted my retinas. I couldn't make out anything through the blinding white at first. As my pupils adjusted to the horrific amount of light pouring in I made out the silhouette of the Blood Countess.

Bathory coated her body with a deep red cream, lathering it on like sunscreen. She hissed with each stroke across her skin. When my eyes could fully focus I noticed the smoke coming off her body. It was made of my blood. Whatever she coated herself with contained a lot of my blood and it still contained enough silver to cause a reaction.

Conry stirred across the hall, barking, howling and then barking more. He crawled to the edge of his cage, careful to avoid the bars and bayed like a new werewolf on their first full moon. Something or someone was coming down the hall.

Elizabeth was in a frenzy slathering more of the bloody cream on her face. The sound of footsteps grew louder. She screamed, something about no one having me. I was pretty sure her sire would have something to say about that.

Conry wasn't snarling or growling at the owner of the boots I heard pounding against the stones but I wouldn't allow myself to hope it was someone other than Caligula.

I hadn't figured a way out of this hell that didn't involve being released from the iron shackles and off the henbane, yet. But I would. One of my captors planned to move me and I was certain they wouldn't do it with me strapped mostly naked to a metal table. I needed to be ready to make my move. I didn't struggle or do anything to draw attention to myself. I had to conserve what little strength I'd gotten back and it wasn't much.

Something rattled the bars of my cell. Someone screamed my name. The voice was familiar but I couldn't place it. Why couldn't I place it? My brain said I knew that voice, knew it and the person who commanded it but I couldn't pull the name. There was a loud bang as something connected with the door. I rolled my head to face the hall. Taking my eyes off Elizabeth was a risk but I needed to know who was out there. A single tear ran down my cheek as relief and embarrassment washed over me.

My father and Mason Hunter were in the hallway. It was stupid given the circumstances to care if my father saw me without my clothes but I did. It was yet another humiliation I would have to endure at the hands of the Blood Countess. Mason kicked the iron bars again and this time they buckled. There was a rush of fabric, a shoe scuffing against the stone floor and I knew Elizabeth had spun around to see the intruders. I didn't take my eyes off of my rescuers until genuine fear flashed in my father's eyes and Mason stepped forward, his palms upturned, sword about to drop to the floor.

"Kill her." I mouthed the plea, hoping he would understand it was more important for her to die than for him to stop her from whatever she was about to do to me.

"Noooo!" Two letters but the hunter roared them with a ferocity that rattled my ribcage. I turned, it felt like an eternity to complete that one physical act but I knew only a second had passed. Horrified and stunned I watched as Elizabeth plunged a piece of wrought iron fencing, the kind with arrow shaped tips, into my chest. My heart sputtered, blood spurting from my between my breast bone. She drove the makeshift spear through me with enough force to penetrate the steel table. It was impossible to breathe. Each attempt to pull oxygen into my lungs was excruciating. I was racked with coughing, blood filling my mouth.

I heard Aidan running down the hall screaming my name. I wanted to call out to him, shout his name until he felt all the passion and despair I heard in his voice but it was impossible. I reached out to him, my wrist twisted, fingers extended straining to touch him despite being cuffed to the table. Mason rushed forward, Aidan on his heels. Aidan tried to shove him out of the way but Mason didn't budge, not even an inch.

He barked orders at Aidan to remove the iron spear so he could apply a special salve to the wound, increasing my natural healing abilities. Aidan dropped a soft kiss on my lips before grasping the metal rod. His breath caused the sweat beading on my face to chill. If I had the strength I would have shivered.

"On three. One." He pulled and if my lungs weren't filled with my blood I would have let out a scream that would have curdled theirs. What the hell happened to two and three?

Apparently my near death state wasn't enough to keep them from arguing. Before I passed out from the pain Mason informed Aidan there was no fucking way Aidan was drinking my blood. He didn't care if it would pull the drugs and any trace of the iron out of my system so I could heal myself. Not one more vampire would taste my blood. I thought I heard Aidan tell him he's already had my blood. Of course he managed to make it sound scandalously sexual. I didn't remember much after my father ordered them both to shut up and scooped me off the table.

I woke in the most comfortable bed I had ever

experienced in my life. Or maybe it was because I nearly died and needed the rest so badly, a box in an alley would have felt like I was on a Sleep Number.

The mattress curved and hugged my body, absorbing the weight of limbs that didn't want to work yet. I wasn't sure where I was but I wasn't on a metal slab, I wasn't hooked up to an IV and the room was iron free. I was out of that dungeon. My father had come for me. Aidan came for me. Because Mason heard you, I reminded myself. I wasn't ready to consider what that meant or the ramifications.

The mattress shifted under someone else's weight. A small smile crept across my face. Sunlight poured in from the open window and I instinctively arched toward it. Once the rays had thoroughly warmed my skin and thawed my brain it occurred to me I was not in bed with my vampire. Again.

My heart picked up a nervous rhythm I didn't recognize. People always say, "my heart can't take it." Seriously, after the last few days I needed a cardiologist.

Both terrified and excited by the idea of being in Mason's bed, I started to roll over. My nerves got the best of me so I kept my eyes closed, feigning sleep. I don't know why it mattered that the hunter had seen me so exposed.

Being a prude was such a human emotion. Most of the supernatural races were as comfortable in their birthday suits as they were a business suit, but it was more than my flesh on display in that torture chamber. He would have felt my fear, my weakness when I called out to him, seen the tracks of my tears.

No one, not Aidan, not my father, not even my adoptive family who I spent most of my life with, had seen so much of me. For reasons I couldn't explain it mattered. Even though I told myself it shouldn't, it mattered what he thought of me.

My arm tentatively slid across the sheet, fingers struggling to make contact with the person beside me, seeking comfort I knew I shouldn't. I needed to be sure, as if touching him would make it easier to look at him. Finally my arm stretched far enough my finger tips were able to graze his fur coat. Fur coat, what the hell? A sigh, heavy with relief, escaped my lungs - which were still really sore, ouch.

"Good, you're awake."

I went ram rod straight at the sound of his voice. The rough and husky timber electrified my nerve endings but I didn't say anything. I was too busy reveling in the onslaught of sloppy dog kisses. Normally I was not a fan of being licked in the face by a dog. I've seen where their tongues have been and the things they indiscriminately put in their mouths, my Conry was the only exception.

I heard the chuckle before Hunter cleared his throat. "I'll inform your father."

I tried to sit up. The wince and small groan had him at my side. His hands slid under my arms and he gently hoisted me. "Lean forward, easy now." After placing a few pillows behind me he helped settle me against the wall. There wasn't a headboard, footboard or even a frame for that matter. The huge mattress sat directly on the floor in the corner of a room and was the most modern fixture in it.

I think his bedroom was bigger than my apartment. Pelts and cushions littered the floor. The embers of a fire still glowed in the large roughly hewn rock walled fireplace, which at one time had been used for cooking as well as providing the warmth living in an old farm house required. The walls were limestone, the floor was slate. The thatched roof was different and suddenly a much needed reminder that we were not in the chamber of horrors beneath Caligula's mansion.

"Thank you." It was barely a whisper, his face was so close to mine. I couldn't ignore the way he closed his eyes, relishing in the proximity of our bodies, my breath a warm caress on his skin. I cleared my throat, still dry from dehydration and from being this close to Mason. "I mean, you know, for coming to get me."

"I will always come for you." He put some distance between us. Enough that he could sit on the mattress next to me but still face me. He never took his eyes off mine. "I should let your father know you are awake. He's been keeping vigil since we brought you here."

"Now that you bring it up, where is here exactly?"

"My home, a few miles outside of Cork."

"Cork? Like as in Ireland?"

"That Bathory woman knows where you live. Your apartment is not safe. Your father feared you would not survive the journey to his home because the wound in your chest wasn't healing fast enough. A combination of the drugs and blood loss. So we brought you here."

"This is a hell of a commute."

"You still have your sense of humor, I see."

"It'll take more than blood loss, my sarcasm is at a cellular level."

"I have a small apartment in Salem, not far from the station."

"Mmm, must be all champagne wishes and caviar dreams living in the city proper." I scrunched my face, trying to figure out how a guy who lived in one of the newly renovated and over priced downtown apartments could be this medieval.

His body shook with the laughter he held back. "It's loud, cramped and insanely expensive but it's convenient. I am a simple creature. I don't need much. Strip it down to the most basic, primal, carnal things. No one needs more than that." His voice dropped an octave, was rougher and hinted at some of those more carnal things.

Just like that we were back to the lion and the gazelle. I tried not to make any sudden movements. Afraid the hunter would pounce. Afraid to acknowledge the part of me that wanted him to. "Maybe you should get my father now." The look he gave me said he would enjoy every minute he spent hunting me.

I was surprised when my father knocked, then walked through the heavy, wooden door instead of appearing at my side. It must have shown on my face. "I didn't want to startle you." He brushed the hair out of my eyes before taking my hand in his and squeezing a little too hard.

It was all the comfort from a parent I had missed growing up. I only had to almost die to get it. I hadn't ever questioned my mother's decision to hide me with mortals until that moment. What would my life have been like, raised with Arawn who was over bearing, old fashioned but obviously loved me as much as any father should love their daughter.

"You wouldn't be the person you are today."

"In the dungeon, I thought, when you didn't respond, I assumed you couldn't hear me. That you couldn't see inside my mind."

"I am afraid that is something I cannot do but I do not need to read your mind to know what is so clearly written on your face. Every time I look at you I am gripped with a sadness for what could have been, what should have been. For all the things I missed. But we must trust that everything unfolds how it is meant to be. We cannot change fate anymore than we should tempt it. We can simply live and allow our lives to progress as gods intend."

"But aren't you a god?"

"Everything is created by something else. Like the gods who ruled Olympus were born of Titan blood, we were born of even older gods. That's enough of that topic for now. One shouldn't contemplate the light of creation when their mind is filled with the darkness that seeks to extinguish it."

I looked at him, certain my face hadn't given me away that time. "I know what hardens your heart daughter but you must not let it consume you. You are my child, born of the Wild Hunt, and because of that your need for justice can easily be consumed by the need for revenge. It is something all who share the hunter bloodline struggle with, succumbing to the darkness when we spend so much time in it."

"Mason said something like that, about light and dark, the first time I met him."

"Hunter is a wise man. He will make an excellent instructor."

Something about the way he said instructor made it sound more like husband. "Where's Aidan?" Guilt washed over me when I realized I hadn't asked about him yet.

My father's face darkened at the mention of my vampire. Apparently he hadn't forgiven him for the whole marking thing. He spoke in clipped words. "He is with his kind. At Agrona's residence I believe."

"What time is it with the time difference? Is it night there? I want to call him." Apparently he had developed a hearing problem in the last thirty seconds. "He was there, he came for me. That has to count for something."

"He's the one who lost you in the first place. Him and that rag tag group you run around with. If he didn't make every effort to get my daughter back I would have staked him myself."

"Hey, those are my friends."

"Friends who should have contacted me the moment they realized it wasn't you but instead a glamoured ghoul who came back from Caligula's."

"How were they supposed to do that? You can't be mad at them for something they didn't have the power to do."

"They have access to Kellen." He had me there, so I didn't bother arguing. Being in the employ of the Council and holding one of the seats would have granted any of them an audience with Kellen, who in turn would have notified my father of my disappearance. I could forgive them the oversight but my father most definitely would not.

"Are you going to let me call Aidan or am I as much a prisoner here as I was in that basement?"

"I will have a phone brought to you." He shook his head. "As much as it causes me grief, I am thankful for your strong will and defiant temperament. It's probably what kept you alive."

"I didn't feel very strong strapped to that table." I didn't bother to elaborate on the depths of the fear and despair I felt watching my blood circulating through Elizabeth's machine.

"And still you reached Hunter. There is much to do. Caligula has gone to ground and his monstrous offspring is using your blood to move through the between. I want you to be careful, Maurin. She's tasted your blood and she'll crave it like no other's. Not just for your power, but your essence. Even if you did not have the gift to move through the between she would crave you. You are my daughter, the blood of a fae lord runs through your veins. Which would be enticing enough but unlike other halflings your blood is not diluted with mortal blood. Your mother was a powerful witch and your blood is all the more potent because of it."

"If I'm so delicious how come Aidan hasn't bled me dry? He's had my blood more than once."

"I suppose he never took too much? He stopped when his wounds were healed, the moment no trace of the

Afrit poison remained in your blood? The urge to drain you dry the night he tried to mark you was only controlled by the fact you would be his forever, to drink from whenever he pleased. I will never understand why you would have bestowed such a gift upon him."

He sighed, taking my hands in his. "Do not waste strength fighting with me about Aidan. He is not the vampire I am concerned about at the moment. Every vampire Caligula sired was a monster, Bathory worst of all. Six hundred and twenty-five young women died by her hand. Over six hundred wrists and throats slit to fill her baths. All that before she was turned. Eternity with an unquenchable thirst for blood. Eternity spent with demons rooted in her mind. Time has neither curbed her blood lust nor healed her shattered mind. If anything she is worse, more blood thirsty, more demented than ever. Bathory has slipped through our grasp before, eluding the Council for centuries. The Hunt is preparing, we will run Caligula and Bathory to ground. They will feel the breath of the Cwn Annwfn on their neck, but for now you need your rest." He kissed the top of my head and left the room.

Conry curled up beside me and I stroked his back. I was about to give him one of the belly rubs he loves so much when my hand grazed the wound in his side. My eyes burned and my throat tightened from the tears fighting to escape.

I had almost lost my guardian, my friend. I would not cry, I would not cry. Elizabeth may have broken me in that basement but they would be the last tears I shed. We made it out and I would make Elizabeth and Caligula pay for what they did to my dog, for what they did to those girls and what they tried to do to me.

When their blood soaked the ground, when their ashes were scattered in the northern winds I would bask in the glory of my kill. The Blood Countess would truly know what a blood bath was when she met the point of my sword. Conry bristled at my agitation, stirring to look for what caused it. He needed to rest as much as I did. I ignored the pain in my chest and slid down in the pillows, curling up with my guardian. I fell asleep petting him.

XV
FIFTEEN

The temperature dropped and I shivered. Conry had moved away during our nap taking his warmth with him. I tried to scoot closer to him and the heat I felt radiating off his body when I realized we weren't in Kansas- or Cork- anymore. The familiar grey of the between surrounded us. Conry had regained enough strength to stand guard. The comfort I usually felt here escaped me. Even as my body absorbed the energy, healing itself in the process, I was on edge. Elizabeth could find me here and as much as I longed to see my sword glistening red from her blood I wasn't ready.

The grey began to shift. Stones took shape in the fog. I felt my chest tighten as the light flickered out and the thatched roof gave way to damp stones. I was back in that room. Medical equipment hummed and beeped in the background. Panic momentarily gripped me, rooting me to the spot at the foot of the metal table that I was strapped to hours ago.

I willed myself to move. The iron cuffs still wore a coat of my crusted blood from my attempts to free myself. I would not end up strapped to that table again. I forced my feet forward, one step, then another and another until I was running out of the cell. The soft glow of candlelight pushed at the darkness. Fully aware of how unarmed and unprepared I was to face my captors I continued to walk toward the light.

The hallway opened into another stone chamber. Unlike the cell where they held me there was no iron anywhere. Thankful for small favors I stepped through the narrow opening. Dead end. The room, if you could call it that was barely six by six. A well took up most of the floor, there was hardly enough room to walk around it. If it hadn't been for the light emanating from the sconces on both sides of the doorway I would have fallen in.

I stepped closer, surprised to find it filled with water instead of sealed with a cement cap once city water had been brought in. I bent down, about to dip my hand in the water when ripples moved across the surface. I jumped back, not wanting to get caught by whatever lurked in the well. Knowing the homeowners it was probably a fucking piranha pit.

A hand broke the surface, gripping the top of the well for support as the rest of the body followed. I watched in horror as eyes peered out of the water like an alligator in a Louisiana swamp. As more of her body rose out of the well it became obvious the water wasn't water at all. It was blood. Red rivulets ran down her naked body as she stepped out of her bath and onto the stone floor. She reached for me, calling my name.

"Maurin." Her bloody hands gripped my arms and I jerked backwards, slamming into the stone wall. The impact vibrated up my spine, rattling my head and snapping my jaws shut. I bit my bottom lip and cursed as I tasted blood. Elizabeth sucked in a breath, hoping to catch a taste of me on the air.

"Maurin." This time my name was a command. Her voice was deeper, stronger and I felt compelled to move toward it. "Maurin, wake up."

I shot up out of the nightmare and into Mason's arms gasping for air. I shook my arms until the sleeves of his pajama top were at my elbows. My mind wouldn't accept this reality until I felt it with bare hands.

I shoved his shirt up and pressed my palms against his back. The skin on skin contact helped me find my center. We stayed like that for a while, my head buried in the crook of his neck, as he supported himself with one hand on the mattress while the other stroked my spine.

His smell was heady and intoxicating, spicy like pipe tobacco soaked in whiskey. It was masculine and incredibly erotic. I took one last deep breath, pulling in the sensory memory as I pushed away.

He watched me scoot back against the wall with a grin that said he knew the effect he had on me. The grin faltered when he saw the haunted look in my eyes. "Want to talk about it?"

I shook my head, offering a thanks instead of the explanation he wanted.

"I told you I would come for you. Even if it's to pull you back from the shadows in your mind, I will come for you."

The intensity of his gaze overwhelmed me. My face warmed from the blush that crept into my cheeks. If I could have moved further from him I would have. It wasn't smart to be this close to Mason, he was an entirely different kind of dangerous. One I wasn't equipped to deal with at the moment.

With nowhere to go since my back was already pressed against the wall, I turned my head enough to avoid the kiss he moved in to deliver. His lips grazed my cheek. Cinnamon scented breath warmed my neck as he chuckled over my attempt to evade his advance. My heart skipped a beat, thankfully my brain put on the brakes.

"Do you have a phone I could use? I really should call Aidan."

He dropped his head, resting it on my collar bone and the sigh he let out had me shivering. It wasn't because I was cold. "He knows where you are. We sent word to the Council once we settled on a location."

"Still, he must be worried. I should call him."

"Oh he's definitely worried." He gave a devilish smile, winking as he produced a cell phone from his pocket. The sleeve of his shirt that I wore had slipped down, covering my hand and I shook my arm to free it so I could take the phone. "I like the way you look in that shirt. It suits you."

I knew he would follow anything I said with something along the lines of liking me out of his pajamas better, so I chose not to say anything. I took the phone and punched in Aidan's number, surprised I remembered it since I had him on speed dial.

"Aidan." There was a long pause and then he said my name, his voice shaken. "It's me. Yes, I'm okay."

I waited for a pause in the jumbled rush of questions and professions of his feelings for me. "I'm not sure how much longer I'll be here. No, they don't think it's a good idea to go back to my apartment."

"You can stay with me." Mason knew full well Aidan could hear him.

"Yes that was him. No. Aidan, did you hear me accept the offer? I'm going to hang up now." Mason laughed, obviously he heard the other side of the conversation as well.

"Maurin wait, don't hang up. I'm sorry. Feckin' hell." His accent was thick and I pictured him raking his hands through his recently cropped hair in his frustration to say things that wouldn't make me hang up on him. He let out a breath and I mimicked him. "We lost communication a couple minutes after you went inside. I wanted to call it off and pull you out of there but Cash wanted to give you a chance. He was confident you'd get the job done, said it would turn into a blood bath if I went in there and you could get hurt." I winced at his choice of words. "I shouldn't have listened to him. I never should have let you go in."

I wanted to reassure him, let him know I really was okay. The pain in his voice was hard enough to hear but the hint of fear mixed in broke my heart. Telling me all of this was important to him. He wanted me to know he looked for me, that he wouldn't have stopped until he found me. I may have lost hope that I would be rescued but not once did I doubt he was searching. Still, rather than interrupt him to tell him I knew he wouldn't have stopped looking for me, I let him get it out. I gave Mason a withering glare and pointed at the door when he muttered something about how you'd think Aidan was the one who was tied up and tortured. He didn't leave, so I turned my back to him while I listened to Aidan.

"But then you came out, so we followed the car back to your apartment. I was already waiting for you at the door by the time the ghoul got out. I don't know who worked that glamour, only the fae can work one that strong. Can't imagine what fae would risk crossing your father by creating a glamour in your image.

"One whiff of that rotting puss bag and I knew it wasn't you. I have been going crazy ever since. We questioned the driver, Cash roughed him up a bit. A lot truth be told but he was compelled, there was no breaking it. Jesus, Maurin, we forced our way back into the house. Caligula was gone by the time we got back. Tore the fecking place apart and never found the entrance. I thought I lost you. Then the Council calls and tells us to meet your father and that *hunter* back at the mansion. Turns out we wouldn't have been able to break the wards on the entrance even if we could have seen it. You were on that table with an iron spear sticking out of your chest. And then they took you from me!"

"Aidan."

"No, don't Aidan me. I told you, you weren't ready to go against him. That he would be prepared for anything and everything. I knew better than to let you go in there alone. You would have died."

"It was a good plan. I could have handled Caligula. What we weren't prepared..."

"Bollocks, it was a horrible plan. You almost fecking died!"

I kept right on going like he didn't cut me off. Normally I'd put him in his place for that and for yelling at me like he was currently doing but in light of recent events and the blame he placed on himself I gave him a pass. "What we weren't prepared for was the henbane and--"

"Henbane?"

Would he ever let me finish a sentence? I was about to revoke his pass. Mason chuckled at my irritation. Why the hell was he still here? I threw a pillow at him. "Think Romeo and Juliet."

"That's certainly one way to describe it," Mason muttered.

"Would you shut up," I hissed.

"What?"

"Not you, Aidan. I was talking to Mason."

"Mason is it? You're on a first name basis with the hunter now?"

That almost sent the hunter into a fit of laughter. "Tell him we've been on a first name basis since you came to my office wearing those knee high boots to tempt me out of that necklace."

"And it worked to. Now shut up or get out."

"You're in my bed, hardly in a position to order me out."

"Maurin." Aidan ground out my name.

I threw another pillow at Mason and he motioned to lock his lips.

"Maurin." I could tell through the phone that Aidan's teeth were clenched and his jaw twitched.

I let out an exasperated sigh. "Ignore him." I gave Mason a pointed stare, making sure he kept his lips locked. "What I've been trying to say is we weren't prepared for the Blood Countess. We thought Caligula killed the girls but it was her."

Something gnawed at me, something Bathory said. "Did you know she was here, Aidan?" Mason leaned forward, very interested in his answer.

"You need to come back to Salem. We have to talk to the Council. If Elizabeth Bathory is responsible--"

"Did you know she was here?"

"I lost her after Reykjavik. I followed her trail of bodies back to the states but there was no sign of her in Salem. My team, your team, has been hunting for her this whole time."

"And you didn't think five girls drained of their blood might be something she was capable of? That she was worth mentioning?"

"No, you found the necklace. Everything pointed to Caligula. This isn't how she normally kills, it was too clean."

"You weren't convinced he was guilty before. Did you know Caligula was her sire? That she can absorb power through blood?"

"Of course not! I never would have allowed you to go in there if I knew that. His line was supposed to be dead. Maurin, please, you need to come home."

"She watched you. She saw me with you. It set this whole thing in motion."

"Maurin, come home. We'll go to Agrona. Get the team together."

"I can't just jump back to Salem. It's not safe for me in the between right now."

"Why? Kellen wouldn't--"

"What do you think she is doing with my blood, Aidan?" The conversation wore me out. I had been in and out of consciousness for the last few days - or was it a week now since I went to Caligula's - but I was exhausted and the wound in my chest started to hurt again. The iron seriously slowed the healing process. I wanted a bath, a meal and a nap. In that order. "Listen, I'll figure out a way to get back to Salem. We'll talk with the Council. I promise. But I'm still not a hundred percent. I can't remember the last time I ate something and I'm exhausted. I need to eat and then go back to bed."

"Alone?"

"I'm going to ignore that. Better yet, I'm going to pretend you didn't say that and you're going to tell me how much you wish you could take away my pain. Followed by how brave and strong and totally amazing I am."

"You are all of those things and more. Maurin, I...you

know that I...you know how much you mean to me."

"I know, Aidan. I'll call you in a few hours." I ended the call, curling back up under the covers. My chest hurt and it wasn't because of the iron recently pulled from it.

The fact that he couldn't say it told me exactly how much I meant to him. Honestly, I was relieved that he hesitated saying those three little words. Relief was immediately followed by sadness. Maybe he was in love with me and decided this wasn't the right time to say it. Or maybe in that moment he realized he wasn't in love with me at all. Either way, if he had said the words I'm not sure what my response would have been.

My feelings for Aidan were a tangled mess. One minute I wanted things to work and the next I looked for reasons we wouldn't. I thought I was in love with him. I had certainly allowed myself to be hurt enough by him to be convinced of it and maybe I actually was at one point. If I was in love with him I would be mad or disappointed when he choked on the words but I wasn't.

I didn't have the energy to analyze my emotional revelation any more today. Mason must have noticed because he didn't fill the silence with smart ass comments about Aidan. He brushed the hair out of my eyes and pulled the covers over my shoulder. He kissed my temple and whispered something in a language I didn't understand. Within minutes I drifted into a dreamless sleep.

I woke up sore all over and with a stiff neck to the sound of running water. Hoping it was a bath being drawn for me, I pulled back the covers and got out of bed. I managed a few wobbly steps before going down.

The cursing I thought was just in my head must have been coming out of my mouth because Mason scooped me up before I hit the floor. He carried me to the bathroom and set me down on the edge of the tub. Some of the aches and pains were gone just from the sight of the streaming water. I couldn't wait to submerge myself in the hot bath. He added Epsom salts and eucalyptus to the water and lit two rosemary and mint scented candles before turning out the overhead light.

He managed to get one button undone on his pajama top. The one I still wore. I grabbed his hand. "Thanks, I can manage from here."

"You're still weak. I think I should stay with you."

"Nice try but I'm fine."

"Your face almost became intimately acquainted with my floor. We obviously have different definitions of fine."

"I've been in bed for a couple days and on a steel table for a couple days before that. I'm not surprised my legs weren't cooperating. If I promised not to drown in your bathtub would you leave me alone?" I threw in a please for good measure.

"If you aren't out of there in thirty minutes I'm coming in."

"Yes, sir." I hadn't meant for my voice to be so husky and had no idea he'd find those two words to be such a turn on. The panty melting stare it earned me had me wishing for a cold shower instead of a hot bath. He saw the surprise in my eyes over his reaction- and my reaction to his reaction, but I'd never tell him that. He gave me that debilitating smile and left me to my bath.

True to his word, before the water had completely cooled he knocked on the door. I barely had time to pull a towel into the water to cover myself when he barged in. His eyes quickly scanned the bathroom before settling on me. The heavy terry cloth towel had absorbed all the water it could hold. My body interrupted the towel's decent to the bottom of the tub and it clung to every curve. It kept me covered but didn't leave much to the imagination. The look in Mason's eyes was enough to boil the bath water.

"I uh, I thought..." He cleared his throat. "I was worried you fell asleep."

I tried not to laugh at the unflappable hunter. He'd seen more of me the other night in that room beneath Caligula's and then again when he obviously cleaned my wounds and put me in bed but this was different. There was no emergency or clinical reason for him to see so much of my flesh and he had a hard time keeping his desire in check. He wanted to do all those carnal things he'd hinted at the first time I met him and it took all of his control not to.

"Wide awake. I was about to get out." He set another towel on edge of the tub. "Turn around and face the wall."

The way he looked at me made me want to drop the soaking wet towel before he turned, giving him full view of the flesh it clung to. I barely resisted the urge, knowing that teasing the hunter would lead to things my body ached to do but my heart wasn't ready for. Once he faced the other way I let the towel drop, splashing into the water. He twitched, fighting the urge to turn around. I wrapped the dry towel around myself and stepped out of the tub onto the plush rug in front of it.

"You can turn around now."

Water dripped from my hair, glistening in the candlelight as it ran down my arms. The tiny flames flickered in his eyes and the man was gone. Replaced by the hunter.

He stalked over to me, pulling me against him. His body was rock hard, all of him. His massive arms engulfed me, pressing every inch of me to him. His mouth crashed into mine, his tongue demanding entrance. I resisted. At least I tried to but my traitorous body melted, deepening the kiss, opening my mouth to him. My hands slid up the hard planes of his chest to lock around the back of his neck.

I moaned into the kiss and he growled in response. Without breaking contact he backed me into the bedroom, moving us closer to the bed. I should stop, I was still with Aidan. This was wrong. So why did it feel so right?

A soft gasp that wasn't from me and was too feminine to be from Hunter broke through my arousal and brought me back to my other more conservative senses. I pulled back despite Mason's efforts to keep my mouth locked with his. Who was she and why did I care so much? Was she his lover or worse his wife? I wasn't in any position to judge. I still had a vampire boyfriend and it hadn't stopped me from ignoring the fact that my moral compass pointed due south, straight to Slutsville.

I couldn't help but compare myself to the copper haired beauty. Her fair skin was flushed, her cheeks and ears flaming a red to rival her hair. She was taller than me, at least five six and her hair cascaded around her toned arms. In a word she was breathtaking. What did she think of me? Raven hair that reflected a deep violet in the sun emphasizing my porcelain skin, brown eyes so dark they looked black ringed with gold. We were opposites, light and dark. I was no slouch in the looks department but I highly doubted she saw me as competition.

Humiliation overrode my jealousy as I looked at her and thought of Aidan. Her face gave away none of the betrayal she must be feeling. That Aidan would feel if he knew. I pushed further away from Mason and gripped the towel, that didn't cover as much of my body as the shame I felt did.

"Begging your pardon, sir." Mason looked at me, humor in his eyes. I turned away, the woman's words not registering. "I set the tray by the fire, there's fresh clothes on the bed for you, miss." She was already backing out the door.

"Thank you, Ryanne." He didn't wait for her to leave the room before trying to close the distance between us.

"Oh my god," I whispered, thankful for the interruption and return to my good sense. "What is the matter with me?"

Of course he chose to only acknowledge the first half of that. "When I imagined you saying those words it was with more passion and while you were on your back, your body beneath mine glistening with sweat."

Things low in my body tightened with his words. "Stop it." My body didn't want him to stop. It wanted to do the things he described. My brain managed to force the words out of my mouth and over traitorous lips that wanted more kissing and less talking.

"I haven't even gotten started yet."

"I can't do this."

"Oh, I think you can. You seemed more than capable a minute ago." He nodded toward the bathroom and my hand instinctively went to my mouth, my lips tingling with the memory of that kiss.

"That's not what I mean and you know it. I can't do this with you." Before he could formulate an argument that would convince me otherwise I kept talking. "I won't bother lying and say I'm not attracted to you. I am. Way more than I should be because I'm still with Aidan." I put heavy emphasis on the last four words. More for my sake than his. "I don't even know you."

"And you know him? Vampires keep secrets, Maurin. It's who they are, they can't help it. You might never truly know him. Ryanne prepared a tray, come sit by the fire." I didn't move. I didn't even look at him or the stupid, romantic fire. "I promise to be the perfect gentleman. You need to eat. Get dressed if it makes you feel better."

I scooped up the clothes on the bed and scurried into the bathroom. The jeans were a little too long and a smidge too tight for my taste, probably Ryanne's. The long sleeve white tee was too small in the chest and thin enough to emphasize the cleavage spilling over the top of the too small bra. Fantastic, Mason's housekeeper was a friggin runway model. "I need to get some clothes before you take me back to Salem. I can't see the Council looking like this."

I was only a size six but I looked like someone shoved me into children's clothes. A very tall child.

"I don't see anything wrong with the way you look." His eyes traced my body, stopping on my chest, when I came out of the bathroom. At my pointed stare he raised his hands in mock defeat. "Sorry, perfect gentleman from here out."

I dropped down on the cushions next to him, ignoring the pinch from French Maid Barbie's damn jeans. I shouldn't be such a bitch, it wasn't her fault she was perfect. I blame the pants. My kind hearted spirit was currently hanging out with my stomach over the top of them. He pushed the tray of fruits, cheeses and sweet breads to me before pouring a cup of coffee. I grabbed a scone and thought better of it, thanks to the damn pants, and popped a couple grapes in my mouth instead.

"You need to eat."

"Not much of an appetite. The jeans are doing their best to curb it."

"Then perhaps you should take them off." I jabbed him hard with my elbow. "I was merely thinking of your health. You'll need your strength. Your training begins tonight."

"Why tonight? Why not now? A few hours isn't going to make much difference."

"A few hours and your body will be almost completely healed. And..." He hesitated.

"And?"

"That is when the vampire is scheduled to arrive."

Aidan. Aidan was on his way. He knew it and was

working over time to get me in his bed before Aidan showed up. I would have been back in his bed doing more than recuperating if it wasn't for the sweet, saintly Ryanne delivering food and her excruciatingly tight jeans. His chiseled body would be working above mine, caging me with his powerful arms as my legs wrapped around him.

No, no, none of that. Imagining that is not helping. I scooted my cushion closer to the fire and further from him. He pushed the tray closer, chuckling when I popped the button of the jeans so I could fit a couple more grapes in my stomach.

"Perhaps I should see to your wardrobe. You'll need clothes you can actually move in for training." He leaned in, his mouth almost on mine when I slipped a grape filled hand between us. I filled my mouth with the fruit to keep his talented tongue out of it. He took my empty hand, kissing my palm before his tongue caressed my love line. It took all of my will power, not to mention conjuring Aidan's handsome face in my mind, not to give in. "Until later."

I don't know if I could survive the later he eluded to. I seriously doubted I would survive the two of them under the same roof. It was hard enough with Aidan and Cash. Aidan wasn't threatened by the alpha but he definitely would be by the hunter. Forget gym mats and heavy bags, what I really needed training for was my suddenly very crowded love life. Actually, the gym mats and heavy bag might come in handy.

XVI
SIXTEEN

I had been escorted to a room off the back of the house outfitted for training by Saint Ryanne, as she will forever be called. At least by me. She blushed when we met outside Mason's bedroom, obviously still embarrassed by walking in on us. She didn't say anything about it so I didn't bother to thank her for saving me from potentially making a huge mistake. It was probably better for all parties if we never spoke of it.

The wooden shutters had been opened letting in the cool evening air. It felt like rain but it was Ireland, didn't it always? I dreamed of seeing this country. It was number one on my bucket list but these weren't really the circumstances I had imagined. I pictured kissing the

Blarney Stone, stumbling from one pub to the next in Dublin, having an Irish breakfast in a bed and breakfast, standing on the edge of the cliffs watching the ocean crash against the jagged rocks below.

Instead I was holed up in a, albeit amazing, stone farm house with sheep and all, honing my fighting skills to kill two vampires and avoid getting into a jealousy induced argument with a third. Not really my idea of a dream vacation.

I rubbed my palms along my leather clad thighs. They weren't quite as absorbent as the yoga pants I typically practiced in. Despite the cool breeze on my exposed shoulders, thanks to the tank top, my palms were a little clammy. When Mason said he was going to get me comfortable clothes to train in I had something else in mind. Primarily cotton. At least the black biker boots didn't have heels. I did a couple deep lunges, surprised by the mobility in the pants.

"They'll give you more protection than the clothes you normally wear."

I spun around to find Mason leaning against the door frame wearing similar clothes. The short sleeves of his black shirt strained against his biceps. He really should be on a calendar. I picked up a sword from the rack on the wall, trying to ignore the pull I felt every time he was around. I let the sword fall under its own weight before swinging it back around. The whoosh of the blade as it sliced the air breaking the awkward silence.

He stepped in behind me. "Who's been teaching you? Your stance is off." He slid a knee between my legs, nudging until they were a distance apart that he was happy with. "So is your grip." His hands wrapped around mine, sliding them along the hilt into proper position.

"I hope I'm not interrupting." Aidan wasn't interrupting anything but his accusation and the way Mason had molded his body to mine, his arms around me holding the sword, it felt like he walked in on us fucking.

He stepped into the room, his long duster brushing the tops of his black combat boots when he moved, his jeans peeking out. The hood of his long sleeve shirt was up, very Assassins Creed and for the first time I saw who he really was- every bit the hunter Mason was. He stalked into the room, his jealousy and anger coming off him in waves.

I broke away from Mason and walked over to him, letting him engulf me in a hug feeling the tension leave his body as soon as he touched me. My stomach churned with guilt over what I had almost done with Mason. I needed to tell him. Not now. Later tonight, when we were alone. Or after training, when we got back to Salem. Or after I killed Caligula and Bathory but I would definitely come clean. I would.

I wrapped my arms around him, breathing in the scent that was uniquely Aidan. He pulled back enough to kiss me, his fangs nicking my bottom lip. I gasped as he licked the tiny beads of blood and tightened his grip on me. This was more passion than I was used to getting from Aidan in front of other people.

Oh he had no problem telling people I was with him, he touched me, kissed me but it was with the comfort of a familiar lover not the uncontrollable passion, the need to touch and be touched like new lovers had. That was always kept behind closed doors. His desire for me washed away the metallic taste of my blood on his tongue. And that had me pulling back. I looked up from our kiss to see his eyes focused on the hunter. I didn't appreciate the fact that this PDA was for Mason's sake.

I pulled him closer and he leaned down into my embrace. I was on tip toes, my mouth on his neck. I should have let him have his moment. It would have been the least I could do after my make out session with Mason but my mouth moved before my conscience could stop it.

"When you kiss me like that you better fucking mean it." I was careful to keep my voice soft enough that my words were only for Aidan.

"And the next time you kiss another man you should brush your teeth or gargle with whiskey at the very least. I can practically taste him in your mouth." His voice was louder than mine and I knew Mason could hear him.

I reeled back, shocked and ashamed. I didn't look back at Mason. I knew he wouldn't be wearing the same guilty expression as me. Triumphant would be a better description for how he probably looked. Aidan pulled me back to him and I whispered my apologies into his chest. His hand was under my chin, forcing me to look him in the eyes. "If it was under any other circumstances I might not be so forgiving. When someone comes so close to death it's natural for them to want to feel alive. I should have expected Hunter to take advantage of that."

"I guess that explains why vampires drink blood every

time the sun sets. They've been mostly dead all day."

That garnered Mason a look from me, one that should have shriveled his tongue in his mouth preventing further outbursts that would start a fight Aidan itched to finish.

He had the last word, except this time it was a whisper in my mind. One word, wrapped in a velvet caress of the between, it was enough to send heat pooling between my legs. *Mine.* I held back the moan as he used our ability to mentally connect with the between against me. My body suddenly felt full to the point of bursting with energy and I needed a release. If Mason or Aidan had their way I would be spending that energy on one of them. I intended to, just not the way they'd like.

"Let's get to work." If I wanted to survive the next few days stuck in this house with the two of them I'd have to spend every second of it training.

I moved to the center of the mat and motioned for Aidan to come and get me. Dropping his carry on and shrugging out of his black duster he joined me on the mat. He dropped the hood and I couldn't help but smile. He was gorgeous and his eyes held a look I hadn't earned and most certainly didn't deserve. And then he pounced.

He rushed me in a flurry of punches and kicks. I barely got my guard up in time, blocking blows with forearms and shins. He continued to press forward, backing me up to the edge of the mat. He moved to sweep my legs out from under me and I jumped in time to avoid being knocked on my ass. Aidan didn't wait for me to land. His palm shot out, connecting with my chest. I stumbled back once my feet were on the mat again, barely keeping my balance. He wasn't taking it easy on me and I got the impression he wasn't quite as forgiving as he said he was.

I couldn't let my emotions or my injuries get the best of me. That shot to the chest really hurt, his palm landing just shy of where I had been impaled. I fought the urge to rub it, knowing full well if this was Bathory she would use my weaknesses against me.

I was always a better counter puncher, finding my openings as my opponents worked offense but Aidan wasn't providing any. He continued to press forward. His arms moving at full vampire speed. There was no way I could strike. It took everything I had to block his blows.

He continued to work us back to the wall. His short inside jabs to the body got through my guard now that I had less room to maneuver. I came down hard on his right foot with two foot stomps. He couldn't really feel them through the steel toe boots but his foot lifted instinctively the next time I moved mine.

I swept to my right, knocking his left leg out from under him. He was quick to recover but not quick enough to stop my knee from connecting with his face on the way down. He backed up an inch and I sent my knee up again, hoping to get inside his guard and catch him in the ribs. He blocked with a downward thrusting palm. Finally giving me an opening.

I came straight up the middle with a short but coiled upper cut. It connected with his chin, snapping his head back. I smirked at the blood dripping on his lip where a fang pierced through. He wiped the blood with the back of his hand and then licked it off. His smirk matched mine, well except for the fangs. I swung with a wide left, hoping to box his ear and throw off his equilibrium. His hand shot out, painfully gripping my forearm as he pulled it to his mouth and fully extended fangs.

So the fangs were out. Two could play that game. No quarter would be given in our first physical fight. He wanted to prove I wasn't strong enough and I wanted to prove I could kick his ass. This was Rocky and the Russian. He may have had me against the ropes but I was about to make a comeback that would make Balboa proud. I spindled enough of the between to jump behind him. Eye of the Tiger blared in my mind as I phased. Before I could land at Aidan's back I was hit with something from the side knocking me flat on the mat.

Mason, who had been content to watch from the sidelines with Conry curled up at his feet until then, hit me with a small ball of his own bundled energy.

"What the hell, Mace? I had him."

His eyebrows quirked in amusement at the nickname I gave him. I rolled my eyes at his wink, knowing he saw it as a term of endearment. I don't know what the hell it was, it just sort of came out. Aidan, however, wasn't smiling. He jerked me up off the mat, my body sliding up against his and then back down as he set me on my feet. He looked at Mason and then back to me, the anger at Hunter softening when our eyes met.

"Stay out of the between. I don't want you in it, not even for the five seconds it would have taken you to come up behind him. Again." Mason was a drill sergeant. There were no breaks while he was in charge of my training.

"Let her catch her breath."

"There won't be any neutral corners with Bathory. She needs to work on her endurance if she's going against a vampire."

"I'm sure you've been testing her endurance as well as her resolve since the moment you brought her here. Give her a minute, she may be immortal but she's not invincible. She almost died, she hasn't fully recovered." Aidan stepped menacingly closer to Mason.

"So you keep reminding everyone. Pissed we wouldn't let you finish the job? Turn her into a bloodsucker, something dark, akin to the Unseelie beasts living in the shadow realms?"

"What?" I moved between them, forcing Aidan to look at me instead of Mason. I shoved him hard in the chest when he didn't answer. He didn't budge but I wasn't trying to get his feet to move, just his mouth.

"You were dying. Even after I pulled the iron bar out of your chest, you weren't healing fast enough. There was too much henbane, too much iron in your blood. I could have pulled all the toxins from your blood."

"I had already lost so much blood, Aidan. That would have killed me."

"You were dying already. I was going to bring you back, give you my blood."

"I don't want to be turned, Aidan. Never, do you understand me? Never."

"You can die, Maurin. You can be killed. You expect me to let that happen if it's within my power to stop it?"

"Yes, I do if it means turning me into something I

wasn't meant to be. Vampires can be killed as easily as you seem to believe I can. In the end it wouldn't change anything but my feelings for you."

"A world where you live to hate me is better than a world where you don't live at all."

"Giving up what I am to become something else isn't living."

"I didn't realize this was how you really felt about vampires. I don't know how you tolerated my hands, my mouth, especially my fangs, on your body for so long." He moved around me, ready to go after Mason. "Satisfied," he bellowed. "I suppose I should be thanking you for exposing her true feelings to the both of us but I won't."

Aidan swung a hand out, gesturing to me as part of the "us" he referred to, not realizing I had moved beside him. When he accidentally backhanded me, Mason pushed off the wall and stepped forward.

Content to watch us beat each other senseless in a sparring session, physical contact outside of that would not be tolerated. He'd have to get through me first. My hand came away bloodied from my nose and lip for the first time since we stepped on the mat and my switch was officially flipped.

Didn't matter that it was an accident. He was being an asshole and that was reason enough. I lunged, my fist connecting with his nose from a bone crunching superman punch. I knew he hadn't hit me in anger or even intentionally but I couldn't stop myself. I punched and kicked until I had him flat on his back and still I didn't stop. I dropped a knee on his chest, about where he had pulled the iron from mine. Breath he didn't need came out as my weight came down. I rained elbows on his face as I screamed incoherently.

The blows slowed down as the past week finally caught up to me again. "How dare you? I've never done anything but care about you. How can you stand there and say those things to me?"

"He's not standing or talking any more, Maurin. You may have just beaten a vampire to death. I'm impressed."

"Shut up, Mason. You've caused enough trouble for one night. Besides, he's not dead. Are you, Aidan? Just an asshole!" I kicked him in the ribs. He was down for the count and it was a dirty shot but I didn't really give a shit, I was too pissed off to care. "You constantly go around making decisions for me. You never discuss anything with me. You impose your will and I make excuses because we care about each other. Or at least I thought we did.

"But if you honestly think I don't want you to turn me because I hate vampires, that I think so little of myself I would give my body and heart to someone I loathe then go fuck yourself because I certainly won't be doing it anymore. I decide how I live and if I die. Not you or anyone else!" I shot Mason a look to let him know he was included in that declaration as well. I stormed out, shouting over my shoulder "I'm going out to get drunk. Alone. That means stay the fuck away from me."

XVII
SEVENTEEN

Alone apparently meant with Saint Ryanne At least they had the common sense to send her to inform me no one was comfortable with me going alone or jumping to the local watering hole. I wasn't surprised they were in agreement or working together to ensure I had an escort. Despite earlier events and the fact they hated each other, I knew they could at least agree on my safety. I argued that I would have Conry with me but they had prepared her counter arguments. Safety in numbers, blah, blah, blah. They obviously told her to save the best for last.

I would still have to jump since I didn't know the area and Bathory could use my blood to locate me if I was in the between for any length of time. I needed someone to drive me. I think they expected me to cave and pick one of them. So of course I nominated Saint Ryanne. Mason was irritated and Ryanne was definitely reluctant but I got them on a technicality. They said I needed someone to drive me but they didn't think to specify anything else. I'd been spending a lot of time with Agrona, I quickly learned the importance of being specific dealing with her.

Dressed in the clothes and weapons Aidan took the liberty of packing for me almost made me feel bad for kicking his ass. Almost. I wasn't sure if he let me or if I actually got the drop on him. I'd worry about it tomorrow night in our next sparring match. I would spend the rest of the night toasting his broken nose and my busted knuckles.

I'd actually be able to drink now that I was in a pair of my own jeans. The Levis induced lap band surgery had thankfully been reversed with pants my own size. I decided on the Flogging Molly shirt with the pin up girl on the front that hugged my curves, my black eight hole Docs and my leather jacket. I slipped a silver dagger into my boot, one on my left wrist and two new hair sticks. It was the most I had felt like myself in days.

Saint Ryanne waited for me in the hall, wearing jeans, a green silk blouse, brown high heeled boots and a brown jacket. She topped the outfit off with a little gold jewelry, simple hoops and chain, and very little makeup. Her red hair flowed behind her in beachy waves while mine was pulled up in a messy bun.

Everything about her said buy me a drink which offset my stay the fuck away look perfectly. We got in her silver Mini Cooper and headed into town. I would say the ride was painfully quiet but that would mean I actually wanted to talk to someone, which I didn't. I was really starting to enjoy being around Ryanne. Her silence was a welcome change. I didn't have to answer a bunch of getting to know you questions or entertain her with stories of my exploits working for the Council.

"So you're here to train with Mr. Hunter?" She signaled the bartender over to take our order, a bee sting for her and a snake bite for me.

I should have known it was too good to be true. I wanted to get drunk, was that so wrong? She hadn't done anything besides lend me her clothes and fix me something to eat so I spared her my typically sharp tongue. Plus I couldn't ignore her since she was my ride to and from the pub.

"Yeah, Mason is working with me on my technique."

"Well there's no one better than Mr. Hunter for that." She gave me a little wink to which I rolled my eyes. "That Aidan fellow, he your ex?"

Why did she have to decide to bond? I liked her so much more when she wasn't talking. I tried to remind myself she was acting like a normal person should but I'm not a normal person. "Right now I'm not sure what he is. It's confusing and apparently driving me to drink. Look, don't take this the wrong way because you seem like a really nice person and everything but I'm not feeling very chatty tonight. I just want to have a few drinks and contemplate my life."

The pub was packed for a weeknight. Locals were crowded around old wooden tables, sharing stories and singing along to the folk band set up in the back corner. We'd be lucky to get a drink, let alone drunk.

I tried to relax, to forget about Caligula and Bathory, strumming my fingers on the bar in time to music that sounded a lot like Van Morrison. Maybe they'd do a cover of Into the Mystic. Ryanne hummed along, watching the band and giving the drummer a little wave. I liked her a little bit more. Everyone always goes for the singer or guitarist. Of course he flashed her a brilliant grin and followed up with a wink. He would have been an idiot not to. I could tell all of the guys in the place hoped to catch her eye.

I wondered again if there was more to her relationship with Mason or if there had been at some point in the past. Two people that attractive would surely be attracted to each other. Visions of little Masons and Ryannes danced in my head and I felt a scowl forming. I wondered why I cared and where the hell the bartender was.

Someone started to complain as the bartender made his way over to us with our drinks. "Shut it, Wallace or that'll be the last drink ye have tonight." Wallace, who apparently thought his refill was ahead of our first round, sank down on his seat. He was a chubby guy, more ass than there was stool, and somehow he still almost missed. "Ignore that one. He's had plenty and waiting will do him good. Besides, you look like you could use this more than him. You're far too pretty to be wearing that frown." The bartender set a glass filled three quarters full of ale in front of me and dropped a shot glass of whiskey in.

"I didn't order an Irish car bomb."

"You're in Ireland. We just call them car bombs here."
I couldn't help it, I smiled. I even managed a chuckle.
"That's more like it, now drink up."

"Well done, James, well done. I haven't seen her smile the entire time she's been in Ireland. Not once." Ryanne nursed her bee sting.

"I haven't had much to smile about lately." I slammed the rest of my drink.

James had my snake bite waiting in the wings and handed it to me. "Let's see if we can fix that, shall we?" His hazel eyes twinkled with a touch of mischief, enough to know he was a healthy dose of fun but totally harmless. I bet he gave the ladies in this bar a run for their money with his down home good looks and all that charm. "Boys play something for my American friend."

Much to my embarrassment James continued to harass the band until the rest of the bar joined in and they had no choice but to toss out their set list. I was uncomfortable with the spotlight until the first few bars of the Who's American Woman belted out of the guitar. When the singer got to the chorus and sang *stay away from me*, while trying not to laugh I was convinced this was my new favorite place. No one but Ryanne knew who I was but I was pretty sure she didn't know what I was or what I was really training for. Maybe I really could have a few drinks and forget for awhile.

The night was finally looking up. We moved from the bar to a table near the band, wedged in between the musicians on a break in between sets. Apparently Ryanne had grown up with all of them and the friendly conversation peppered with teasing was contagious. It had been too long since I'd done this. Not since my split with the coven. Well, at least I had Conry. You're not really drinking alone if you're with your ethereal dog, right?

Eighties pop music wafted out the speakers and laughter filled the air. James came over with another round as I considered flagging myself after singing along to not one but two Blondie songs. I couldn't carry a tune and probably made an ass out of myself.

I took the drink to wash down the embarrassment and prevent my defense of Debbie Harris and her ground breaking rap effort from coming out after the drummer asked James to turn that shite off. I didn't bother to learn all their names, certain I wouldn't see them again after tonight so I kept them straight by instruments. When the bassist asked how I even knew the words to that song I credited my vast lyrical knowledge to Pop Up Video on VH1.

Apparently Ryanne forgot she was my designated driver because she threw drinks back like it was sorority initiation night. If it wasn't damn near impossible for me to stay drunk, a cab would definitely be in our future. If I cut myself off now, my metabolism would burn off the alcohol and I'd be fine to drive us back to Mason's place. Staying on the right side of the road would be the real problem and by right I mean left. Maybe we should walk.

I pushed my half empty glass to the center of the table, laughing when the guitarist slammed it down instead of his own.

"Bloody hell, what did you do to it? You ruined a

perfectly good beer."

Before I could explain the perfection that is Black and Tan mixed with hard cider (or James's equivalent) Conry bolted out from under the table, knocking over glasses and bottles. Chairs screeched against the floor as everyone pushed back from the table in an effort to get away from the huge puddle of spilled drinks spreading to the edge of the table.

Chaos erupted as Conry tore through the bar leaving a wake of turned tables and flipped chairs behind him. I shoved through the crowd and ignored the shouts of *what the hell is that, how the bloody hell did that pony get in here* and some other more colorful complaints as I followed him toward the front door. Ryanne was right behind me, shoving her hand on the door before I could pull it open.

"Maurin, I've already called Mr. Hunter. His instructions were to stay inside. He and that vampire fella are on their way."

"I think James is going to have a serious problem with that plan." The happy go lucky bartender from moments ago was replaced by a surly, cursing man trying like hell to keep the place from being completely destroyed. I watched as he knocked one guy flat on his ass for trying to make a run on the bar. That'll be the last time he tries to steal when James is behind the bar.

Ryanne's face went slack, eyes glazed over like a Krispy Kreme. I snapped my fingers in front of one eye and then the other. Nothing. I gave her a firm shake. "We don't have time for this, Ryanne. Wake up!"

Someone yelled, *would somebody please get that damn dog*

out of here! Conry growled as a few of the bigger guys tried to back him in a corner. "You don't want to do that boys, trust me. Ryanne, seriously wake up. I'm going to slap you but I want it duly noted I had no other choice since you didn't respond and I'm fairly certain you'd rather I slap you than ruin your makeup and blouse by throwing whatever it is that's left in the closest glass I can find." I reeled back and was about to make contact when she came to. My breath came out in a rush. I really didn't want to smack Saint Ryanne.

"I'm back, I'm back. Jaysus, don't slap me."

"I appreciate your desire to follow orders, what with Mason being able to fire you and all but going catatonic is taking it a bit far don't you think? He said stay inside not stay still. What the hell is the matter with you?"

"I have a touch of the sight. Wee bit of fae blood thrice removed on my mother's side. Not enough to help anyone, just enough to be a danger to myself. I practically turn to stone when a vision hits me. It's why Mr. Hunter took me on as his housekeeper. He'd never admit it but he felt bad for me, wanted to help me somehow."

"You have visions, nothing to feel bad about. When we finally coral my dog and get out of here, away from whatever has him spooked, remind me to tell you about the weird shit that has become my life." I gave a soft, low whistle hoping Conry would hear it over all the commotion he started and know that I wanted him to fade. "When my dog disappears we go, got it?"

"Your dog's been in here the whole time, hasn't he?"

"I never leave home without him."

"Mr. Hunter said to stay inside."

"We're not staying inside. We're getting the fuck out of here, now!" Conry ferreted out a vampire, who made his presence known at the entrance to the men's room. We weren't the only ones out for a drink. He tossed the drummer out of the way, slowly moving toward us. His eyes and body language said this vampire was looking for a fight."Out the front door, now. Move."

"We're not going out the front."

"I don't care what Mason said."

"Maurin, we're not going out the front." Her voice was an octave away from panicked scream.

"What did you see?" Something spooked her, something from her vision.

"I saw him." Her arm shot out pointing at another vamp outside. "That's why I didn't want to go outside."

"This is why it's so important to be specific about these things." Okay, think Maurin. The vampire inside is more of a threat. Take him out, wait to see if his buddy still wants to come in after that.

Two stakes, two silver daggers, two vamps. Time to party. These mother fuckers are ash. "Get behind the bar with James. I'm betting he's got a shot gun back there. It should help buy us some time." I pulled the dagger from my boot and slid the other out of its sheath.

Ryanne scrambled across the floor on hands and knees, looking over her shoulder once to see where I was. "Right behind you." I reassured her. Only, I wasn't. I closed the distance between me and the vampire. Ryanne cried out my name but James already had the Dutch door open and dragged her behind the bar.

With her out of the way and as secure as I could get her, I focused ninety percent of my attention on the vamp in front of me. I still needed to keep an ear out for the one outside. He would come through the window or the pile of people who'd jammed chairs and tables in front of the door and then themselves on top of that. I guess they liked the odds with the vamp inside better than trying to run away from the one outside.

Conry positioned himself at my back watching the one outside. My hands clenched around the daggers as I kicked a chair out of the way. Some of the locals huddled into corners praying they went unnoticed.

The drummer snapped off the rounded tip of his drumstick under his boot and lunged for the vampire. I didn't even have time to yell for him to stop. The vampire snatched him out of the air. The drummer's blond ponytail came loose and his shoulder length hair fanned out around his face. His hands instinctively went to pry the vampire's hands from his neck. It was over before it started.

With a loud snap the vampire broke his neck and tossed him aside. A woman screamed, others sobbed but I didn't look for any of them. I kept my eyes on the vamp in front of me. He obviously wasn't a music lover because he snatched the guitarist off the floor. Fangs extended. The guitarist didn't scream or beg, hell he didn't even flinch. I liked him, with his black faux hawk, smiling brown eyes and easygoing personality but I couldn't save him.

His eyes slid to me as the vampire's teeth tore through his neck. Before his eyes went flat and the life was drained from his body the guitarist stabbed the vampire in the stomach with one of the jagged drumsticks he had picked up off the floor. The guitarist was dead before he knew if he even hurt him.

The vampire barely flinched as he pulled the makeshift stake out of his gut. The wood was all wrong and it wasn't a kill shot but it was a distraction. Bought me a couple seconds. I circled around a table and moved closer to the vamp. It shrugged out of his leather coat, giving him better range of motion. He didn't think he needed the protection from me or my blades. That was his first mistake.

His second mistake was lunging for me. I dropped down on my knees keeping one dagger slightly raised. He over-shot me by a few feet but I managed to slice through his jeans and his leg, if the darkening fabric was any indication, as he sailed past. He still managed to land on his feet, running his hands over his slicked back, dish water blond hair. He kicked the edge of another table hard enough to send it sliding toward me. I couldn't move out of the way fast enough and it crashed into my pelvic bone, folding me in half.

My upper body hit the table top hard expelling all the air from my lungs. The vampire grabbed the back of my head and slammed my face into the table, splitting my cheek. He grabbed my hair and used it to drag me across the table, pulling me against him. He licked the blood running down my face, breathing deep as he savored my complex taste.

I drove my dagger up, trying to reach the heart but I was too close, the angle was wrong. I pulled out and aimed higher but was hit in the side with a hard right that definitely cracked a few ribs. I tensed my abdominal muscles in an effort to lessen the blow aimed for my solar plexus and hold on to some of the air in my lungs. I heard the shotgun blast and felt the vampire jerk. James pumped the shotgun again and took aim to the left of the vampire. The windows shattered.

A vampire with a hole in her stomach from James's gun climbed through. Where the hell did she come from? And where was the other guy? I tighten my guard, tucking my left elbow in, favoring that side because of the cracked ribs. I could still end up with a punctured lung if I took another hit before they had time to heal.

With short quick thrusts I stabbed the vampire holding me in the chest. The last one almost hit its mark, nicking his heart leaving him immobile. Still holding the dagger I used all my body weight and leaned against him. He went down on his back with me straddling him. One palm over the other I pushed down, forcing the dagger through his heart and out his back. The tip wedged into the wooden floor boards so I left it where it was.

The vamp bitch had already made her way to the bar. Blood pooled on the teak wood where James was slumped over the top, the right side of his face was smashed in. She reached behind for Ryanne when Conry clamped down on her leg.

Sounds of a fight spilled in from the parking lot, more vampires were out there and I prayed to whoever listened that the people outside weren't slaughtered. Ryanne stood up from behind the bar with her boot in her hand. She swung hard, jamming the heel in the vampire's eye. Conry pulled, his teeth tearing through the vampire's calf, shredding muscle. She shrieked, the boot making a wet sucking sound as she pulled it free, part of her eye clung to the heel like chewing gum.

Ryanne backed up to the end of the bar. I still had one hair stick. Yanking it free of my knotted, tangled hair I slammed it into her back, wishing I paid more attention in biology. I wasn't sure I pierced her heart until she crumpled to the floor. I didn't bother pulling the mini stake free, backing up before the body turned to ash. I was in no mood to be covered in vamp ash - that shit itches. I was down to one blade and by the sounds of it there was more than one vampire outside.

Ryanne crawled over the bar with James's shotgun in hand and moved down beside me. With Conry leading the way we crept to the window, or what used to be the window. A few people yelled at us to get back, to stay inside. Ignoring them we pressed forward. I was about to poke my head out of the hole in the wall to see how many vampires were out there when one slammed into the siding. Before he could push off and get back in the fight, Aidan was on him. He connected with a right hook that would have knocked a norms head clean off when he caught sight of me in his peripheral.

"Stay inside."

"Like hell. On your left." I crawled through the opening with my dagger in hand as Aidan blocked the blow from the vampire he fought.

Aidan landed three sharp left jabs, hitting the liver

with laser precision before moving up and working his ribs. Bones crunched as Aidan continued to work the body. He threw an upper cut that snapped the vamps head back and probably popped a couple vertebrae. His fist was through the chest and out the other side before my feet touched pavement. The heart beat once in Aidan's palm before the body hit the ground. I stood there gaping like an idiot and got a mouth full of ash.

"I should have told you to get out, to run for your life. Maybe then you would have stayed inside, since you always do the opposite of what I say."

I would have told Aidan to fuck off if I wasn't so busy gagging on ashes. The itching I wouldn't be able to scratch since it was in my mouth set in. I tried rubbing my tongue against the roof of my mouth but it made it worse. I'd just have to deal until I got water and an antihistamine.

Scanning the parking lot for Conry, I caught sight of him taking down a vampire under the street light. Mason threw a dagger burying it to the hilt in the vampire's chest, hitting the heart on the first try. Conry took off but he wasn't fast enough. With a muzzle full of ash he sneezed the whole way as he cleared the distance to join Mason.

The last vampire, totally succumbed to blood lust, stalked Mason. The hunter was now the hunted. If he got his fangs in Mason, he was as good as dead.

Vampires that far gone didn't make two neat little holes, lapping the neck when they're done to remove any trace of the feeding. They ripped, gnawed their way through, tearing out huge chunks of flesh and swallowing it along with the blood. I gripped my dagger tight enough to feel my nails dig into my palm and slowly stepped around Aidan.

"Where do you think you're going?" Aidan grabbed my arm, careful to avoid the silver blade. "The hunter has it well in hand."

The air cracked as Mason unfurled a black snake whip fashioned into a blackjack from his side. Muscles flexed as he controlled the silver laced leather, splitting the vampire's skin each time the tip made contact. After the third strike the vampire was able to maneuver his way in out of the whip's danger zone.

Certain Mason was in trouble I struggled against Aidan's grip needlessly. A whip was useless in close contact but the blackjack handle wasn't. The vamp never saw it coming. He swung the buckshot loaded handle out, smashing the vampire's skull. Mason stood over the stunned vampire and drove his bowie knife into the heart. The vampire, head and all, was ash before he pulled out the blade.

"We need to clean this up." I couldn't risk people getting caught in the cross fire or my location being compromised - probably should have thought about that before I decided to hit the bars.

"I already spoke to the local Regulator. A team is already here to take care of it."

"I want the night totally scrubbed, Aidan. They can't remember me, that I was here."

"I think this is simply a case of wrong place wrong time but I will be sure any memory of you is wiped from their minds."

"You really think this is a coincidence?"

"There's been a few attacks, nothing serious. Sounds like a sire has been neglecting the children. Not everyone should be allowed to have children."

Aidan helped Ryanne out of the window, wincing once he held her full weight in his arms. She didn't weigh much so I knew he was injured. His shirt bunched as he moved to set Ryanne down. Muscle and skin knit back together around the piece of a blade, a switch blade if I had to guess from the width that had been snapped off in his side.

I caught the hem of his shirt before he could smooth it down and lifted up to fully expose the wound. "We're going to have to cut that out." My fingers traced the healing skin and he sucked in a breath at my touch. "You need to feed."

He cupped my chin, forcing me to look at him. He didn't see whatever he was looking for as his thumb barely touched the bruised and broken skin on my cheek, the disappointment evident in his eyes. "You should tend to your own wounds, a chuisle." He walked away, leading Ryanne to the black H2 waiting in the shadows of the parking lot.

I felt Mason's eyes on me, watching me as I watched Aidan. I knew I shouldn't but I couldn't help myself, I hadn't been able to since I first met Mason. I turned, meeting his gaze. My breath hitched in my throat, my body tightening, responding to him even though I felt torn in two. Ignoring the urge to run to him I headed to the H2.

"Maurin."

I turned slowly so he wouldn't know how much hearing him say my name affected me. He stood in between the open driver door and the car, arms crossed, resting on the roof of the Mini Cooper. His black hair stuck out in every direction, blood, ash and grime covered his face but he had never looked sexier.

"Ride back to the house with me." "If for no other reason than to watch you fold yourself up in that little car."

I probably shouldn't. I should probably go with Aidan but I didn't want the lecture I knew he would give me. Aidan's lectures usually turned into arguments because I was too stubborn for it to go any other way. I was too tired to deal with that. The Mini Cooper held the promise of peace and quiet. I glanced at the Hummer. Aidan and Ryanne were already inside. Aidan was brooding behind the wheel, watching me with an intensity the prospect of a car ride didn't deserve. I put a finger up, telling Mason to wait a second and jogged- well more like briskly walked, since I was more than a little sore at the moment- to the driver's side of the Hummer.

Aidan lowered the window. "Maurin, we should go. Get in."

"I'm going to ride with Mason. It's probably better if we split up, no one should go alone."

"He's a big boy. He can take care of himself." You'd think I just told Aidan that Mason and I were going steady.

"It's a car ride, Aidan. It's not like I'm going to perform fellatio on the way back." His jaw actually dropped. "My ribs are too sore. I don't think I could manage to position myself across the front seat and under the steering wheel."

XVIII
EIGHTEEN

"So, does this happen every time you go out?" Mason relaxed his grip on the steering wheel.

"Actually this was the first time a band sang to me." I saw the look out of his peripheral. "Oh you mean the part where vampires decided to attack us? No, vampires in Salem don't make a habit of eating the tourists."

"I was actually talking about having guys fight for your attention?"

"Nobody was fighting over me except for vampires trying to drink my blood."

"Based on the look Aidan gave me when you decided to ride with me, I'm going to disagree with you. Do me a favor, next time don't wait for Ryanne to call me. You can trust me, Maurin. You can count on me. I meant what I said, I'll always come for you. No matter where it is, especially when you're in danger."

"I was so focused on getting Conry out of the bar I totally missed what set him off in the first place. I didn't feel the vampires. I didn't see the first one until he wanted me to."

Mason didn't push or take the fact that I didn't respond to his vows as a slight. He didn't expect a response because he knew I didn't have one. "They were cloaked. If you open yourself up to it you can sense them. We'll work on that tomorrow night."

The first time I met Aidan he had cloaked me, helping me break into a crime scene, so I knew I'd be partnered with him again for training. Maybe we could get through the night without hurting each other for real this time. There was an instant attraction and everything about him, about the way I felt for him, was different than Oberon.

Of course that whole thing with Oberon was basically a magical hallucination courtesy of Mahalia so every relationship I ever have will be different than that one. Aidan was exciting, he took risks and almost died for me. That was our first night together. Everything since then was like an emotional roller coaster. We were never on the same track or the same speed.

"Where'd you go just?"

"Hmm?"

"I was telling you about your training with me tomorrow morning but you were off someplace in your head that I can't follow."

"Sorry, it's nothing. I guess I'm just tired." Afraid he would sense the lie I turned the conversation back to him. "So, sensei, what will I be learning tomorrow?"

"Ahh, grasshopper, now you will have to wait and see."

I stumbled into Mason's house, pressing my back against the front door to close it and resting for a minute. Exhaustion took hold now that the adrenaline had worn off. Most of the injuries would be gone by morning. A few fading bruises and tender ribs would be the only physical reminder of my run in with the blood crazed vamps.

I didn't want to think about the team coming in to clean up the mess from my night on the town. I didn't want to think about the waste of youth and talent, the two sweet band members, Ryanne's friends, dead. I really didn't want to think about the fact it was a crazy coincidence that we were at the same bar as the vampires because I don't believe in coincidence.

What I wanted was sleep and maybe a burger. My stomach rumbled in confirmation. Unfortunately food and sleep would have to wait. Triage would have to come first.

I looked around the living room where everyone had collapsed into chairs and couches, apparently feeling the same as me. Ryanne fared the best out of all of us. Having spent most of the scuffle behind the bar she only had a few scrapes and bruises. Still, she was probably emotionally exhausted at this point.

I got the feeling she led a pretty normal life despite her employer and her visions. Not many bar fights with vampires. Aidan sat next to her and winced when she repositioned herself causing the cushions to shift. Shit, I almost forgot he had a blade broken off in his side. The skin had already healed over it by now.

I pealed myself off the door and walked to the couch, stopping in front of Aidan. "Take off your shirt and lie on the floor."

"If I knew fighting vampires turned you into such an exhibitionist, I would have taken you to work with me months ago." His hand glided along the outside of my thigh.

I saw Ryanne, looking ready to flee as a blush crept over her face, from the corner of my eye. I didn't dare look at Mason. Aidan did as he was told, slowly standing and pulling the blood stained charcoal grey shirt off.

Bruised and battered as he was, he was still breathtaking. Every inch of him muscle, from perfect pecs to that well defined V dropping below the waistband to his jeans. I'd seen it before but it was still impressive. Ryanne seemed to agree, her face was so flushed she looked on the verge of heat stroke.

He lay on his back looking up at me with half lidded eyes. He knew me well enough to know whatever I was about to do was far from sexual but that didn't stop him from putting on a show.

I stood over him, and started barking out orders. "Ryanne get me a bowl of warm water and some clean towels. I need a knife, one that isn't silver or serrated." I moved to step over Aidan so I could kneel beside him when he grabbed my ankle. His hands slid up to my knees, with a hard jerk on my jeans he had me straddling him.

"I thought this would go differently."

"No you didn't."

"Okay, I hoped it would go differently." He tried to sit up, wincing a little, so I pushed him back down. He grabbed the front of my shirt and pulled me to him. My hand flew out, bracing against the floor so our faces didn't collide. His lips barely touching mine, "Go easy on me." He kissed me. Just a brush of lips but before it was over his fangs grazed my bottom lip. What used to fill my body with anticipation, an aching need, had me reeling for an entirely different reason. My father's words about my blood echoing in my ears.

"Here," Mason shoved a blade in my face. "Use mine."

If I wasn't so thankful for the interruption I might have been a little pissed to have a knife that close to my eye. "I can't use silver."

He must have seen something in the way I looked at him, relief maybe, because his eyes softened a little. "It's not."

Ryanne came back with bandages and towels and placed them on the floor around Aidan. "Water is on the stove, almost ready." She rushed back to the kitchen before I could even thank her.

"While I appreciate your concern for sanitation, I'm a vampire remember? I don't have to worry about infection. Let's get this over with." He looked at my shaky hands. "What are you so nervous about? It's not like I'm going to die on the operating table."

"I don't want to hurt you. You're awake. Maybe we

should knock you out first."

"I'll do it."

I knew Mason wasn't serious, still I couldn't help but laugh at his comment and that was all the motivation I needed.

With my left hand pressed against Aidan's stomach I pressed the tip of the knife against his side like a scalpel with my right. Mason obviously took care of his weapons because the knife cut through skin and muscle like butter.

Blood poured from the incision. Ryanne was already at my side, dipping a towel in the water, ringing it out and wiping the area so I could see. I slid two fingers in with all the gentleness one might show a virgin and started feeling around for the broken switch blade. The incision wasn't long enough. I could feel the end, rough from where it had snapped off. My fingers, slick with blood, slipped easily out of his side. Wiping them on a towel I grabbed the knife again.

"I thought you said you didn't want to hurt me."

"It's deep, Aidan. I need to make the incision bigger. Mason do you have any pliers? Preferably needle nose."

"There's a toolkit under the sink." When Ryanne moved to get it he told her to stay where she was. "Maurin needs to see what she's doing. I haven't forgotten where things are kept or what needle nose pliers look like since you've been working for me."

Ryanne wiped away the blood and I opened Aidan up a little more. He finally let out a groan, clenched teeth the only thing preventing a full blown scream. He might be immortal but he wasn't impervious to pain. None of us were.

"Fecking hell, Nurse Ratched. I said take it easy on me."

"Ryanne, hold his shoulders, on your knees, cradle his head in your lap."

"Right, like I can hold a vampire down."

"He won't struggle, in fact he'll lie perfectly still. Won't you, Aidan?" He nodded his head yes. "He'll be so focused on not moving, not struggling, so he doesn't hurt you that he won't be paying attention to what I'm doing."

"Oh I'll still be paying attention to what you're doing with the fecking pliers but it will be a welcome diversion."

Ryanne positioned herself so that she was on her knees sitting on her heels, Aidan's head in her lap as I instructed, pressing down with a hand on each shoulder.

"A welcome diversion indeed." His eyes moved from her perfect breasts positioned above his face and back to me, with one of those *what? I'm a guy looks.*

Mason handed me the pliers and I slid my fingers along with the tool into the muscle. I wasn't nearly as gentle the second time. When I felt the blade again I slid the pliers into position and pulled my fingers out. I pried the pliers open and clamped down on the steel in one swift movement. I tried to tug it free but the muscle had healed around it already. I slid off Aidan and grabbed the knife.

"What are you doing? Just pull it out."

"Shut up, Aidan. Mason hold the pliers. I can't cut the muscle away and hold them at the same time." Mason relieved me of the pliers and wiped a towel across Aidan's stomach so we could both see what we were doing.

"I saw Giada do this once on Food Network." I pulled back on one side of the incision so I could see deeper into the cut and set the tip of my blade next to the end of the piece of steel.

"If Giada did this someone needs to have a serious talk with the people at the network about their programming."

"Shut up, Mason." With all the precision I could manage I cut the muscle away using the fillet technique I'd seen on TV.

"I'm impressed. Maybe you should have been a chef." Mason pulled the broken knife out of Aidan's side and dropped it in the bowl. He wiped his side one more time before I taped a bandage on.

I shrugged my shoulders. "I can fillet a steak, doesn't mean I can cook it."

We each took an arm and carefully helped Aidan off the floor. "I think I'll lay down for awhile, like until the next sunset." He started toward the hallway.

I had a hand on his arm, stopping him before he got two steps away. "Hey, you lost a lot of blood. You need to feed if that's going to heal tonight."

"Volunteering? Coming to my rescue again, like the night we met?" He turned, moving to pull me into an embrace.

"I think we rescued each other that night."

I didn't fall into his arms, afraid for the first time that he would see it as an invitation to take my blood. The night he tried to mark me had been the most incredible, most erotic night of my life. I could become addicted to that as easily Aidan could my blood. I could so easily become a blood slave, giving myself to him over and over until the night came when he lost control. Until the night he fully succumbed to the addiction, drinking until the beast was sated and I was dead.

Sensing my hesitation, he closed the distance, wrapping his arms around me. "I have synthetic in my bag. It will hold me over until I can find a surrogate. You need to see to your own wounds, Nurse Ratched." With a sorrow filled kiss he left me standing and went to the spare bedroom.

My body was almost as sore as my heart. I gave myself a quick once over. I was a mess, literally and figuratively. The cut on my cheek from where it smashed against the table was deep but already closing. My ribs were broken but mending. I was covered in blood, mine, Aidan's and the other vampires.

"I'm going to grab a shower and go to bed." I stopped walking when I realized that going to bed came down to two options. In the spare bedroom with Aidan where I might give in to feeding him if he's in pain or not healing. I might still be mad at him for almost turning me but I still cared about him. I couldn't turn it off, even if it would make my life easier.

Or I could stay in Mason's room where I might give in to other needs. I'd been drawn to him from the moment I met him. I wanted him and I knew he wanted me but it would only complicate my life more than it already was. And right now my life felt pretty complicated.

Mason chuckled when he saw the panic stricken look

on my face. "You've already spent the night in my bed. More than one night in fact and I have yet to take advantage of you. Well, I may have pressed the advantage a little. I'll sleep on the floor by the fire or out here on the couch like I have every night you've been under my roof. I'm going to speak with your father. He'll want to know what happened tonight."

"Maybe I should come with you." My stomach growled in objection.

"Maybe you should feed the monster that has taken up residence inside your stomach. I'll only be gone a couple of hours." He cupped my face in his hands before pressing a kiss to my forehead. "Besides we can't drive to your father's and it's still not safe for you in the between."

I watched Mason wrap himself in the between and jump to wherever it was my father actually lived. I had yet to see the place for myself. I was on my way to the kitchen when Ryanne called after me.

"Go grab your shower. I'll take Aidan some fresh bandages and bring you something to eat. After cleaning this mess up I don't feel like cleaning another one in my kitchen." She gave me a little wink and shoved the blood soaked towels into a basket. She set the bowl of bloody water on top of the basket and headed toward the laundry room across the hall from the training room.

I ripped the Flogging Molly shirt over my head and dropped it in the tub. The jeans didn't come off as easily. They were soaked with blood so I had to sort of roll them down my legs before they joined my shirt. I was tired of tossing my clothes. Maybe Ryanne had a trick for getting blood stains out. At some point in the night the strap on my bra broke so I tossed it in the trash with my socks.

I stepped out of my underwear and into the shower, hissing when the hot water hit my skin. Normally I liked the water set to melt your skin off but the little scratches and cuts I didn't notice until after the water hit them had me dialing back the temperature.

Once all the blood and grime had rinsed away I opened the shower door to grab the sugar cookie scrub Aidan packed for me. As soon as I had the gritty scrub in my hand I changed my mind. I might as well wash my cuts with sand paper. There was a new bar of soap in the shower caddy. Certain Mason wouldn't mind I lathered up with the soap. The steam filled the shower stall with spearmint, citrus, lavender and something else I couldn't place. It was spicy, smoky. It smelled like Mason.

Afraid mere thoughts of him while I was naked in the shower would conjure him, I tried to scrub the images of him from my mind as I shampooed my hair. It was damn near impossible since his scent still filled the shower. I rinsed my hair. The water sluicing down my body, rinsing the bubbles away and with it some of my tension. My stomach rumbled again, reminding me I hadn't been paying nearly enough attention to it but it would have to wait until after I conditioned. Otherwise it would be hell getting a brush through my hair.

Turning the water to cold I rinsed my hair, careful to leave a little of the conditioner behind and got out. I threw my hair up in a turban using one of the fluffy terry towels and wrapped another around my body.

After digging in my bag until I found a pair of yoga pants and my Beastie Boys tee shirt, I quickly threw them on and went into the bedroom hoping to find a dinner tray. I wasn't used to having someone bring me food. I was far from spoiled despite my adoptive parents being filthy rich, but I admit to being a little disappointed when there wasn't anything waiting for me. Perfectly capable of fending for myself however, I decided to head to the kitchen. Poor Saint Ryanne had probably fallen asleep on a stack of clothes before she could get out of the laundry room.

I was on my way to the kitchen when I stopped in front of the door to Aidan's room. I should check on him, make sure he had enough of the synthetic blood to at least heal himself. He wouldn't feel a hundred percent without fresh blood but with enough synthetic he wouldn't have a huge wound in his side. If Ryanne passed out before she made it to the kitchen she probably hadn't checked his bandage. He should be healed beyond the point of bleeding but I wanted to clean the incision for him before he went down for the day.

Guilt over my torn feelings for Aidan and Mason, not to mention my inability to give him my blood, the one thing he needed most tonight, had me hesitating. My hand was on the door knob but I couldn't seem to turn it. Would he want to see me after I had basically rejected him in front of Mason and Ryanne. I had to at least explain why. He deserved that much, even if he didn't want to hear it.

And I deserved the apology I knew he wanted to give. I just needed to let him. He knew I cared about him, not whether or not he was a vampire. What he didn't understand was why I would rather die than be one. We needed to have a talk about my fae blood and whether or not our relationship could survive it, whether or not we could survive each other.

A noise on the other side of the door sent me flying into the room. If Aidan was in pain none of that mattered. I would figure out a way around the feeding, figure out a way to make him better without giving him my blood. Only it looked like someone beat me to it.

Aidan found his blood surrogate all right and Saint Ryanne wasn't looking all that saintly at the moment. I guess she forgot who she was supposed to bring dinner to. Which was fine, I wasn't really hungry anymore.

I stood frozen, unable to turn away never mind turn and run. She was draped across his lap. Her shirt was unbuttoned. One hand caressed a breast, the other slid beneath her jeans caressing other things. The sound I heard, had mistaken for Aidan's pain was actually Ryanne's pleasure.

Fangs pierced her neck, her blood filling his mouth as endorphins filled her body. I knew from experience the sensations he could send through every nerve ending until it felt like you would burst out of your skin. I was intimately acquainted with the hands that held her as he fed. There was nothing inappropriate in his touch, one hand supporting her neck, the other beneath her legs. Almost clinical as far as feedings went. My eyes told me there was nothing sexual about it, at least not for him, that it was just another feeding. A necessary feeding if he wanted to heal the stab wound.

He was a vampire and vampires needed blood. Blood that I couldn't give him. Hadn't I been contemplating that exact thing only moments ago? Was this the universe's way of answering my question? Aidan's had my blood but I wasn't feeding him. Until recently he hadn't wanted that to be a part of our relationship. I knew he wasn't living entirely off synthetic, not with the injuries he sustained in his line of work. Was it like this with all the surrogates? Could I handle this? Even if Aidan wasn't doing anything, could I deal with women having this reaction to him?

So many thoughts ran through my mind but I couldn't process anything with Ryanne writhing on his lap. It may have been just another meal for him but did he have to make it so fucking erotic for her? He could control what she felt. The level of pain or pleasure was totally up to him, he'd told me as much. And by the sounds Ryanne made the level of pleasure was pretty high. Jealousy spread through my body faster than Ryanne's climax. I needed to get out of here before I did something I would regret tomorrow, like punching that ginger bitch in her face.

I backed up, easing out of the room when I wanted to run. My back bumped the door making a soft thud. Barely audible, unless you were a vampire. A vampire who would have heard my heartbeat from the hallway. A vampire who would have smelled me, sensed every emotion before I even opened the door.

His eyes flicked to me, finally acknowledging me even though he had to have known I was there the whole time. There was nothing there, no emotion. No lust or passion for the half naked woman on his lap. No pain or remorse for what he had to know this would do to me, to us. Detachment. That's what it was. He was completely detached from everything happening right now.

"Fucking bastard." I managed to choke back a sob. "You bastard." Before I turned to slam the door behind me something flickered in his eyes. Sorrow? As quickly as it came it was gone, leaving his beautiful eyes blank again. The door hit the jam so hard when I left the room I was certain I heard mortar from the solid stone walls rain down on the floor.

I was at the front door before I knew it. Stepping into my boots and grabbing a coat off one of the hooks, I stormed out of the house. The cold, damp air seeped into my clothes, threatening to chill my bones. I was hardly dressed to be out in this weather, I didn't even have socks on, but I didn't stop. I couldn't be in that house right now even if it did cost me my toes. I needed to think, clear my head, instead of acting on my first emotion - which was usually anger. My teeth chattered as I paced the back yard.

He wanted me to see him with her. Why? Because he wanted to hurt me like I hurt him? I didn't mean to but I had basically been flaunting the attraction Mason and I had in front of him. I had already broken his trust when I kissed him. But he had broken mine when he decided he would turn me without my consent. Of course I didn't know that at the time my tongue was entangled with Mason's.

I started to lose feeling in my fingers and toes, I paced harder hoping that getting my blood pumping would keep the frostbite at bay. I couldn't stop imagining him with all those surrogates, all those women. And I knew it was women because Aidan preferred pleasure to pain. If he ordered dinner in it wouldn't be a man.

But feeding didn't mean fucking did it? He certainly wanted me to think that, but his hands weren't on her breast, between her legs. Ryanne gave herself physical release because of what Aidan made her feel. Of course he could be up there right now, balls deep, releasing himself into her for all I knew.

Conry joined me but I wouldn't take comfort in the warmth radiating off of him. Sensing I needed to be alone he wandered off but I knew he still kept watch. My dog was the one constant in my life. I walked in circles until it felt like my skin was being pelted with shards of ice.

After a couple hours in the elements the only conclusion I came up with was Aidan had decided to cut me loose. Sometimes love isn't enough, no matter how much you want someone, care about them. It's entirely possible to fall in love with someone who isn't good for you. Wasn't I going to have a conversation with Aidan about that very thing before I walked in on them together? Wasn't I about to ask him if a vampire could have a relationship without blood? Ask myself if I could share him if he said yes?

He had already figured out why I hadn't offered my blood to heal him. That first night, when he was shot repeatedly, I hadn't hesitated to feed him. He had to know. Just like he knew if we tried to sit down, go over the pros and cons, we'd end up talking ourselves out of ending it because we both desperately wanted it to work no matter how many signs told us it couldn't.

He wanted me to think he cheated on me, to hate him for it. He was wrong. I could have forgiven him. It wouldn't have been as fast as he had forgiven me for kissing Mason but I would have gotten there eventually.

I would have worked through it- the fact that his feedings were based in pleasure, that he was weak from his injury and things had gotten out of control. I would have remembered how much he loved me, that I was his a chuisle - whatever the fuck that meant. If that's what had really happened I could have forgiven him. But what I couldn't forgive, would never forget, was how he used my insecurities against me. He used something I secretly feared to purposely hurt me. And I let him do it. Again.

I whistled for Conry, spindling the between before he was even by my side. I let it fill the holes in my heart and spirit until I couldn't hold any more without stepping through the veil. It felt so good, better than I'd felt in weeks. This was who I was. This was what I was supposed to be. I needed to forget about the disaster that was my love life and focus on the bitch who kept me out of the between, away from the one thing that completed me. I was the daughter of Arawn, Lord of the Other World. It was time I accepted my heritage and did what I was born to do. Hunt.

"And just where do you think you're going?"

I spun around, startled by the sound of Mason's voice. I lost my concentration and the between's energy in my body uncoiled, became something wild. I needed to release it. I tried to force it out but nothing happened. I screamed, it hurt. Oh god, it hurt.

Before I could ask, Mason was there, trying to help me ground the energy before I fried my brain. "Give it to me, let it go." His arms wrapped around me, he tried to leech the energy from my body. "You need to stop resisting me. You're blocking me. I can't help you if you don't trust me. Let me all the way in."

His voice was gentle, whispering all the right words in soothing tones but I was past the point of trusting anyone, at least tonight. Hell maybe forever. I needed to control this without Mason's help. I had to do this. I never held the between inside any longer than I had to. It was stupid to pull so much and hold on to it for so long knowing I couldn't use it.

Chills racked my body, while a fever scorched my brain. *You can do this.* I opened myself up to the between again, fighting the rush of power as it tried to claim every cell in my body. I was a wide open channel and I needed to reverse the flow of energy and then close it off.

I focused all my concentration on one thought, sending the energy back into the between. My head flew back, slamming against Mason's collar bone, my back arched as my chi was drawn to the source of the energy filling it. Releasing this much unused, raw energy hurt like a son of a bitch. I felt the ripple as the first ounce of power returned to the between. It surged to the point of a tidal wave by the time the last drop left me. I think I blacked out for a second.

Mason scooped me up and carried me back inside the house, over the threshold and straight back to his room. When he tried to set me down on the bed I clung to his neck, too exhausted to manage anything but muttering the word fire. He set me on my feet while he spread out a few heavy blankets like a makeshift mattress. I was already curled up on the floor in front of the fireplace before he could set out the last blanket. He covered me with it instead and sat down next to me.

"Want to tell me where you were going?" He made lazy circles with his hand on my back.

"I wasn't going anywhere."

"You spindled enough energy to move the Emerald Isle to a tropical location. You were going after Bathory. Now tell me why."

"I wasn't going after Bathory. Not yet anyway. I haven't moved through the between in so long. I miss it. It's a part of me, you know? I only meant to pull a little, enough to fill the holes." I whispered, "To stop the hurt, the ache in my heart."

"What was that last part?"

"Nothing."

"I know you want to go after Bathory and Caligula. And we will. Soon. But you've got to be able to sense a cloaked vampire, sense when someone else is moving in the between and cover your own trail so no one can follow you when you jump. Promise me you won't try to jump again until then."

"I said I wasn't going anywhere. I wasn't jumping."

"Then tell me what had you so upset you didn't realize you pulled enough energy to fry your brain like an egg if you didn't release it."

I didn't have the strength or the desire to verbalize

what happened. I rolled away from his comforting touch, closed my eyes and pretended to be asleep.

"Okay, Maurin. I'll let you off the hook tonight but we are going to talk about this in the morning." He brushed the hair out of my face. Tucking a strand behind my ear, he leaned in. "You smell like my soap. I like it." With a kiss behind my ear he was gone.

Conry quickly took his place, his massive head resting on my hip. I fell asleep with the warmth of the fire on my face and my guardian at my back.

XIX
NINETEEN

The smell of freshly brewed coffee was enough to have one eye cracked open. They both wouldn't open until I actually drank some. I was about fifty percent functional after my second cup. Was that bacon?

"Out of bed sleepy head." He ruined his dark and smoldering image with all this morning sunshine.

"What time is it?"

"Seven thirty."

"Not even coffee and bacon will get me out of bed before eight."

"What about coffee, bacon, eggs and rye toast with raspberry preserves."

My stomach sent out a distress signal, growling loud

enough to be mistaken for a grizzly bear. I sat up, shivering when the warmth of my blanket cocoon pooled around my waist.

The plate was five star hotel quality, complete with orange garnishes and a bowl of fresh strawberries and blueberries. Once I saw it, there was nothing that could come between me and that breakfast. For the first time in - probably ever - I ate before I had coffee, shoving an entire piece of bacon in my mouth. I washed it down with black coffee. "Oh my god, it's real bacon." I moaned my satisfaction over the pork perfection. How could something so good be so bad?

"I'm suddenly jealous of the bacon."

I almost choked on my coffee from laughing. "I switched to turkey bacon a couple of years ago. I forgot how good it is", I said around a mouthful of eggs.

"Either I'm a better cook than I thought or you never ate dinner last night."

"I was too wound up to eat."

"One more reason you weren't able to control the energy you pulled. Ready to tell me what had you so upset?"

"You made this?"

"I'll take that as a no. Ryanne isn't feeling well so I told her to stay home. I can manage breakfast."

"I bet she isn't feeling well." Mason looked at me for an explanation but I shoved toast in my mouth to prevent saying anything else. I would not have this conversation before my third cup of coffee if I could help it.

"Did something else happen? Something besides the

vampires?"

"It's totally vampire related." I shoveled in the last of my eggs and poured another cup of coffee from the carafe, adding cream and sugar this time. "So what's on the training agenda for today?"

"First you're going to get dressed. I've laid out something for you to wear on the bed. Then we're going to jump somewhere I can show you how to sense other people in the between."

I picked at the last piece of toast. "I thought you didn't want me jumping. What about Conry?"

"You're not doing the jumping, I am. You're just going along for the ride." He took my plate with one hand and helped me up with the other. "Conry will hold down the fort while we're gone. Get changed. I'm going to make a quick call. I want to touch base with Masarelli, then we can go."

"You need to get back. This is stupid, I can train at home. We don't need to be in another country for me to learn any of this."

"The only thing I need to do is keep you safe and your apartment is definitely not the safest place for you to be right now."

"Aren't you supposed to be running a department? You can't do that from here."

"I'm on leave."

"Leave? You just started."

"How about you let me worry about SPTF, okay?"

"You're going to get fired."

"I'm not going to get fired but if I did it'd be worth it.

You're worth it."

"You barely know me. How can you say that?"

"I know enough. I'm part of the Hunt, I don't need that job, or any other job for that matter. But I need you. I needed *you* before I ever met you." He left me standing, mouth hanging open like an idiot. "You've got ten minutes to get ready." His called out from halfway down the hall.

I went to the bed to see what he picked for me. "I am not wearing this!" I knew he heard me. I heard him laughing. Where the hell were we going that I needed a bathing suit.

A deep purple, crocheted bikini specifically. I definitely owned underwear that covered more than this. No way in hell would those strings hold up my boobs. I don't care what you saw on TV, if they were real you needed a little more than two triangles and two pieces of string.

I dug in my bag until I found a pair of black boy shorts and a black cotton bra. It could almost pass for a bathing suit. It would have to pass because while I appreciated the fact that Mason thought I could fit in that bikini, it was so not happening. I held it up again, confused. Where the hell were we going?

Mason pulled me in tight, my back pressed against his front. "Ready?"

"As I'll ever be. Are you going to tell me where we're going?" I had thrown on a pair of jeans and tee shirt, my docs and put my hair up in a top knot.

"No. You're not wearing the suit I picked out?"

I laughed. "Did you actually think I would?"

He shrugged his shoulders. "No, but you can't blame a guy for trying."

"Yes, I can."

He cleared his throat, trying not to laugh. "I don't want you to pull on the between when we cross over. Just feel. Concentrate on my movements, my energy."

Mason's arms tightened around my waist as the familiar sensation of calling up the between swirled around us. Instead of the rush of power I usually experienced it crept lazily over my body. The between slowly rolled over me and while I desperately wanted it to fill me from the tips of my toes to the top of my head it still felt amazing.

It felt like eternity, like we had all the time in the world. I wanted to stay here, linger with him in the place where time and distance was irrelevant, where we had the power to change reality.

Everything he did, all of his movements in the between were different than mine. My style felt like jumping, the force of the push, the propulsion, the impact on the landing. This was like being weightless, riding the current of the between. A familiar drop in my stomach, like when you go over a hill a little too fast in a car, was the only sign we reached our destination.

The veil pulled back, revealing the bustling streets of a quaint town filled with tourists. No one seemed to take notice of the two people who literally appeared out of thin air. They stepped around us as if we'd been there the whole time.

"Where are we? In England?"

"Nice to see you know your geography. Welcome to

Bath. Come on." He grabbed my hand, leading me across the street and past a massive modern building that while beautiful clashed with the Abbey styled buildings around it.

We came to a small building, dwarfed by the large modern architecture to its left. The Roman structure may have been smaller but it took my breath away in a way modern architectural design never would.

"Aquae Sulis, Cross Bath, it's ours for a few hours." Mason swung the door open to reveal a stone room with glass walls opening to a stone patio surrounding a hot mineral spring bath.

"You reserved this? For us? Why?"

"It's a source of power. Sul, has blessed the waters in her temple. Even the Romans recognized her, Sulis Minerva, during their occupation of the Celts. She was a warrior like you, a goddess of retribution. The Hunt has found solace and a source of rejuvenation here. It's the best place outside of the between to show you how to feel other people moving through the grey. Besides the mineral bath will do your muscles good. Loosen you up before your training with Aidan tonight."

I stifled a groan. "Nothing short of elephant tranquilizers will loosen me up right now." I tried to shake off the tension and apprehension brought on by the mere thought of training with Aidan.

I should tell Mason everything that happened last night while he met with my father. Tell him what his precious Ryanne did with my quasi boyfriend, excuse me, ex boyfriend. He would no doubt cancel my training or bring in another vampire - which was unlikely given the unrest in the local vamp community.

Either way it would put me further behind, Caligula and Bathory's trail getting colder with each minute we wasted trying to replace Aidan. So as much as I hated the idea of working with him I didn't see an alternative because catching them, serving justice with the tip of my sword was now my only priority. I wasn't going to think about anything or anyone else. That was until Mason started to undress.

Steam rolled off the crystal clear water, leaving a hint of the minerals it contained in the air. Mason dropped a small backpack I hadn't noticed he was carrying on the floor. He kicked off his boots while he undid the button fly on his jeans. I couldn't take my eyes off the denim, watching it slide down muscular thighs and calves- until he pulled his black thermal shirt, exposing perfectly chiseled pecs and abs.

Tattoos like mine covered most of his body, some dipping below the waistband of his black board shorts. He looked at me expectantly as he yanked off his socks. There was something nerve racking about deliberately undressing in front him so I ripped my clothes off like a Band Aid and walked into the bath in my bra and underwear.

The one hundred and seven degree water stung like thousands of tiny needles against my chilled skin as I waded out until the water was chest deep.

"Close your eyes."

"Why?" If this was a lesson on trust I would seriously fail. Generally speaking, I had trust issues.

"Do you plan to question me the entire time? Close your eyes."

"It's possible. Why do I need to close my eyes?" I spun around, the movement sluggish in the water. I jumped when I saw he was right next to me- I couldn't help it.

"Do you really think I'm going to hurt you?"

Of course I didn't, but that didn't make closing my eyes any easier. He took my hands in his, kissing the tips of my fingers before placing one hand over each of my eyes.

"Relax. Take a deep breath. That's it, in out. Good. Now, see if you can sense my movements. Feel my location. And no peeking."

"You brought me all the way to England to play Marco Polo?" I totally peeked, by the way.

"Maurin, we only have the bath for a few hours."

"Fine," I huffed, squeezing my eyes shut.

I couldn't feel anything and I struggled with keeping my eyes closed. I always sucked at Marco Polo. I moved, turning in a half circle listening for any sounds in the water. *Be still*, Mason's voice was a whisper in my left ear. I threw my hand out, expecting to catch him beside me but was left grasping at air. *Be still*.

Instead of using his voice to zero in on where he was, I listened to his instruction. I stilled my body, my mind and spirit. The sounds from the city outside the bath house fell away as I slowed my breathing. My hands rested palms down on the surface and I became one with the water. I couldn't rely on my eyes, stopped relying on my ears and concentrated on my sense of touch. I felt every ripple, every lap against my skin and that's when I had him.

This time my hand connected, clamping down on his bicep. "Gotcha!"

"Don't be so pleased with yourself. If I was Bathory you'd already be dead."

"If you were the Blood Countess the only mineral in this bath would be iron." I made the ba da dum dum cha, drum sound and chuckled at my own lame joke.

"You have a sick sense of humor, has anyone ever told you that?"

"I may have heard it once or twice."

"Try again. The water is the between, you need to be able to feel my movements. Preferably before I am close enough to kill you."

It went on like that, over and over until my fingers were well past pruned and our time in the restorative pool was almost up. We worked through lunch and had run out of bottled water an hour ago. I was exhausted, dehydrated and ready to get the hell out of the steaming water. I'd drastically improved over the last forty-five minutes. Hopefully that meant we'd call it quits.

Mason couldn't get within arm's reach of me anymore. Of course this wasn't the Matrix and a bullet could still do a lot of damage an arm's length away but I wasn't worried about being shot. Not really. Bathory didn't want me on the ground bleeding out. She wanted me trussed up, bleeding into her bathtub.

"Last time, come on." Mason snapped his fingers. "Don't start daydreaming now."

I wiped at the sweat dripping down from my hairline.

"Sshh, I'm having fantasies about drowning you right now."

"At least you're fantasizing about me. One more time and then I'll take you to dinner. Anywhere you want."

I already knew he wasn't in the bath with me anymore. He didn't try to hide it when he walked up the stairs and got out. The last two times he managed to get waist deep before I felt him in the water. The idea was to catch him the second he broke surface tension. Dinner sounded amazing. I was so hungry he could have offered me Slim Jims and a Coke and I would have rated it a five star meal.

"Anywhere I want?"

"One of the little perks of being able to do what we do."

Food and more specifically coffee was excellent motivation. I wanted Rhode Island clam chowder and clam cakes followed by dough boys with coffee. The possibility of giving in to my fried fantasy had my mouth watering and me feeling especially confident. I practically smelled the warm donuts covered in granulated sugar. Pushing the thoughts of fried dough out of my mind I found my center and focused on the water.

The water is the between had become my mantra the last half hour. This time when I sent my senses out the wisps of steam thickened to a familiar fog. The crystal clear water darkened until completely replaced with a soupy grey.

The momentary excitement of the challenge, of actually being done with training for a few hours wasn't enough to counteract the exhaustion. I had accidentally opened myself to the between. Wholly and completely in a way I hadn't felt before, power oozed into every pore

The second Mason pulled back the veil to follow me in I knew he was there. I pulled him to me, ready to claim my prize for winning when two things occurred to me. One, the reason I felt Mason was because he moved like a gale force wind to get to me, and two we weren't alone.

The imprint on the between was familiar. It felt like mine, like a tainted version of me. Bathory. So she hadn't used all the blood poultice. Not that I wanted anyone else to fall prey to the Blood Countess but I was kind of hoping she would have used up all her reserves of my blood by now.

It would have been a hell of a lot easier if we were the only ones using the between. The feel of her in the grey made my skin crawl and stomach turn. It was wrong, her very presence defiling the particles that made up possibility. She closed the distance, moving easily through the decay she caused by being here. Thanks to my blood. I left Mason's side and moved to meet her, to put an end to this. Right here, right now.

Mason slammed into me, tackling me and forcing a rip in the veil that separated one reality from the next. It was lacking the finesse of our first trip but he managed to elude Bathory by taking control of the energy and jumping us back to his house. We landed in a tangled heap, arms and legs entwined, on his bed.

Thank the gods he had good aim because hitting the floor with this momentum would have left a hell of a mark. We stayed that way, with me on top of him, bodies pressed together, until I caught my breath.

"She was right there, Mace. We had her. We could have ended it." Frustrated, I shoved an elbow in his ribs.

"And what were you going to stake her with in just your underwear?"

"*We* could have done it." I struggled against him and might have elbow him again.

He grunted. "She's stronger than those vampires at the bar, smarter too. Do you really think she would let you rip her heart out?" He shifted to avoid another elbow, his body rubbing against mine. This close I knew he suffered from a different kind of frustration. "I like it when you call me Mace, by the way."

Yeah, that much was obvious. I started to climb off him, to find clothes before all this flesh on flesh led to something that could end up hurting my heart as much as Bathory wanted to hurt my body. Mason wrapped one long muscular leg around mine and pulled me back down, trapping me in a cage of bare limbs that had me hotter than the one hundred and seven degree water.

I really needed to get up and get dressed. Cotton and denim were my only defense against giving in to the urges I felt every time I was this close to Mason. I knew what I felt, what were both feeling but I also knew it would be a mistake to do this now. Too much had happened and all of it involved vampires.

Caligula, Bathory and Aidan. The first two were easier to deal with than the last. I would kill the two murderous vampires but as much as I wanted to kill Aidan it would cause more problems in the long run. He made the decision to end it and deep down I knew he was right. I needed to deal with the way he ended it before I could start something else. Of course right now I still needed to deal with the incredibly sexy, mostly naked man under me.

"It's time for your training but I see the hunter is schooling you in a different subject." Aidan sounded upset. He wasn't entitled to feel angry, as far as I was concerned.

Well that was certainly one way to deal with Aidan, I thought, feeling a little satisfied that he got a taste of his own medicine. It was glaringly obvious by the dark look in his eyes and the menacing sound of his voice that last night's show was exactly that.

He still fed from Ryanne, pumping her full of endorphins until she begged for release but pleasure wasn't his goal. Of course part of him enjoyed it, the vampire and the man, but his plan had been to hurt me, to convince me that despite how much we cared about each other it wasn't meant to be. And it worked. Better than he thought if I had to guess by his mood.

I hadn't realized the sun was down and it was time to practice with Aidan until he darkened my door. Maybe I'd get off the hook since Bathory was so close. Maybe we would step things up and go after her. Maybe they'd both make me train harder. This should be fun. And by fun I mean tortuous.

Nothing happened between Mason and me. We hadn't acted on the attraction we - even Aidan - knew was there but I was happy to let Aidan think we had. I pressed my lips against Mason's, a gentle kiss that hinted at more. He didn't seem to mind playing along, kissing me back. He deepened the kiss for a moment, letting me know when I was ready there would definitely be more, before pulling back and helping me off with an easy push.

"I guess I should change into something…" I looked down at my underwear, "less revealing." Catching the duffle bag Mason tossed to me I headed into the bathroom.

XX
TWENTY

Aidan and Mason waited for me in the training room- as far away from each other as possible. Aidan moved to the center of the mat when I came in. Without looking I knew Mason had positioned himself against the back wall, assuming his position from last night.

I joined Aidan on the mat, practically tripping over Conry who had been glued to my side since I got back. "Did Mason tell you what happened?"

"I am over three hundred years old. I do not need a hunter to have the sex talk with me."

"I was talking about what happened today, with Bathory. She was in the between."

"Exactly why you are not supposed to be." He glared

at Mason. "All the more reason for this training."

I spent the next ten minutes listening to Aidan give me instructions that sounded a lot like the ones Mason gave in the bath house. "Ready?"

"If you are."

Mason gave a short, low whistle and Conry obediently padded over to sit beside him. If I didn't know better I might have thought my guardian liked Mason better than me. I pondered the fact that my dog never listened to anyone other than me but had no problem taking orders from Mason.

Aidan disappeared from the mat. Damn, I forgot how good he was at this. I cracked my neck, first to the right then the left and rolled my shoulders. I bounced on my feet a few times, shaking out my arms and the urge to spar that had been building since I walked into the training room.

I needed to calm down, center myself, if I wanted to catch Aidan before he got close. Mason and Aidan seemed to be in agreement that when we faced Caligula and Bathory they wouldn't be alone. I had to be able to sense a cloaked vampire before we could go after them. I would master this tonight. I was sick of waiting. That bitch was after my blood. I was going to kill her.

Unlike my training with Mason, Aidan didn't take it easy on me. He swept my legs from under me, knocking me hard on my ass the first time he came at me. Standing up hurt but I didn't so much as wince from the pain radiating out of my tailbone.

"You'll have to do better than that. You should have spent more time on your training and less time cuddling to your new boyfriend."

He was already gone, lurking in the shadows, waiting to pounce. Since I still couldn't pin point his location I shouted my retort. "How's Ryanne?" His answer was a palm in the middle of my back. I stumbled forward, coming down hard on my right knee. "Son of a bitch." I slammed a fist on the mat.

Aidan snatched me by the hair, snapping my head back. He licked his lips, fangs slightly extended. "She's a delight." He shoved my head forward, letting go of my hair.

His tone didn't match his eyes but I wasn't backing off now. Brushing myself off, I stood. My blood had been replaced with piss and vinegar and it pumped hard through my veins, my temper well out of control. "Don't you mean delicious?" That earned me another shot from the shadows, this time behind the knee. My legs buckled and I went down again.

"What's the matter with you? Concentrate. What we practiced in Cross Bath, Maurin. Come on," Mason shouted from the sideline. He still didn't know exactly what happened last night but he pieced it together. "He's using your anger against you. Clouding your perception with emotion."

"No shit. Tell me something I don't know." For the third time I picked myself up off the mat, determined to put Aidan flat on his back. With a deep, cleansing breath I pushed away the hurt and anger.

Reeling in my temper was harder and taking longer than I thought. Aidan didn't wait for me to finish composing myself. He came at me from the left but this time I felt him before he touched me. Barely, but still it was an improvement. I spun to my right, his hand grazing my shoulder. He was relentless but each time I improved, gaining enough distance to defend myself. When I felt him come from behind I threw an out elbow, ramming him in the solar plexus.

His grunt of pain was the best praise I'd had all day. This time I even felt him move away. He displaced air the same way I moved in the between. Once I knew what I was feeling for, it was easier to follow him. I closed my eyes and waited for the disruption in the atmosphere.

My left hand shot out, connecting with a hard throat chop. If I had to guess by the gurgling sounds coming from him I might have crushed his wind pipe with that hit. Not that it would slow him down since vampires didn't need to breathe.

"It's training remember? Stop trying to break my fecking bones." His wind pipe was apparently fine even though his voice sounded like he had been gargling with razor blades. With a parting shot - a hard shove on the shoulder - he was in the shadows again.

Mason watched me intently, analyzing my every move targeting my weaknesses. I felt his eyes on me. I turned to face him. There was a subtle change in his expression.

I was surprised by the realization that I had paid enough attention to Mason to pick up on those little differences. Even without the minute increase in the angle of his eyebrows or the single twitch in the corner of his right eye, I would have felt Aidan move. The moment he was close enough I positioned myself, throwing him down with a technique I had learned in Aikido a couple of years ago.

I sent him ass over tea kettle, slamming him down on his back. Wasting no time, I pounced on his chest, pinning him with all my weight. I pretended to stake him and declared myself the winner.

He grabbed my wrists, pulling me close so our faces were inches apart. "Why didn't you tell me? Why did I have to hear it from him?"

"What are you talking about?" I had a sinking feeling I knew the answer.

"Don't play coy with me. Your father and I had a little heart to heart last night."

"Arawn told you about my blood," I said, barely a whisper. Last night suddenly made sense.

"I don't know what pissed me off more, that I heard it from him and not you, or that he's right. Your blood isn't the only thing that calls to me but I can't separate thirst from desire with you. Even if you could share me with another it wouldn't be enough. I would always crave more of you."

So Arawn had been there. Mason wasted a trip going to talk to my father because Arawn already knew. He had been watching us from the moment we got back from the bar. He had been there waiting for the right moment to talk to Aidan.

His injury provided the perfect opportunity. Arawn probably made it back in time to meet with Mason. And then Ryanne provided Aidan the perfect opportunity to irrevocably end things when she stopped in to check on him.

I wrenched my hands free. Pissed at my father for telling him before I had the chance, pissed at Aidan for choosing to end things the way he did, I used his chest as a spring board and stood up. The more I thought about it the more pissed off I got. I was furious they both knew me well enough to know things wouldn't have, couldn't have, happened any other way.

And I was really fucking pissed that out of all the mean things I could say, should say, because he deserved them, I wanted to say I'm sorry. Instead I turned my back on him and walked out.

Mason found me a few minutes later in the kitchen, water bottle in one hand and a pack of pepperoni slices in the other, raiding his fridge. "Make it to go. I just got word the vamps from the bar were Caligula's. The local Regulator is making a move on the remaining hive. If they know where their sire is hiding, I don't want local authorities killing everyone before we can find out."

Music to my ears. Finally we were mobilizing, going on the offense. I was so fucking ready to kill something.

XXI
TWENTY-ONE

Mason was reevaluating who was a bigger threat to getting information out of the vampires, me or the local Regulator, as he followed me to the H2. I was definitely throwing off a kill first ask questions later vibe with my sword strapped to my back, silver daggers on my wrists and stakes tucked into my belt. All the gear I wore would make for an uncomfortable ride but I wasn't walking into a vampire lair without being armed to the teeth. These assholes already tried to kill me once, I didn't plan on giving them a second chance.

Mason turned off the headlights and slowed to a crawl as we approached the location of the hive. People moved in the shadows as he backed us into an alleyway across the street. Tensions ran high when we met up with the team the European Council had put in place.

The one in charge was a witch and a powerful one at that if she was able to rise through the ranks of a cleaning crew to become Regulator. Her team was compiled of two more witches and three weres- all of them in black camo and heavily armed. I was surprised and to be honest, a little relieved, to discover there wasn't a vampire among the local team.

Never having worked with them before, their lack of fangs was reassuring. I had been contemplating the possibility we were walking into a trap. If a vampire was on the team I'd be worried they were compromised. Brief introductions were made. Mason tacked on my title of Regulator for the eastern United States which earned me a respectful nod from the team.

Sinead, the Regulator, filled us in on the situation inside the ramshackle house which sat in a rundown part of town. Most of the houses at this end of the street were connected, slightly wider and shorter than the townhouses back home. The hive house sat at the end of the dead end street with a high brick wall surrounding the back and right side of the unkempt yard. The tall, crumbling bricks made it difficult to gain entry from the back door unnoticed.

If we breached it would have to be through the front, costing us the element of surprise. I could already tell she was not a fan of any plan that involved going through the front door.

Her intel said at least a dozen vampires had been seen coming and going since sunset. Best they could tell, the vampires inside the hive were mobilized, gearing up for something big.

Seven were confirmed inside by the dark blue spots on infrared. The other five left an hour ago, with a tail. All of them, her tracker included, were unaccounted for. It was a gamble. Did we go in now, try to take out the vamps inside, possibly leaving ourselves open to an attack from the missing vamps or wait until they rejoined the party and move in then?

"We could be waiting until sunrise." I may have mentioned before that I have zero patience when it comes to waiting. I'd never make it on a stake out. Ha, we were all watching a house full of vampires I guess this was the ultimate stake out.

"It would make our job easier if the sun was up," Sinead said.

"They won't be able to answer questions if they're dead. I need the location of their sire."

"Look, Mason, we brought you in as a courtesy. And frankly speaking, with a hive this large we could use the backup. But this isn't the first time they've attacked like they did last night and I'm fresh out of warnings. We're not here for reconnaissance. My orders are to take them out. You want to snatch and grab one of the vamps after they go down when the sun comes up I'll turn a blind eye but you're on your own with disposal."

As much as I liked Sinead's no nonsense attitude her plan sucked big time. I'm talking golf ball through a garden hose sucked. I didn't get dressed for the ball only to have someone tell me I wasn't allowed to dance. I pulled the

Retaliator from its sheath and stepped out from behind Mason.

"I don't have time to wait for the rest of them to finish snacking on your tracker and come back home. There is a psycho bitch running around with a stock pile of my blood contaminating the between. The vampires inside that dilapidated house have information that could put me one step closer to stopping her. We're moving in. You want to sit outside and keep watch fine but you're on your own with the clean up. And just so you know, things tend to get messy when I'm around."

"Yeah, I got that from your mess at the bar."

"Oh that wasn't me, that was all them," I said pointing across the street. "My mess involves a lot more blood."

"This is who you were passed over for? You're joking." She looked at Aidan while throwing her thumb in my direction.

"She did take down an Afrit and a rogue high priestess about six months ago."

"Don't forget the An Chap Bain and the goddess I beheaded last year." Bolstered by my past exploits I was feeling pretty bad ass at the moment and ready to take charge. There was one five foot eight, blue eyed, spiky blond haired obstacle in my way.

"You're not risking my team just so you can ask a couple questions. They're armed, heavily, which is insult to fucking injury in my opinion since vamps don't need guns. The vampires in there don't just feed, they torture their victims. Exsanguination has been the most common cause of death, they pump the victims full of anticoagulants before the bodies are inflicted with multiple bite wounds. They're also fond of cat o' nine tails and other weird shit that's left a couple bodies looking like they were run through a meat grinder."

"Apples don't fall far from the tree." Mason was right. There wouldn't be a vampire left alive if we hadn't moved in. The killers in that house crossed a line, becoming the monsters depicted in horror movies. Deemed unfit for cohabitation with other species by the EC, the only outcome was the death penalty. I looked at Mason and then Aidan. We were in agreement. We were going in. "Caligula and Bathory are rebuilding his line, making more vampires in his image. We can't let that happen."

"I have my orders, they don't involve Caligula or Bathory. We wait until sunrise."

I lost precious moonlight getting into this pissing contest with her. "You can wait until sunrise after you set up a perimeter. You might want to get out your phone and google those two vampires. I think you'll be seeing things our way before you get to the part about their undeath."

Mason took over from there, being a part of the Hunt meant being a strategist. He knew what positions to put Sinead's team in that would give us the best tactical advantage should things go bad once we were inside.

Before everyone could move into position a black cargo van with tinted windows pulled up to the house. The missing vampires got out to unload their cargo.

One of them opened the rear doors, after pulling a key from his pocket he unlocked a thick chain from the floor of the van. Another moved in, grabbing the chain and dragging it behind him. We all watched in horror as people in shackles started falling out. Most of them looked like they had been scrapped up off the streets, vagrants that wouldn't be missed but three or four of them were clean cut, probably at the wrong place at the wrong time.

"They're bringing back dinner." Aidan's voice dripped with disdain. As a strong supporter of cohabitation before the shift, he had helped more than one vampire meet their true death over the centuries. It's how he ended up working for the Council in the first place. He abhorred this behavior, spent his life ensuring vampires lived in accordance with the jus sanguinis inter gentes. He had been the one to bring in Caligula before, been hunting Bathory for months. He was more than ready to go in.

"That's Conall" Sinead pointed to a guy with a wiry frame, matted brown hair and a seeping cut on his temple.

"Your tracker?" I had a feeling she would see things my way - now that one of her teammates was on the menu.

"Who's the red head? I've seen her before. Isn't she one of yours, Mason?"

We all focused on the woman Sinead pointed to. The familiar shock of red hair covered most of Ryanne's face but I saw the bruises and swelling. Her head hung low as she was dragged behind the other people, who looked less like dinner and more like bait.

"There's a very real possibility that we're walking into a trap." Just as I suspected Sinead was on board with storming the hive.

"It changes nothing. We're going in." Aidan stepped out of the alley. I grabbed the back of his shirt and pulled him back into the cover of darkness provided by the surrounding buildings.

"Nobody said differently and it's more than a possibility. It is a trap. So before we go all gangbusters and kick in the front door we need to revamp our plan."

One of the weres snickered at my choice of words while Aidan and I stared each other down. He finally backed down, leaning against the brick wall with his anger focused back where it should be - on the vampires in that house.

"When did you become the voice of reason?" Aidan watched the front door close behind the last of the hostages.

"I thought since you decided to play me in this little drama that left the role of brooding conservative vampire for me." Seeing Ryanne beaten and shackled had Aidan riled up and me left wondering if he liked her more than he let on. Not that I cared. "So how are we doing this?"

"Follow me."

Sinead crept out of the alley, staying low to the ground and hugging the walls. When she was close enough to the house she tossed two grenades through the front windows shattering the glass. We heard commotion inside as the vampires scurried to take cover from the explosion. There was a loud bang followed by a blinding flash of light.

"Move!" With that one command her team fell into position on the front steps, kicking down the door and splitting off into smaller groups once they breached the door.

"Flash bangs?" I seriously needed to add those to my

arsenal.

"Made them myself. They give off low grade UV, not enough to kill them but it'll give one hell of a sunburn."

Aidan's shouts from inside the house had Sinead and me hitting the floor as we got in the door. Conry had taken point so I threw as much of myself as I could on top of him, taking him down with me. In the initial rush someone tripped a Bouncing Betty.

I watched helplessly from the floor as silver shrapnel ripped through the room and the three werewolves. Aidan managed to dive behind a couch, narrowly missing the worst of the blast of metal that could have killed him. I stood slowly, carefully, in case there was trip wire or another makeshift landmine somewhere. The Bouncing Betty had certainly leveled the playing field. The half dozen vampires Sinead managed to scorch and stun were already getting up while we were down three werewolves - half her team obliterated. The couch couldn't have provided much cover against the shrapnel. I was about to call out to him when he grabbed the back of the shredded cushions and hauled himself up. He took a few hits in the shoulder and a few looked like they grazed his cheek but it could have been worse. Much worse. Bits of wolf and man covered everything and everyone.

Mason scraped blood and tissue out of his eyes in time to see the vampire at his feet come around. He pulled a stake from his belt and drove it through the shoulder, using the momentum to force him down and pin him to the floor. "Stay there, I'll be right back."

That was our cue. We only needed one vampire alive

to question. If he didn't have the answers we needed there were more waiting in the basement. I pulled the Retaliator from its sheath and made short work of decapitating the vampire closest to me. Her head hit the floor, rolling to Conry who huffed at it before pushing it away to lunge at another vampire charging towards us.

His teeth clamped down around the vampire's throat, shaking back and forth like he had a squeaky toy until he ripped the throat out. Sinead finished the vampire off with a stake in the heart.

We moved, slashing, tearing, staking our way through the room until only the vampire Mason trapped and the one being roasted from the inside out by a witch were left. The cooked vamp made an audible pop as his skin split, spilling blood and useless organs on the floor. The heart still beat, hopelessly pumping blood to a body that couldn't be repaired.

Looking at the disfigured, gooey vamp I couldn't help but think of Mercy Brown. A woman who was the object of a vampire's obsession, driven crazy by it in the undeath she never wanted, trapped in suspended state - like this vampire- until the Council took pity on her.

Even now after meeting the sun all those years ago she still couldn't rest. He wouldn't let her memory die. I would kill him, satisfied that not only would I rid the world of a madman but when I drove my sword through his chest he wouldn't see me. In his twisted mind he'd be looking at Mercy.

Aidan and Sinead took off, scanning the rest of the first floor for hostages. I knew they found them and a few vampires when I heard fighting, screams and a bang loud enough to temporarily deafen any norms in the house - percussion grenades. Sinead must have been in the IRA. She was seriously into explosives.

"If you don't cooperate and tell me what I need to know I'll let the little witch over there boil you up, from the inside out." Mason jerked the vampire's head in the direction of the soupy vampire remains and the witch, who wiggled her fingers and said boo.

The vampire whimpered, actually whimpered. "They'll kill me. They'll kill me."

I laughed as I knelt beside him. "Why do people always say that when facing this scenario? They'll kill you, we'll kill you. Death is eminent. You can tell us what you know and we kill you quickly or I throw you down the steps to join your fucking friends waiting to ambush us. I doubt they'll give you the option of a quick death since no matter how many times you deny it they'll never believe you didn't tell us where your sire is."

"They say absence makes the heart grow fonder. It must be true if you're this desperate to find me."

Mason was already standing in a Kali fighting stance with a blackjack whip in one hand and a dagger in the other. Everything slowed. Heartbeats felt like minutes. The witch's hands flared with an ethereal blue flame. Conry growled, sitting back on his haunches preparing to lunge. All in the time it took me to stand and face him.

"Oh, I couldn't agree more. Since you drugged me and gave me to your little protégé I've grown fonder and fonder of the idea of killing you. I guess I don't need him anymore, now that you're here." I plunged the tip of my sword into the chest of the vampire on the floor. The Retaliator wasn't silver, sun, or rowan wood, but nothing, not even a vampire, healed a wound from my blade. It was one of the few things that killed an immortal.

"Yes, I suppose he's out lived his usefulness for both of us. It was an elaborate plan just to get you here, but they are the best kind. It would have been so mundane to snatch you from the farmhouse. Elizabeth could have grabbed you any number of times you slipped up and entered the between but where's the fun in that. All these puppets dancing on a string, it's too delicious."

"Sounds like you've been busy."

"So have you." He waved his hand to encompass the room and the carnage around us. "Why don't we bring your friends out here to join the party?"

Vampires casually filed in, dragging Aidan and the others behind them. I thought Sinead had turned the tide with her grenades but I was wrong. There were too many of them.

We were out numbered and quickly running out of options to get ourselves and the hostages out of this house alive. Our intel had been way off. How did we not know he was here siring all these vampires? There had to be at least twenty, making it close quarters for a fight should the opportunity present itself.

The spot where Caligula had been standing seconds ago burst into flames. The witch was good but he was better. The sound of her neck snapping was almost as loud as her body hitting the floor. The fire snuffed out when her heart stopped beating. Someone threw up, one of the norms no doubt. Two of the fledglings rushed her body before the blood had a chance to spoil. Then all hell broke loose.

For once the man who prepared for everything, even his own death, hadn't accounted for something. A veritable feeding frenzy broke out as the newbie vamps went after the still viable blood.

If they drank too long after the blood went cold and coagulation began, we'd have a serious problem on our hands - like berserker vampires problem.

Caligula shot across the room, yanking his children off the corpse only to have them dive back in like little piglets fighting for the teet. If piglets snarled, were deadly, and had fangs that is.

We needed to take advantage of the chaos to get the norms out of there. I grabbed the old piano stool being used as a side table and threw it out the window, motioning to Aidan and Sinead to get everyone out. Aidan fought the burn of his silver cuffs, the skin on his hands sloughing off as he broke free of the bonds. There wasn't time to undo everyone's restraints so he freed Sinead and a couple more who were strong enough to lift people up and out the window.

With the hostages out of the way, Mason, Conry and I could fight without worrying about mortals getting caught in the cross fire. The local Regulator wasn't the only one with a few tricks up her sleeve.

I pulled a handful of small glass vials out of my pocket and tossed them on the floor at the edge of the vampires piled on top of the dead witch. Smoke and the acrid smell of burning flesh filled the air as the holy water worked its magic.

The fledglings scratched and clawed at the holes the blessed water bored into their skin. Mason's whip cracked the air, the silver corded blackjack splitting the face of one vampire as he drove a silver dagger through the heart of another that had come up beside him. Conry jumped into the fray, tearing away at the undead, while I went after Caligula.

I swung the Retaliator with enough force to cleave his head from his neck, almost falling when the blade didn't connect. There wasn't time to apply my training. Caligula didn't need to cloak, he moved that fast.

What I wouldn't give for one of Cash's guns right now. Melee weapons weren't any good when your opponent could be out of blade reach in the blink of an eye - literally. I may be unrefined when it came to swordsmanship but I was effective. I needed to change tactics. One good hit and it was over.

Deciding that being on the defensive was actually a better strategy when going up against Caligula with a sword - even a deadly fae relic - I waited for him to come to me. Muscle recall had my legs in the stance Mason showed me and my hands in the proper grip.

Caligula moved forward. I sliced the Retaliator horizontally, hoping to eviscerate him. He jumped backwards, his back arched and stomach pulled in, voiding the strike at the last second. The loose hair hanging around my face lightly brushed my neck as the air shifted with his movements.

This time I felt him move and was ready when he came up behind me. Thrusting backwards and down with my sword had the pommel connecting hard with his knee cap. He instinctively crouched forward to grab his knee, providing the opening I hoped. With as much force as I could muster I slammed my elbow into his face breaking his nose. My victory was short lived however. He swung wide with a left that slammed into my temple like Thor's hammer, splitting the thin skin along the brow bone. Blood pooled into my eye, blurring my vision.

Mason threw the vampire he fought against the wall hard enough to shatter her skull. She wasn't dead but definitely down. His Kali whip and knife technique was extremely effective. The dangerous tip of the black snake whip kept most of them back, while he slashed the vampires who were able to get close with his silver blade. Clearing a path to get to me, he pulled his Bowie knife from the chest of a fledgling with a roar, lunging through the ashes.

I spun to face Caligula and almost vomited in the process from dizziness. Pawing at my left eye, I tried to reset my stance. His hand shot out, fingers clamping on my throat, he pulled me to him.

A mangled cry tore from my throat as his tongue lapped at the blood flowing from the cut above my eye. His crushing embrace had the Retaliator wedged firmly between us. With my arms pinned and my blade trapped I would never be able to deal a killing blow.

Caligula's fangs viciously ripped into my neck as the

air shimmered behind him. Elizabeth Bathory stepped through the veil, encircling us with arms stained red from the blood poultice. Mason's fingers slipped through my hair, grasping the air left in my wake as the three of us fell into the between.

XXII
TWENTY-TWO

Bathory released us once we were alone the between. While I was distracted with training, the Blood Countess had been busy carving out a piece of the grey for herself.

Without my blood she'd never be able to hold onto it. Even now the between fought the contamination like an infection. Small sparks, like from an arc welder, rained down around us as the untainted particles of the between clashed against her circle.

Sensing she was losing control of her stolen powers she pried Caligula's mouth from my neck leaving two parallel gashes from below my ear down to my collar bone. With the silver out of my system, nothing would stop her from going straight to the fount. Her power surged as she covered herself in the undiluted blood flowing freely from my wounds. With renewed strength she could keep us blocked off from the rest of the between.

Still trapped in Caligula's arms I was unable to stop the crush of his mouth against mine. His tongue forced its way in, coating my mouth with the coppery tang of my blood while Bathory's hands slid across my blood slicked skin, stopping to unfasten the blades at my wrists. My stomach lurched. And as much as I despised throwing up, in that moment I prayed I would.

He loosened his hold as his hands roamed my body. He cupped my ass, grinding his erection into my pelvis. I pivoted my wrist and the Retaliator. I felt the razor sharp edge of the blade slice through his clothes and into his flesh before he realized what happened.

Throwing me down, he clutched his chest and stomach in a move that mirrored my own. He collapsed, landing hard on his side. No amount of infusions would staunch the flow of blood from a wound by my sword. I watched the light fade from his eyes as darkness crept into mine.

With a double edged blade there was no way to cut Caligula without cutting myself. My hands, covered in blood and pressed against my stomach, were the only warm part of my body. Cold seeped into my extremities as my body pulled blood in to keep the vital organs functional. I tried to stand only to fall again. Lulled by the ebb and tide as the grey flowed in and out of my wound it became more difficult to stay awake. Unconsciousness threatened to take hold. If I gave in, my death wouldn't be far behind.

Bathory was lost in a blood craze, oblivious to everything around her. Kneeling in a pool of my blood she painted her body, occasionally stopping to lap at her fingers.

The sight of her, every inch of her exposed skin covered in my blood, was enough to stave off my death for a few minutes more. I had to find the strength to kill her. I would not die before I killed her.

My arms shook as I strained to lift the few pounds of perfectly balanced steel. As weak as I was I'd never be able to swing the blade in a horizontal strike. Pulling the hilt back even with my hip, I put all of my weight and the last of my energy into a forward thrust. She must have felt my shift in the air as she rolled at the last second, moving out of my strike zone.

Swing and a miss, I couldn't stop the momentum and ended up landing hard on my knees. Searing pain shot though my knee cap. The Retaliator plunged into the veil and was almost swallowed by the swill surrounding us. The rot she created in the between continued to spread. I struggled to free my sword from the detritus.

The residue from Bathory's contamination destroyed my sword. Rust pitted the exposed portion of the blade. I pulled on the hilt one more time, the between finally loosened its hold but too late. Bathory latched onto my back, her heels hooked into my side.

She fisted her hand in my hair, yanking my head back. Her fangs tore into the base of my neck. I bucked, pulled her hair and tried to flip her over my shoulder but she held on.

Too afraid the Retaliator's blade would snap, I gave up using the melee weapon. I clawed at her eye, pressing with my fingertips until I felt them slide behind the soft tissue.

She continued to maul my neck until I ripped out her right eye. Bathory unlatched her fangs but stayed firmly attached to my back. Her right hand connected with my jaw and I heard something pop. It was definitely dislocated.

I didn't have the time or energy to heal it. My face was swollen, my neck shredded and I had a serious laceration on my stomach from a blade that inflicted mortal wounds. I was knocking on death's door. If I didn't do something quick, death would answer.

I tried to spindled enough of the between to jump us back to the spot where she had appeared, back to where I left Mason at the vamp house. Bathory felt my pull on the veil and slammed her fist into the base of my skull.

I went down, face first. She got up, flipped me over and dragged me by the ankles like a rag doll to the center of her circle. She dug her toes into the gash in my abdomen. I would have screamed if my jaw worked. I clamped my hand on her calf, in a futile attempt to keep her from smashing my intestines.

She slowly wiggled her toes out of my insides and sat on my pelvis. Under her full weight I felt something dig into my back. I still had a small stake on my belt. I slid my hand around and tried to work it free. Bathory clawed at my chest. Her fingernails pressing around my heart. She was knuckle deep in my flesh by the time I unfastened the stake from its holster. This was it. I had one stake, one chance to kill her. My heart pounded and I imagined it bumping against the tips of her fingers as they pried through my rib cage.

I aimed for her heart and drove the rowan wood into her chest. She swatted my hand away, snapping the stake before I could pierce her heart. The splintered wood punctured her lung. It wouldn't kill her but it was enough to incapacitate her. Paralyzed, she collapsed on top of me.

It would have been so easy under the dead weight of the vampire to give up and let death claim me. I needed to move before I passed out.

I fought the blackness at the edge of my vision and pushed Bathory off. I rolled her onto her back. The shards of rowan wood weren't long enough. I needed something else. Too afraid to damage the Retaliator more, I scrambled to find one of my daggers. Blade on hand and completely exhausted I crawled back to the immobile vampire.

With my head on her chest I listened to the gurgling sound in her lungs as she uselessly gasped for air. I tightened my grip on the dagger and drove it into her heart. I fought the pull of unconsciousness until I was certain she was dead. Lying face down in a pile of ash, I closed my eyes and welcomed death.

The between already reclaimed the grey spoiled by Bathory's manipulation of my powers. Matter shifted as the layers of reality settled back into place.

The ash and blood I spilled were absorbed as an offering, payment for the damage done and the cost to repair it. I felt the vibrations from hooves pounding through the between - my ride to the Other World.

I should stand or at least sit up but the idea of moving

exhausted me. Shouldn't I be healed? I mean wasn't that part of the deal when you died? If I had to suffer through eternity with these wounds I would be pissed. If I could stay awake long enough to be pissed, that is.

It was true, what they say about your life flashing before your eyes. Images of a lonely and unloved childhood, my sister Frankie the only bright spot in an otherwise bleak upbringing. My adoptive mother would be more upset that I met my escort to the Other World in tattered, blood soaked clothes, than my actual death. My time with SPTF, followed by a quick flicker of Matthison and Massarelli's faces. Arawn, my father. I finally had the parental love I craved all my life and now I was dying.

Aidan's face flickered in my mind. My heart hurt more than any other part of my body as I watched the memories of us play out like a filmstrip in my head. We wasted so much time hurting each other. It was Mason's turn to make an appearance in the movie of my life. Tears streamed down my face as I imagined all the things that could have been. And then there was nothing, nothing but blackness and the physical pain that wracked my body.

***

Why did everything hurt? I was dead for fucks sake. I thought I lived a fairly decent life. I only used my powers for good. Well, except that time in high school, but Janie Bennett had it coming. I would think stopping Bathory and Caligula would have evened things out. I'm guessing not because this had to be what purgatory felt like.

"Open your eyes, Maurin." Groaning in protest, I swatted at the hands stroking my face. "Come on, open your eyes. I know you hear me."

"Mace," I croaked. My throat was so dry and I sounded like I suffered from laryngitis.

"There you are."

"Are you my escort?"

"I've been a lot of things but an escort isn't one of them."

"Then what are you doing here? Who's going to help me cross over?"

"You mean to the Other World?" He chuckled. "I hate to be the bearer of bad news but despite your best efforts you didn't die. You came pretty close, we thought we'd lost you for a while there."

"What? But the Retaliator... How?" My brain felt foggy and I had trouble stringing complete sentences together.

"The Retaliator will not inflict a mortal wound against the fae who wields it. Leave it to you to test the limits of that safe guard."

"So I'm not dead?" Blinking a few times, my mind cleared and I took in my surroundings. There was a familiar crack in the ceiling next to the water stain from the melt after the last blizzard. The dark purple comforter I bought on sale at Bed Bath and Beyond a couple of months ago was pulled up to my neck. I was back in Salem, in my apartment, in my own bed. Home. It was enough to bring tears to my eyes.

"No, you're not dead but if you ever do something like

that again, I'll kill you." He ran a finger along my collar bone. My body trembled as he traced the scars from Caligula's fangs. "Vampires are more of a threat to you than your sword. If Caligula hadn't taken so much of your blood you would have healed on your own."

"I dreamt of horses and the Cwnn Anfwnn. It was so beautiful. They were going to lead me to the Other World."

"I'm sorry to say, the Other World's not as quaint as you imagined. That was your father's idea of a rescue mission. He rode out with the Hunt, searching the between for you. It wasn't until after Bathory died and the darkness she created shifted that we found you."

"So you rode in on your white horse to rescue me?"

"Something like that." He gave me a little wink that had my stomach flipping flops.

"Do I smell coffee?"

Mason grabbed my favorite mug - the one with all the sugar skulls on it - off the night stand and held it out for me. "You really are a knight in shining armor, aren't you?" I pushed myself up so I could take the mug, wincing a little from the sharp pains in my abdomen.

"A noble knight wouldn't let his lady throw herself on her sword."

Finally positioned against the headboard for support, I took the mug. Amalie might be out of a job. The coffee was amazing. Or maybe everything tastes amazing when you wake up after you should be dead.

If I was a brave woman I would try eating anchovies to test that theory. Thankfully I knew it was stupidity and not bravery that had me doing most of the things I did because I hate anchovies and I seriously doubt a near death experience would change that.

"For the record, I didn't throw myself on my sword."

"Duly noted. Now let's have a look at that wound." He peeled back the covers and lifted my shirt - the same pajama top I slept in when at his house. "It looks better already. A couple days and you'll be good as new."

"So, your lady, huh?"

Mason's hand shook a little as he poked at the tender, healing skin. He looked up at me expectantly. "Would you like to be?"

"Maybe we should start with dinner and a movie."

XXIII
TWENTY-THREE

Aidan sat on the steps outside my apartment building looking a little worse for wear. It had been almost four weeks since I watched him hoist the last of the hostages before climbing out the window himself.

I'd given two statements to the Council on Caligula and Bathory. I'd met Amalie at the Daily Grind twice, had lunch with Cash a few times, hell even my father had been by to visit every week.

But the person who professed his love for me five weeks ago couldn't be bothered to check in on me after I almost died. It wasn't like I expected flowers and balloons or anything. I knew we were over. So I shouldn't have been disappointed when he never came by and the phone never rang. But I was.

I kept waiting for closure - that mystical thing grown-ups talk about when love ends, the thing that is supposed to tell you it's okay to move on.

After a month of mourning a relationship that wasn't meant to be, of stalling and postponing every time Mason asked me out, I decided I wasn't getting closure. I convinced myself that a respectable amount of time had passed and I was actually ready to accept Mason's dinner invitation - the hunter had finally caught his prey. So of course Aidan sat on my stoop waiting to have a heart to heart when I was supposed to be getting ready to go out.

"I don't have anything to say to you, Aidan."

"You don't have to say anything. Just listen."

"What could you possibly have to say tonight that you couldn't have said a month ago?"

"Hear me out, please."

I glanced at my watch. "Two minutes."

"Can we at least go upstairs to your apartment?"

"One minute fifty seconds."

"Jeysus, I see your stubbornness came back with you from the brink of death."

"You know, I wasn't sure you knew at first but after I reported to Agrona there was no way you hadn't heard what happened. A minute thirty seconds."

"I wanted to see you, to make sure you were okay. Especially after the way things ended."

"One minute."

"Would you please stop doing that?"

"Then get to the fucking point, Aidan. You wanted to know if I was okay but what?"

"Jus primae noctis."

"You didn't bother with so much as a phone call because you've been busy deflowering virgins on their wedding night?"

"What? No! I turned Ryanne. Jus primae noctis for a fledgling refers to their first feeding. It's the sire's responsibility to ensure their child can feed on their own."

I didn't know what to say. That wasn't what I expected to hear. I didn't know exactly what I expected to hear but Ryanne being turned into a vampire, his vampire, definitely wasn't it. "Fatherhood isn't everything you remembered?"

"She would have died that night."

"And you felt obligated to save her. A stranger, for all purposes. Looks like our taste in vampires isn't the only thing Ryanne and I have in common then."

"Maurin, don't. I had already turned her when I found out what happened to you. Even if Ryanne's turning went perfectly - which it didn't by the way - I couldn't follow you into the between."

"You know what, you're right. We're not even together anymore. So why I'm so pissed off at you?"

"The same reason a phone call wouldn't be enough for me. Because you still care."

"I'll always care about you but if you came here to salvage things, please don't. Don't say all the things I wanted to hear weeks ago. I don't think I'm strong enough to walk away from you if I'm not angry. You'll tell me all the things I want to hear and I'll believe you because you mean it. In the end we'll hurt each other again. You should go. Mason is picking me up in thirty minutes, I'm going to be late."

"I just wanted to say I'm sorry."

I'm sorry. They were only words but my heart softened at the sound of them. I didn't need to hate him to let him go. "Me too, Aidan." And I was, sorry for what happened and what could have been. So this is what closure feels like. I let him pull me into a hug. He moved in to kiss me and I turned so his lips landed on my cheek, to afraid to get caught up in emotions. He lingered in the embrace longer than necessary, breathing in my scent one last time.

"Am I interrupting something?"

"Mace." I seemed to be out of breath every time he was around me lately. My heart picked up its pace, beating wildly in my chest.

"It wasn't that long ago your heart beat like that for me." Aidan brushed one last kiss on my temple. "I was just saying goodnight."

"Don't you mean goodbye?" Mason was telling, not asking.

"No, I meant exactly what I said. Maurin is the Regulator of my cleaning crew and I report directly to her. So it's not really goodbye now is it? See you around, Hunter." And just like that he was gone, leaving Mason and me standing awkwardly outside my apartment. I would bet next month's rent he knew I was going out with Mason tonight. It was too much of a coincidence and I don't believe in coincidence.

"Are those for me?" I pointed to the flowers, desperate to get our night back on track. "They're beautiful."

"Wildflowers. They reminded me of you."

"Come on, you can put them in water while I get ready." I took his hand and led him up the three flights of stairs to my apartment like we were any normal couple. "So where are we going?"

"You'll have to wait and see."

I left Mason with the task of floral arranging while I jumped in the shower. I was determined not to let Aidan ruin this. I had been putting Mason off for weeks. Tonight was his night and I wanted to show him that I was worth the wait.

Wrapped in a towel, I headed to my closet to figure out what I was supposed to wear on our mystery date. He dressed up his black tee shirt and jeans by putting them on his body. I needed to step it up. Band tee shirts wouldn't cut it tonight.

A little glimmer on my bed caught my eye. Laying next to a familiar string bikini was a silver chain with a delicate apple branch charm hanging from it. I didn't normally wear jewelry but this was beautiful. There weren't any stone adornments on the matching silver charm. It wasn't over done. Its simplicity making it the perfect necklace for me. I fastened it on before holding up the string bikini that had been laying next to it.

"I'm still not wearing this!" I called out, loud enough for him to hear me over the TV in the living room.

A few minutes later I stepped out of my room in a pair of black wedges, skinny jeans and a black tee shirt fitted around the waist and hung off the shoulders. My hair was up in a messy bun. If we were headed where I thought we were it would be a waste of time styling it.

"Ready?"

Mason stood, his eyes fixed on the dark purple strings tied around the back of my neck. He stalked across the room, his desire heavy in the air. He didn't even notice I wore the necklace he gave me. He was too busy imagining what I looked like in the bikini.

"Cross Bath?" I squeaked as he backed me up against the wall.

"You're wearing the bikini. We might not make it to the baths." His mouth burned a trail of kisses along my neck. "You smell like apples and honey. It's nice but I liked you better covered in my scent."

"I would have worn the bikini this time even if you hadn't given me the necklace." I ran a finger along the chain and then the charm, stopping at the rise of my breasts.

"Necklace?" He dragged his eyes away from my chest to the charm dangling above it. The small silver apple branch was dwarfed by his large hands as he examined it. "This isn't from me. Where did you find it?"

"What do you mean it isn't from you? It was on my bed with the bathing suit." Mason rested his forehead against mine. "What is it?"

He looked down at my mouth, watching me nervously pull on my bottom lip with my teeth. "A problem for tomorrow." His hands clutched my hips, pulling my body against him as he claimed my mouth. His tongue demanded entrance as he deepened the kiss until we both had to come up for air.

"Tomorrow," I said breathlessly. I pulled him in for another kiss as we slipped into the between.

Dear Reader,

I hope you enjoyed reading Blood Bath. I love hearing from readers. Your feedback is extremely important to me, so please leave a review on the site where you purchased this book.

Want to know more about new releases, events, contests and giveaways? Be sure to check out my Facebook page www.facebook.com/TheMaurinKincaideSeries. It's a great way to keep in touch and I try to interact as often as I can on the page.

Thank you so much for your continued support.

Rachel Rawlings

www.rachelrawlings.com
twitter: @rachelsbooks
www.facebook.com/TheMaurinKincaideSeries
www.tsu.com/rachelsbooks
www.hallowread.com
www.facebook.com/hallowread